THEATERS AND THREATS

An Isle of Man Ghostly Cozy

DIANA XARISSA

❀ Created with Vellum

AUTHOR'S NOTE

Now that I've reached book twenty in this series, we seem to be running out of alphabet! I have a lot more planned for Fenella and her friends, though. I haven't yet started to think about what I'm going to do when I reach Z with this series. I'll let you know more when I know more.

As with all of my series books, I recommend that you read them in order. This series runs alphabetically and the characters and their relationships change and develop as the series progresses. Each story should stand alone, however, if you prefer not to read them all.

While the story is set on the Isle of Man, a UK Crown Dependency, the main character grew up in the US, so I use American English for the story. The only exception is when the other characters are speaking. They speak in British English, unless I mess things up, which is increasingly likely the longer I live in the US. I do apologize for any errors.

This is a work of fiction and all of the characters are fictional creations. Any resemblance that any character may bear to any real person, living or dead, is entirely coincidental. Similarly, the businesses mentioned in the story are fictional establishments located where convenient to the story, rather than where any actual businesses on the island may be located. Again, any resemblance that they may share with any real business, on the island or elsewhere, is coincidental.

The Gaiety Theatre, on the other hand, is a beautiful Victorian theatre on the Douglas promenade. Originally opened in 1900, it was purchased by the government in 1971 and then restored to its original glory. Events that take place at the Gaiety in the story, however, are entirely fictional.

I hope that you enjoy the story. If you want to get in touch, all of my contact details are available in the back of the book. I'm active on Facebook and I always answer e-mails. Thanks for spending some time with Fenella and Mona.

"Wear the blue dress," Mona Kelly suggested.

"Daniel has seen me in the blue dress," Fenella Woods replied. "I wanted to wear something different."

"So wear the red dress," Mona said with a yawn. "Daniel will love you, regardless."

Fenella grinned at her aunt. "I know," she said happily. "We're stupid in love."

"Indeed."

Fenella flushed. "Or maybe just stupid," she muttered as she pulled the red dress out of the wardrobe.

"I wouldn't say that. I think it's lovely how much you've come to care for one another."

"If you would have asked me a few years ago where I'd be right now, I never would have imagined any of this," Fenella said thoughtfully. "My life has not gone at all the way I expected."

"In all the very best ways," Mona suggested.

Fenella nodded. Two years earlier, she'd been working as a university professor at the same university where she'd earned her degrees, including her doctorate in history. She'd been involved with another professor, Jack Dawson, for nearly a decade and had no plans to end the relationship, even though both she and Jack knew it was going nowhere. Even after all that time together, Fenella had still lived on her own in a little house in the suburbs of Buffalo, New York. Jack had his own home, and the pair rarely spent nights together. Everything had changed when Mona had died, though.

While Fenella had vague recollections of her mother's sister visiting the US on one or two occasions, she'd paid little attention to the woman who lived on the Isle of Man. Fenella had been born there, but her parents had moved the family to the US when she'd been no more than a toddler. John, the oldest of Fenella's four older brothers, had kept in touch with the woman, sending Christmas cards on behalf of the family after Fenella's parents had died. No one had been more surprised than Fenella, therefore, when she'd been informed that she'd inherited Mona's estate.

With little idea of what she'd actually inherited, Fenella had used the inheritance as an excuse to change everything in her life. She'd sold her house, quit her job, and ended her dead-end relationship. When she'd first arrived on the island, she'd discovered that she now owned a luxury apartment right on the promenade in Douglas, the island's capital city. Doncan Quayle, Mona's advocate — the Manx term for a lawyer — informed her that she'd also inherited some bank accounts and other things, and suggested that she get herself settled on the island and then come to speak with him about Mona's estate.

Days had turned into weeks and then months before Fenella finally made an appointment with Doncan. She'd been shocked and delighted to discover that Mona had been considerably wealthier than she'd ever imagined. In addition to her apartment in Douglas, Fenella discovered that she owned properties all over the island. She'd also been left stocks, bonds, bank accounts, jewelry, and a fancy red sports car that she'd struggled to learn how to drive.

There were two reasons why it had taken her a while to make that initial appointment with Doncan. The first was that she kept getting herself tangled up in murder investigations, something that was still happening with alarming frequency. The second reason was more complicated. While Fenella loved her spacious and gorgeously decorated apartment, she hadn't expected it to come with its own resident ghost. While Mona had died, she seemingly hadn't gone far, and it had taken Fenella some time to adjust to sharing her apartment with the dead woman.

Now, however, she'd come to appreciate the many benefits of having Mona around. One of those benefits was the large wardrobe in the master bedroom. It had been left full of Mona's gorgeous clothes, and even though Fenella and Mona had very different body shapes, everything in the wardrobe seemed to fit Fenella as if it had been made for her.

As she slipped on the red dress, Fenella wondered if it would fit. Very occasionally, when she and Mona disagreed about something, a dress would be too tight. The red dress fell into place perfectly. Fenella twirled slowly in front of the mirror.

"What do you think?" she asked Mona.

"I think the blue one would be a better choice."

"Katie, what do you think?" Fenella asked the tiny kitten who was stretched out on the bed.

Katie had walked into the apartment right after Fenella had moved in. While Fenella had been trying to find her owners, Katie had made herself at home. Although she'd never intended to get a pet, Fenella was grateful now that no one had ever come looking for Katie. When the animal heard her name, she looked up at Fenella and made a noise.

"She said blue," Mona said.

"She was just making noise," Fenella countered.

"She said blue. But wear the red if you must. Just don't stand too near the curtains on the box or you'll disappear."

Fenella frowned. "There are curtains on the box?"

"Of course, in case privacy is desired."

"But who would go to a show and then want privacy? That doesn't even make sense."

"Perhaps some people prefer privacy during the interval."

"Is the interval the same as intermission? Is this going to be different to going to the theater in the US?" Fenella asked.

"Yes, the interval is the intermission. Beyond that, I've no idea, as I never went to the theater in the US. You've booked a box for tonight. Did you used to sit in boxes in the US?"

"Of course not. I couldn't afford such luxuries when I lived in New York."

"So it will be different in that respect."

"I just don't want to do anything that might embarrass Breesha."

"Then be on your best behavior."

Fenella nodded. "Of course. But now I need to get something to eat before Daniel gets here."

Mona sighed. "You should have insisted that he take you out for dinner before the show."

"I suggested it, but he had to work. I'm fortunate that he'll be finished in time for the show."

"He works too much."

"He has a very important job."

Daniel Robinson was a CID inspector with the Isle of Man Constabulary. Fenella had first met him after she'd almost literally tripped over a dead body right after her arrival on the island. Over the past year and a half, their relationship had developed, with some stops and starts, into a romance. In August, while in the US for Jack's wedding, Daniel had proposed. Neither of them was in any hurry to set a date for their wedding, but they both enjoyed spending as much time together as Daniel's demanding job allowed.

"He should quit his job and travel the world with you," Mona suggested.

Fenella swallowed a sigh. She loved the idea of traveling, and she had the resources to do it in luxury, but Daniel was as uncomfortable with her money as he was devoted to his job. "Maybe one day he'll take early retirement, and we'll be able to travel," she told Mona. "Today, though, he's been dealing with break-ins at two different retail shops in Braddan."

Fenella wandered into her modern kitchen and began to open cupboards. "There's nothing to eat in here," she told Katie.

"Merooww?"

"Oh, no, there's plenty of cat food," she assured the animal. "There just isn't a great deal of people food."

As she spooned Katie's dinner into her bowl, someone knocked on her door.

"Shelly, hello," Fenella said to her next-door neighbor and closest friend.

Shelly Quirk was a widow who'd taken early retirement from a lifetime of teaching. Immediately after her husband had passed away unexpectedly, she'd bought the apartment next to Mona's. Mona had helped the woman learn to embrace life again. Shelly had been one of the first people that Fenella had met on the island, and the two had quickly become very close.

"Hello," Shelly replied. "Tim and I were in the lift, on our way to get a nice dinner somewhere before the show, when his mobile went off. He had to go into the office to deal with some sort of emergency. Would it be terrible of me to ask if I can join you and Daniel for dinner?"

Fenella laughed. "Daniel is working. I'm on my own as well. Let's go together and get something wonderful."

"Do you want to change for the show first?" Shelly asked, glancing at Fenella's jeans and T-shirt.

"Yes, I'd better, hadn't I? Do you want to come in? I don't need long."

"Thanks. I'd rather not go back to my flat and upset Smokey. I'd just told her that I was going to be out for the evening."

Fenella nodded. Smokey was an older cat that Shelly had adopted shortly after Katie had appeared in Fenella's life. The two cats were close friends now, too.

Back in her bedroom, Fenella put on the blue dress and found the matching shoes and handbag. It only took her a few minutes to touch up her makeup and pull her hair into a neat twist at the back of her head.

"You look lovely," Mona told her as Fenella headed back toward the living room.

"Thank you," Fenella replied as she left the room.

"You're welcome," Shelly said, looking confused from her seat in front of the huge windows that showcased the promenade and the sea below them.

Fenella laughed. "Just muttering to myself," she said.

Behind her, Mona chuckled. Fenella was the only one who could see and hear Mona, and she sometimes forgot not to reply to the ghost out loud when there were other people in the apartment.

"Be a good kitty," Fenella told Katie. "I'll be back after the theater. It might be later than usual, but it won't be too late."

Katie jumped down from Shelly's lap and stretched. "Meeooww," she replied.

"Where shall we go?" Shelly asked as Fenella locked her door behind herself.

"We've plenty of time to go somewhere nice," Fenella replied. "Although, I don't know if I want to eat too much before the show. If I eat too much, I'll be too sleepy to enjoy the performance."

Shelly nodded and then suggested one of Fenella's favorite restaurants. "They have a new menu of what they're calling 'lighter' options," she told her. "Tim and I went there last week and I tried one. It was delicious."

"That sounds good, although I may get something not very light, as I love their food."

"Don't let me talk about the wedding," Shelly said as they walked the short distance to the restaurant.

"Oh?"

Shelly laughed. "I'm afraid I've become rather obsessed with the entire thing, and I'm trying to stop myself from talking about it all the time. If you want to talk about it, though, of course we can, especially considering the circumstances."

After having been on her own for over a year, Shelly had met Tim Blake, an architect who played in the local band, *The Islanders*, about a year earlier. Tim had proposed in June, and the pair was planning for a January wedding. It had taken Fenella a great deal of time and effort, but she'd finally persuaded Shelly to let her pay for the couple's dream wedding. That didn't mean that Fenella was interested in every detail about the big day, though.

"I don't mind what we talk about," Fenella replied. "Although, I'd like to talk about the play we're going to see, if you know anything about it."

Shelly shook her head. "I'd never even heard of it before you asked if Tim and I wanted to join you for the performance."

Fenella nodded. "I don't think it's a particularly well known play," she said. "I looked it up on the Internet, and I couldn't find any mention of it."

"*Three Gentlewomen from Bologna?* I can't believe it hasn't been on the West End," Shelly laughed.

"I asked Breesha for a plot summary, but she said she didn't want to spoil anything for me."

Breesha Quilliam had been Doncan's assistant for years. She and Fenella were friendly, occasionally meeting at a nearby pub for a drink and a chat. When Fenella had learned that Breesha was taking part in a play, she'd been determined to show her support for the woman.

Fenella opened the door to the restaurant and held it open for Shelly. Inside, they were quickly seated at a table in a corner.

"Just the new menu, please," Shelly told their waiter. "That way I can't be tempted by any of the things I shouldn't have."

He nodded. "And for you?" he asked Fenella.

"Just give me the new menu, too," she replied. "If I can't find anything I want on that, I can always request the full menu, but I should get something light. We're going to the theater after dinner."

"I've heard it's a very good show," he said, handing them each menus and then walking away.

"Do you think he's really heard that or was he just being polite?" Shelly asked Fenella.

"I think he was just being polite. Tonight is opening night, after all."

Shelly shrugged. "I can't believe Breesha wouldn't tell you anything about the show."

"She didn't really want me to buy tickets. She said she thinks she'll be extra nervous, knowing that I'm in the audience. Well, not just me, but all of us."

"She does know that you're coming, though, doesn't she?"

"Sort of. She knows I bought tickets for one of the shows, but I didn't tell her which performance. I sort of hinted that I'd bought tickets for one of the shows next weekend. I don't want her to be extra nervous if I can help it."

"Didn't you say that she's the assistant stage manager as well as having a part in the show?"

"Yes."

"So she may well be taking tickets and showing people to their seats when we arrive. Having said that, she's probably been given a list of ticket sales as well, including which nights will have VIP guests."

"We aren't VIP guests."

"You bought a box. That makes us VIP guests."

Fenella opened her mouth to argue just as the waiter returned. By the time she and Shelly had ordered, she'd decided it wasn't worth disagreeing. Whatever she thought, Shelly was probably correct in that the theater management probably regarded her and her friends as VIPs.

"I'm sure the box was expensive," Shelly said after a moment.

"It wasn't terribly, actually. In fact, I think it was less costly than I would have paid for four tickets to a Broadway show back home."

Shelly laughed. "This isn't a Broadway show, though. This is a local production of a play no one has ever heard of before."

"Maybe it's an undiscovered classic."

"More likely, the director's daughter wrote it, and he's promised to get it seen at least once. You were probably smart to get tickets for tonight. It might close after a single performance."

"Surely not. It's supposed to run for three consecutive weekends."

"I don't know what will happen if they don't sell enough tickets," Shelly said thoughtfully. "I mean, it isn't as if they can book another show into the theater on such short notice, but putting on the show to an empty room won't be inexpensive."

"Everyone involved in the production is a volunteer, according to Breesha. The only person who makes any money is the playwright. He or she received a payment up front to give the company the rights to put on the show, and he or she will also get a small percentage of the ticket sales."

"What happens to the rest of the money raised through ticket sales?"

"Some of it goes to the venue, and the rest is put back into the company to help pay for the next show they want to produce," Fenella told her. "Breesha said this show was fairly inexpensive, as shows goes, which may explain why no one has ever heard of it."

"But she said it was going to be a good show, right?"

Fenella frowned. "That isn't exactly what she said. She said some of the performers are excellent and that she's always happy to be part of an artistic experiment, whatever that means."

"It's experimental theater? Is it too late to catch a bad cold?"

Fenella laughed. "If you truly don't want to come, you don't have to. I want to be there to see Breesha's first ever performance, though."

"I thought you said she's been involved with the theater company for years."

"She has, but always behind the scenes. She started out taking tickets and whatnot, and she's moved up to being the assistant stage manager, but she's never appeared on stage before."

"My goodness, not even when someone fell ill at the last minute?"

"She did say that she read lines once for someone who'd fallen ill. She sat on the corner of the stage and they pretended that the conversation was being conducted by telephone, just for that one performance. Apparently, it worked out okay, because the missing actress had only a very small part."

"But tonight she's going to be on stage properly, isn't she?"

"She is, but again, it's only a small part. Apparently, the director couldn't find anyone who was willing to take such a small part because of the demands of rehearsals and everything. Since Breesha was already there, stage managing everything, he persuaded her to take the role."

"So if we blink, we may miss her," Shelly suggested.

"I hope it won't be that bad," Fenella laughed.

The waiter arrived with their meals a moment later.

"Every bit as delicious as you said it would be," Fenella told Shelly after a few bites. "It doesn't taste light at all."

"But hopefully you won't be too full to enjoy the show," Shelly said.

"What are you seeing?" the waiter asked as he refilled their water glasses.

"*Three Gentlewomen from Bologna*," Fenella replied.

He shrugged. "I'm sure it will be very good," he said before he walked away.

"He's never heard of it either," Shelly said.

"I don't know that anyone has," Fenella replied.

They finished their meals and after some debate, decided against dessert.

"We can always get something sweet later, after the show," Fenella said as she got to her feet.

"That sounds good," Shelly said. "But we have an hour before the show starts. Do you think we dare go to the pub?"

"I think the pub is the perfect place to go."

While there were many pubs along the Douglas promenade, there was no doubt in either woman's mind as to which pub they meant. The Tale and Tail was only a short walk from the restaurant. On the way there, Fenella texted Daniel and asked him to meet her there. Shelly sent the same message to Tim.

As they walked into the Tale and Tail, Fenella smiled broadly. The pub was one of her favorite places in the world, and when she was there she couldn't imagine why she wanted to travel anywhere else.

The huge room had once been the library of an enormous mansion. When the building was sold, the new owners had converted the mansion into a luxury hotel. The library had been left largely intact. A bar with a few bar stools had been installed in the center of the room, and comfortable chairs and couches had been added to the upper level. Additionally, a dozen or more cat beds had been distributed throughout the entire space so that the pub's many rescue cats could make themselves at home.

As far as Fenella was concerned, the cats were the second best part of the pub. Her favorite thing about the Tale and Tail was that the library's books had remained on the bookshelves that were nearly everywhere. Customers were encouraged to browse the shelves, to read books everywhere in the building, and even to borrow titles if they so desired.

As she and Shelly walked toward the bar, the bartender waved. "Your usual?" he called.

They both nodded, and when they reached him, he handed them each a glass of wine.

"We'll be upstairs. Daniel and Tim should be here soon," Shelly told him.

He nodded. "I'll send them up."

"We won't be staying long," Shelly added. "We're going to the show at the Gaiety."

"What's showing at the Gaiety?" he asked.

"*Three Gentlewomen from Bologna*," Shelly replied.

His surprised look nearly made Fenella laugh out loud. "I've not heard of that one," he said after a moment.

"It isn't a very well known play," Fenella replied. "But Breesha is in it."

The man smiled. "I should get tickets, then," he said. "Breesha is one of my favorite people."

"Maybe wait until we've seen it," Shelly suggested. "We'll give you an honest review."

"Let me know. I like to support our customers in their endeavors," he replied.

Shelly and Fenella headed up the winding staircase that led to the upper level. There was a large group sharing several bottles of wine in one corner of the room.

"How far can we get from them?" Shelly asked in a whisper.

"Maybe not far enough," Fenella replied.

They found a table in the opposite corner of the room and settled in. Even at that distance, they could hear every word of the loud conversation that the other party was having.

"...three or four times a week," a dark-haired man said. "And then she ran away with the gardener."

Everyone laughed loudly.

"More wine," one of the women shouted. "Lots more wine."

"We shouldn't drink too much," another woman said. "We won't want to be running to the loo in the middle of the show."

"Why not?" the first woman asked. "It isn't as if we really want to see the show."

Everyone laughed again, and then someone began to refill everyone's glasses.

"It sounds as if they might be going to Breesha's show," Shelly said in a low voice during the slight lull while everyone was drinking.

"I hope not. They seem as if they'd be very noisy."

"What show is it anyway?" one of the men asked.

"*Two Gentlemen of Verona*," someone told him. "It's Shakespeare."

"Yawn," the first man replied.

"No it isn't," a woman said. "It's *Three Gentlewomen of Bologna,* and it isn't Shakespeare at all."

"It isn't some sort of feminist retelling of the Shakespeare play, is it?" someone demanded. "I haven't had enough to drink yet to put up with that sort of nonsense."

"It isn't," was the reply from somewhere in the group. "It's an original play by a very talented young playwright named Dorothy Gilbert. Her father just happens to be the theater manager, but I don't think that had anything to do with her play being selected to be performed."

"Oh, good heavens," one of the man snapped. "This is going to be dreadful."

"It might be very good," someone said.

"It won't be very good," he replied gloomily. "It might be just barely tolerable, if I drink enough before the curtain goes up."

Before anyone else could respond, Daniel appeared at the top of the stairs. He was a handsome man, now approaching fifty, but to Fenella, at least, he looked a good deal younger. He smiled at Fenella and then glanced over at the crowded table of drinkers. The smile faded as he nodded in their direction.

"He's a police inspector," one of the women whispered loudly.

"Do you think the management rang them because we're being too loud?" someone asked.

"Nah, that's his girlfriend over there," was the reply. "She's Mona's niece, the one who inherited her fortune."

Fenella felt her face flame as every person at the other table turned to stare at her. Shelly reached over and patted her hand.

"Hello," Daniel said, stopping in front of Fenella and deliberately blocking all of the curious stares.

"Hi," she replied.

"Maybe we should get a drink somewhere else before the show," he suggested.

"Maybe we should just head to the theater," Shelly replied. "They have a bar."

"Do they? How lovely," Fenella said, getting to her feet.

The trio took the elevator to the ground floor. They were nearly at the door when it opened and Tim walked into the room.

"We're leaving?" he asked in surprise.

"There's a very large, noisy, and annoying group upstairs," Shelly told him. "We thought we'd get a drink at the bar at the theater instead."

"Sounds good to me," Tim replied, taking Shelly's arm and dropping a kiss on the top of her head. "Hello," he said softly.

"Hello," she replied.

The Gaiety Theatre was only a short walk away. Mona had told Fenella all about the historic Victorian theater, including the fact that there were at least four ghosts in residence in the building. There was a short queue of people waiting outside the building as they approached.

"The doors aren't open yet," a man told them.

"Good thing it isn't raining," Fenella said, glancing up at the dark skies.

"They'll be open any minute now," he assured her.

Sure enough, only a few minutes later the doors at the front of the building opened.

"Please have your tickets ready to be scanned," the man in the doorway said loudly. "The bar is open on the ground floor. The curtain will be going up in exactly thirty minutes."

"That doesn't give us much time for a drink," Tim said.

"Fenella and I already had a drink," Shelly told him. "We can wait for the interval for another."

He shrugged. "I'm so happy to be away from work that I don't care if I get a drink or not."

"Do you want a drink?" Fenella asked Daniel.

He shook his head and then gave her a gentle kiss. "I'm just happy to see you," he whispered in her ear.

Fenella held out the ticket that she'd printed for the man to scan with his handheld scanner.

"Oh, you're in the boxes," he said loudly. "Let me get someone to show you the way." He looked around and then shouted "Kyle" loudly.

The young man who was directing people toward their seats jumped and then rushed over. "Yes?"

"Can you please show Ms. Woods and her party to Box B?" the man asked.

"Of course," Kyle replied. "Right this way."

He led them through the crowded foyer and then down a short corridor. A moment later, he opened a door that was labeled "Box B."

"Here we are," he said. "If you want anything brought up to you, just use the telephone on the wall."

"Anything brought up to us?" Fenella asked.

"Drinks from the bar or anything," he explained. "You can order by phone and someone will bring you what you want. You can use a credit card or pay cash."

"How nice," Shelly said.

"Did you want drinks?" Kyle asked. "I mean, I can get you whatever you want, save you having to ring downstairs."

"Maybe a bottle of wine?" Daniel suggested. "I'm not working tonight and, unusually, I even have the weekend off."

"I do too," Tim said. "A bottle of wine and four glasses, please."

Both men had their wallets out before Fenella could object. They split the cost of the bottle between them, giving Kyle cash and a generous tip. They were barely settled into seats when he was back with the wine and an entire tray of glasses.

"Thank you," Daniel said as he took the tray from the young man.

"If you need anything else, please ring," Kyle replied before he dashed away.

"This is very fancy," Shelly whispered as she settled back in one of the padded chairs.

"It's very nice," Fenella agreed. "The view of the stage isn't the best, though."

"I've never understood why boxes in the theater are built the way they are," Tim said. "We definitely don't have the best view."

"I think, traditionally, getting a box at the theater was more about being seen than seeing a show," Shelly told him.

They watched as the seats below them slowly filled.

"Oh, look, our friends from the pub," Fenella said to Shelly as the loud group took seats in the middle of the room.

It was obvious that they were still shouting back and forth to one another, although Fenella couldn't hear what anyone was saying. A few minutes later, a man came up to the box and handed them all programs.

"Sorry, we were supposed to be handing these out at the door," he said as he passed them around. "We had a problem with the printer, and they've only just arrived."

Fenella glanced through the handful of pages, noting that the play had indeed been written by Dorothy Gilbert. There was nothing in the program that suggested a link between her and the theater manager, Harry Gilbert, though.

"I still have no idea what the play is about," Shelly whispered to Fenella as the lights were dimmed.

"We're about to find out," she whispered back.

Forty minutes later, as the lights went up, Fenella was ready to apologize to her friends for dragging them to the show. The first act had been nearly incomprehensible. While the actors appeared to be doing their best, the plot seemed to meander along in one direction before suddenly veering in another, and then stumbling into a third. When one of the characters suddenly appeared as a ghost with no explanation as to how she'd died, Fenella gave up on trying to follow the plot.

"I think I drank too much before the show," Shelly said. "I couldn't follow that at all."

"It wasn't just you," Daniel told her. "I was lost from the second line."

"You followed it further than I did," Tim muttered.

"The man in the next box appears to have given up and gone to sleep," Fenella said, nodding toward the box on their left. A man's head was just visible, seemingly resting on the banister at the front of the box.

Everyone chuckled.

"It was pretty dreadful," Fenella said. "I'm really sorry that I..." she stopped because it was clear that Daniel wasn't paying any attention to her.

He'd stood up and crossed to the wall between the two boxes and was staring intently at the seemingly sleeping man.

"What's wrong?" Fenella asked, a sinking feeling in her stomach.

"Maybe nothing," he replied. "But I think I need to check on our neighbor."

He walked to the door and opened it. Fenella was expecting him to object when she followed him out of the room, but he didn't say a word. It took only a moment to walk to the door to the next box. Daniel knocked loudly. After a moment, he knocked again.

"Police," he said in a voice that was just below a shout. "Is there anyone in there?"

He looked at Fenella and shrugged. "I hope they don't lock the doors," he said before he tried the knob. The door swung open under his touch. He and Fenella walked into the box. They'd only taken a few steps forward when Daniel held up a hand.

"I think we need a crime scene team," he said grimly.

Fenella could only stare at the body that was slumped in a chair near the front of the box. From where she was standing, it was clear that the head that was resting on the banister was at a very odd angle. What was worse was the blood that seemed to be everywhere. As she stared at the scene in front of her, from somewhere in the theater a woman began to scream.

2

"There's no chance he's alive," Daniel said tightly. "Go back to our box and use the telephone in there to request help. I want the theater manager and at least one other person, if at all possible. We need to find out where the screaming is coming from as well."

Fenella nodded and turned around. Daniel was already on his mobile, calling the station to request assistance. When she opened the door to leave the box, the three men standing outside of it all gasped.

"What were you doing in there?" someone demanded.

"What's happened in there?" one of them asked.

"We've rung the police. You need to stay where you are," another added.

"I'm Fenella Woods," she began.

"We know who you are," the first man said darkly.

This isn't going well, she thought. "When the lights came up, my friends and I noticed that the man in the next box didn't look well. My, er, fiancé and I came over to check on him, to make sure he was okay."

"And just a short time later, blood started dripping from this box down into the seats below," one of the men told her.

Fenella frowned. "There's a great deal of blood around the body," she explained. "Daniel has called the police. Someone will be here soon."

"Who's Daniel?" someone asked.

"Her fiancé," the first man replied. "Inspector Daniel Robinson, Douglas CID. I suppose, if someone had to get murdered, we should be grateful Inspector Robinson was in the audience."

Fenella took a deep breath. "Daniel wanted me to find the theater manager," she said.

"That's me," a short man with a bald head and a small goatee said. "I'm Harry Gilbert, manager of the Gaiety and its associated properties."

"And I'm Josh Bailey," a much younger man with a long, dark ponytail told her. "I'm the stage manager for this particular production."

Fenella looked curiously at the third man. He scowled at her and then sighed. "I suppose I don't have a choice," he muttered. "I'm Adam Manning. No doubt you've recognized me from the show."

Adam had thick, dark hair and Fenella thought he was blandly handsome. If she'd been twenty years younger, she might have found him attractive. He was probably getting close to forty, but it was difficult to tell because he was wearing heavy stage makeup. Clearly, he'd been in the play, but as Fenella stared at him, she couldn't remember seeing him in the show.

"I'm playing Mr. Harrison," Adam told her as if that explained everything. "I'm also second man from the left in the third act, but that's simply because some people are incapable of casting a sufficient number of actors to fill the demands of a given production." He glanced at Josh as he spoke and then quickly looked away.

Josh laughed. "I've told you at least a dozen times that it's simply impossible to find people who are willing to give up hours and hours of their time for rehearsals and shows for a nonspeaking part in an amateur production. That's especially true for the first performances of a brand new play by a new playwright."

Adam sighed. "Let's not get into that right now," he said. "I could talk all night about playwrights who fail to understand how casting works or, indeed, how plots work, but I won't." This time, his remarks were clearly directed at Harry Gilbert.

Harry flushed. "The second act is due to begin in three minutes," he told Fenella. "Can we simply hold the police in the foyer until after the show?"

Fenella opened her mouth, ready to explain about how murder investigations worked, when the door behind her opened suddenly.

"Ah, Inspector Robinson, your, er, lovely lady friend was just telling us that the show could go on in spite of the disturbance," Harry said to Daniel.

"That's fine," Daniel told him. "Do you have a key to this box?"

Harry nodded.

"Please lock the door and then meet me back here after the show," Daniel told him. "We'll take things from there."

Fenella watched as Harry locked the door. Daniel checked that it was locked tightly.

"I'll want to speak to everyone from the show once it's over," Daniel told Harry. "Please don't let anyone leave."

"You don't need the audience?" Harry checked.

"No, I don't believe so," Daniel replied.

Fenella knew she was staring, open-mouthed, at Daniel, but she was too shocked to care. What was he saying?

Harry and the other two men turned and disappeared down the corridor.

"What is going on?" Fenella demanded when the three men were out of sight. "You can't leave a murder investigation until after the show."

"You know I wouldn't do that," Daniel replied.

"So what is going on?"

"The more I looked at the body, the more I realized that the angles were all wrong," he explained. "So I took a much closer look. It's a mannequin of some sort, not a real person."

"No one is dead?"

"No one is dead, but whoever set that up wanted to make a huge mess and cause a scene. That suggests that the theater or the acting company is being targeted. I have half a dozen constables coming to help with questioning everyone after the show, along with a crime scene team to process the scene. For now, though, we can enjoy the second half of the play."

"Oh, goody," Fenella replied, wondering if a murder investigation was such a bad thing.

Daniel laughed. "It has to get better," he told her. "It can't get worse."

"I'm not sure about that."

"Whoever set up that mess in there must have been hoping to interrupt tonight's performance," Daniel told her. "I think it may be useful to disappoint that person. The woman who was screaming from below us is already being questioned, and the mess down there has been cleared away."

"You think this was an attempt to sabotage the show?"

"I can't imagine why anyone would want to do that, but I can't think of any other reason why anyone would have done what's been done otherwise. Judging by the amount of fake blood spilled everywhere, he or she must have expected it to start dripping on the people underneath the box."

"Presumably, he or she was waiting for exactly what happened — a bunch of people racing up here to find out what was going on."

"And if we hadn't been here, they would have burst into the box and started screaming. No doubt they would have rung the police, and the rest of the performance would have been cancelled."

"Except now it won't be."

"And we'll get to see Breesha's performance."

"I suppose it's worth sitting through the rest of the show for that."

"Maybe the second half will make more sense."

"It can't make less sense," Fenella told him.

An hour later, she was willing to admit that she'd been wrong. "That was, um, interesting," she said as the lights went up.

"Was it?" Shelly asked. "I stopped paying attention after the man began to cry on the corner of the stage."

"Was he meant to be there, or had he simply forgotten his part?" Tim asked.

Shelly shrugged. "I've no idea. None at all."

"Maybe we should get Breesha to explain the plot to us," Fenella said.

"I think she didn't want to tell you in advance because she's as confused as we are," Shelly replied.

"But someone must know what the play is about," Fenella insisted.

"That someone isn't me," Daniel told them. "Having said that, I was probably distracted by the problem in the next box."

"What happens now?" Shelly asked.

"Now I go in with a crime scene team and take a better look," he told her. "And then I interview all of the cast and crew from the show."

"You aren't going to need to interview the audience?" Tim asked.

"Not at the moment. Whoever set it up must have done so before the theater opened to the audience. I didn't see anyone in that box while we were waiting for the show to start," Daniel said.

"I'm surprised we didn't notice the man's head before the show started," Fenella said.

"I suspect it wasn't left where it is now. I think it slowly slid into that position during the show," Daniel told her.

Shelly shuddered. "Who would do such a horrible thing? And why?"

"Both are questions that I'm going to do my best to answer," Daniel told her as he got to his feet.

"So Shelly and I can go?" Tim asked.

Daniel nodded. "If I were you, I'd go and have another drink at the pub," he told them.

"That's an excellent idea," Tim said, offering Shelly his arm.

"What about me?" Fenella asked.

"You're welcome to go as well," he replied. "Or you can make your way backstage to congratulate your friend on her performance. If you do that, please keep your eyes and ears open."

"I'll go and see Breesha, then," Fenella told him. "Good luck with the crime scene."

"I'll be down to start interviewing people soon. Constable Corlett is down there somewhere. If you have any difficulties, ask for him."

Fenella nodded. Howard Corlett had been the first constable on the scene when she'd discovered her first body. Daniel thought very highly of the bright young man.

They walked out of the box and into a crowd of crime scene investigators. Harry Gilbert was standing in the middle of the group. Fenella gave Daniel's hand a squeeze, and then she slipped past him, down the corridor.

"Mr. Gilbert, the key, please," Daniel was saying as Fenella walked away.

Fenella made her way back to the foyer and then followed the signs that said "Cast and Crew Only," fully expecting to be stopped somewhere along the way. A tall, blond, uniformed constable was standing in front of the door that was labeled "Stage."

"Ms. Woods? You've been cleared," he said, pulling open the door for her.

Fenella walked through it and found herself standing in one of the wings. It was dimly lit, and she could hear low voices coming from somewhere in front of her, but curtains blocked her view. She took a step forward and pushed aside the curtain. The audience had mostly gone, and Fenella could see what looked to be a dozen people at work in the box where the dummy had been found. Letting the curtain fall back into place, she turned in the other direction and pushed another curtain out of her way.

The large backstage area seemed to be full of people. There were a dozen chairs scattered across the room, and clusters of people were gathered around each chair. It took Fenella a minute to find Breesha in the crowd, in part because Breesha was still in costume and didn't look at all like herself. Taking a deep breath, Fenella crossed the room to her friend.

"Hello," she said brightly. "You were wonderful."

Breesha flushed. "Thank you, but I don't think any of us were at our best during the second half. Do you have any idea what happened? We were all back here, and we could hear someone screaming in the audience. Harry left and then came back, but he wouldn't tell us anything."

Fenella glanced at the men and women who were standing nearby. They were all clearly listening to every word.

"I can't tell you anything," she said apologetically. "But the police are here. Daniel will be here shortly."

"Was someone murdered in one of the boxes?" asked a pretty brunette who appeared to be in her mid-twenties. Her face was still covered in stage makeup.

Fenella looked over at her and then shook her head. "I truly can't say anything," she told her.

"Fenella, this is Brooke Blake," Breesha said. "Brooke, this is my friend, Fenella Woods."

"Yeah, great, but what happened?" Brooke asked. "I thought things were going really well when the curtains closed on the first act. Then someone started screaming and, well, the mood in the theater changed completely."

"You'll have to ask the police for an explanation," Fenella replied.

"What did you think of the show, then?" Brooke asked.

Fenella flushed. "It was different," she said after a moment.

Brooke nodded. "I think Dorothy did some incredible things with the storyline. The nonlinear plot was a real challenge for me, as an actor, but I believe it also allowed me to showcase some of my strengths as a performer."

"We all thought you were wonderful, Brooke," an older woman said in a sarcastic drawl. She had black hair that was streaked with grey, and she was wearing thickly applied stage makeup.

Brooke looked as if she'd been slapped.

"Fenella, this is Susan, Susan Lucas," Breesha said quickly. "Susan, my friend, Fenella."

"It's lovely to meet the island's richest woman," Susan said. "If you ever run out of things to spend your money on, a fund for poor actors who need work done would be much appreciated."

Brooke made a noise. "Faces are so much more expressive when they're natural," she said.

"That's easy to say when you're twenty-six," Susan told her. "I'm two decades older, and I'm not getting good parts any longer."

"I'm twenty-four," Brooke snapped. "And I truly believe that parts go to the most talented performers, regardless of age."

Susan laughed harshly. "It always helps when you're willing to sleep with the theater manager, the stage manager, the director, and every actor in the company," she said.

Brooke turned bright red. "I haven't, that is, I didn't..." she began.

"Ladies, let's not argue," another woman said. "Ms. Woods will be thinking that we don't like one another, and nothing could be further from the truth."

The woman looked to be in her mid-forties, with short brown hair and bright green eyes. Her face appeared to have just been scrubbed clean. She stepped between Susan and Brooke and then turned to Fenella.

"Ms. Woods, I'm Eileen Harris. I'm sure you understand that everyone is upset. Actors are, of necessity, very sensitive people. We were all upset by the screaming during the interval and, well, I suppose confused when everyone refused to tell us what was happening. It's very difficult to perform when one's mind is elsewhere."

"Especially in a play as complicated as this one," Brooke added.

Eileen glanced at her and then smiled as she looked back to Fenella. "This play has its own unique challenges. The plot is, well, complicated, let's say."

Fenella nodded. "It definitely seemed complicated."

"The question is, were you able to follow the story?" Susan asked.

"I'm sure Ms. Woods enjoyed the show very much," a familiar voice said.

Fenella smiled gratefully at Josh Bailey, who'd crossed the room to join them.

"Of course," she murmured.

"Any idea how much longer we'll be stuck in here?" he asked her.

She shook her head. "I just came down to congratulate Breesha on her performance."

"Of course, because Doncan Quayle is your advocate," he said. "I should have made the connection and realized that was why you were at the show. You don't typically come to live theater performances, do you?"

"I used to go to a lot of shows when I lived in Buffalo. I've missed it," she said honestly. "I'm going to have to start making more of an effort to get to shows on the island now that I'm settled here."

"Of course, you could fly to the West End to see shows whenever you want," Susan said.

"I'd rather support local theaters," Fenella replied.

"And our little community theater efforts, I hope," Josh said.

"Yes, of course," she agreed.

"But what's going on?" another voice interrupted.

Fenella smiled at Adam as he joined them.

"I can't tell you anything," she told him. "I just came to congratulate Breesha."

He looked surprised and then laughed. "I wish I'd had fans back when all I had was tiny parts. It took me years to build up my following. Of course, you'd never know I have fans tonight, as no one has been allowed to come back and congratulate me."

"Congratulations," Eileen said dryly. "You were amazing, as ever," she added while rolling her eyes at Fenella.

"I worked hard on my character," Adam told her. "A bit more support from the supporting cast would have been much appreciated."

"We all did our best with the drivel that we were required to perform," Susan said.

"Drivel?" Brooke repeated. "If you can't appreciate the beauty and magnificence in what Dorothy wrote, why are you even in the show?"

"We weren't given a script before we auditioned," Susan told her. "I thought we were going to be doing a real play."

"It is a real play," Brooke said crossly. "It's a genius retelling of every classic love story ever written."

Adam turned his laugh into a cough. "Brooke, my dear, I appreciate your unbridled enthusiasm, but even I, the star of the show, will admit that the play has some, um, difficulties."

"The second act didn't work tonight because we were all distracted," Brooke told him. "It will be much better tomorrow night."

"Unless someone gets arrested and we can't go on tomorrow," Susan suggested.

"Why would someone get arrested?" Brooke asked.

"Something happened in Box A tonight," Susan reminded her. "From the size of the police presence, I'm going to guess that someone was murdered."

"No offence to Ms. Woods, but she does make a habit of turning up at murder scenes," Josh said. "But as long as no one from the cast or crew is dead, the show will go on tomorrow."

"What if I'm arrested for murder?" Adam asked in a dramatic tone. "The show could not go on if I were unjustly incarcerated."

"I'm sure the police won't be unjustly arresting anyone," Josh told him.

"Of course we won't," Daniel said as he walked into the space.

"What happened?"

"Is someone dead?"

"Why are we all being kept here?"

Several people shouted questions at Daniel. He held up his hand. "Ladies and gentlemen, we greatly appreciate your patience. There's been an incident in the theater. No one has been injured in any way. We are dealing with criminal damage, though, which is a serious crime. We're going to need to speak to each of you in turn. We'll be working as quickly as we can, but we're going to need you to remain patient as you wait for your turn."

More people shouted questions, but Daniel simply shook his head. When the room was quiet again, he resumed speaking.

"I'll be sending for each of you, one at a time. Please wait here," he said.

A few people muttered under their breath, but no one spoke as Daniel turned and left the room.

"And now we wait," a voice said dramatically from one of the corners.

Fenella looked over as the large man got to his feet and strode into the center of the room.

"My dear thespians," he said in a booming voice. "Tonight has been a difficult and trying one for all of us. After our many months of rehearsals, struggling with a complicated and emotionally over-whelming script, we finally made it to the starting line. The place where the words on the page come to life and then take on a life of their own. Tonight we were to rediscover why we toil for hours and days and weeks and months and years to create, to produce, to craft a performance that transcends our pitiful existences and soars as something larger and something magnificent. Tonight, our opportunity to achieve this was cruelly snatched from our eager grasps."

Fenella looked at Breesha.

"Alfred, the director," she whispered.

He looked in their direction and frowned. "You all did your best tonight. I'm aware of that, and I believe that the audience was able to enjoy an above average performance, but we can and we must do better as we go forward. We can and we must learn to put tonight's distractions out of our minds. We can and we must rise above anything and everything that takes us out of our performance. The play is every-thing. Say that with me, please."

"The play is everything," a few people muttered.

"Again," Alfred demanded. "You must mean it. It must come from your very souls. The play is everything," he shouted.

"The play is everything," Brooke said passionately.

"Whatever," Susan muttered in a low voice.

"We cannot allow what happened tonight to derail us from presenting our show," Alfred told them. "I shall be informing that police person that he must speak to each of you quickly so that you can get adequate rest before tomorrow night's show. We will be having an extra rehearsal tomorrow at two o'clock. There are no acceptable excuses for not being there."

"Sorry, but I already have plans for tomorrow," Adam said.

"There are no acceptable excuses," Alfred replied. "Change them."

Adam stared at him for a moment and then laughed. "We're a community theater group. No one is getting paid for his or her time. We've all put hours and hours into this ridiculous play that doesn't even have a plot. If you think I'm giving up even one extra minute of my life to rehearse this nonsense any further, you're sadly mistaken."

"It's a wonderful play," Brooke said.

"And Adam can be replaced," Alfred said in a careless tone.

Adam laughed. "Good luck with that," he said. "Although I doubt you have anything to worry about, really. I can't see anyone coming to see any more of the shows, not after tonight. I had friends in the audi-ence. They all left during the interval because they had no idea what was happening — and they didn't care, either."

Alfred shook his head. "This play will be the talk of the island tomorrow. The significant police presence has made us big news. The rest of the performances will be sold out. I'd stake my reputation on that."

"Sadly, he's probably right," Breesha told Fenella in a whisper.

She nodded. "It almost seems as if he had a motive for what happened," she whispered back.

Breesha's eyes went wide. "He's slightly bonkers, but I don't think he'd do anything completely crazy."

Before Fenella could reply, a uniformed constable walked into the room. "Mr. Josh Bailey?" he asked.

Josh waved. "That's me," he said.

"Inspector Robinson would like to speak with you now."

Josh shrugged. "I feel so important," he said as he began to cross the room.

"Constable, you are a constable?" Alfred asked.

The man nodded.

"Constable, why is Mr. Bailey being questioned first?" was Alfred's next question.

"I'm sorry, but I've no idea. I was just told to go and find Mr. Bailey," the man replied.

Alfred sighed deeply. "I simply don't understand why I've not been questioned yet. I know the company better than anyone does, and I'm privy to so many secrets. The things I could tell the inspector — well, but I'll wait my turn, I suppose."

"I thought the point of secrets was keeping them," Susan drawled.

"Of course, darling, your secrets are safe with me," Alfred told her.

"As if I've told you any of my secrets," Susan replied.

Alfred chuckled. "But we'll talk together about all of this tomorrow," he said. "We'll work through a few exercises, talk about tonight's catastrophe, and then run the play from beginning to end. I'm certain we can improve everywhere. I took extensive notes tonight."

"Oh, terrific," Susan muttered.

"You'll be fine," Eileen told her. "You were very good tonight, even after the interval."

Susan gave her a small smile. "You may think so. I'm pretty sure Alfred doesn't agree."

"Eileen is right," Brooke said. "You were great tonight. I, well, I let myself get too distracted. I wasn't at my best."

"You were splendid," Adam told her. "I could sit and watch you read the telephone book, though."

Brooke flushed. "That's very kind of you, but I don't want to read the telephone book. I want to bring amazing stories to life. There are so many incredible playwrights working right now. I want to share all of their stories."

"I much prefer the classics," Eileen said. "And by classics, I mean anything written ten years ago or more. I'm not suggesting we should only be doing Shakespeare, but then again, there's a reason why his plays are still performed today."

"Because people think that his plays are inherently better than anything written since," Adam said. "People are wrong."

"What did actually happen in Box A?" Breesha asked Fenella in a whisper.

Fenella took Breesha's arm and they walked a short distance away from the others.

"I'm not entirely certain, but it looked as if someone put a mannequin or a dummy of some sort in the box and then arranged it to look as if a man had been murdered in there," she told her quietly.

"I heard that the woman who was screaming in the audience had blood all over her," Breesha said.

"Daniel said it was fake blood, but there was definitely a lot of it."

Breesha shuddered. "Why would anyone do that?"

"Daniel thinks someone was trying to disrupt the show."

"But why would anyone want to do that? I mean, I know this show isn't exactly great theater, but it's a community theater production put on by a bunch of enthusiastic amateurs. I can't imagine anyone wanting to stop us from performing."

"Maybe someone read the script," Fenella muttered.

Breesha laughed. "I kept hoping, at every rehearsal, that the story would finally start to come together once we'd rehearsed enough. Then I just about convinced myself that it would all make sense to the audience, even if I couldn't totally follow it. I'm going to guess I was wrong."

Fenella nodded. "I couldn't follow the story. I don't know why half of the characters were dead sometimes, and I don't even know if there was a happy ending or not."

"I don't know why half the characters are dead sometimes, either," Breesha confided. "The author, Dorothy Gilbert, came and talked to us about her vision, but I couldn't follow what she was saying any more than I could follow the script."

"Who selected the play?"

"It was selected by committee," Breesha replied. "Although I believe some of the committee members have more than one vote."

Daniel walked back into the room and looked around. "Alfred?" he asked.

"Yes?" the man replied.

"I'm afraid I didn't get your surname," Daniel told him.

"It's just Alfred. In homage, if you will, to one of the world's greatest directors. Of course, my humble efforts are nothing compared to his masterpieces, but at least I can share my name with the man who changed the world with his work."

Daniel nodded slowly. "I'm ready to speak to you now," he said.

"Excellent. Good night, darlings. I will see you all tomorrow afternoon. Remember, no excuses," Alfred said as he followed Daniel to the door. "And Adam, I really mean it," he added before he swept out of the room.

"He can't possibly replace me at this point," Adam said loudly.

"Do us all a favor and don't give him an excuse to try," Eileen suggested. "We've enough problems now without having a major cast change in between shows."

"He can't replace me now," Adam repeated. "No one else knows the part, and no one else can learn it by tomorrow night."

"I think Josh knows all of the parts," Susan told him. "He's been reading for everyone at rehearsals, and he hasn't been using his book for the last week or two."

"Yes, but Josh? He isn't an actor," Adam argued.

"Just show up to the damned rehearsal," Susan snapped. "We've only a few more weeks of this nightmare, and then we'll be done with *Three Gentlewomen from Bologna* — and maybe, just maybe, we'll be able to do some sort of proper play again."

"Gee, thanks," a voice said from the doorway.

Fenella looked over at the woman standing there. She appeared to be close to thirty, with long brown hair that was pulled back in a low ponytail. Her face was bare of makeup, and she was wearing thick glasses, jeans, and a sweatshirt advertising a West End show.

"Dorothy Gilbert," Breesha whispered.

❧ 3 ❧

"**D**orothy**,**" Brooke exclaimed. "I'm so sorry that I lost focus so badly in the second half. I never meant to dishonor your vision."

"Were you in the audience?" Adam asked.

Dorothy looked at him and then slowly shook her head. "I came, but I couldn't stay. It was, I mean, the more I thought about it, the more difficult it became. I simply couldn't stay and watch. Too many of my hopes and dreams and fears were tangled up in tonight's premiere. I had to go."

"So you missed the show and the accompanying drama," Susan said.

"I sat on the promenade and watched the theater doors. I thought, maybe, if it was terrible, that people would leave after the first act. And then, people did leave. Seventeen people left after the first act. I didn't know what to think. I couldn't stop crying. It wasn't until the police started going in that I began to realize that something else had happened," Dorothy told them.

"So you rushed back over here, just ninety minutes later?" Susan asked.

Dorothy flushed. "I rang Mr. Gilbert. I asked him what was happening. He told me that something was wrong in one of the boxes, but that the show was going on as planned. I, well, I wanted to come back, but he suggested that I stay away."

"I thought Mr. Gilbert was her father," Fenella whispered to Breesha.

"He is, but she always calls him Mr. Gilbert, at least at the theater."

"How odd," Fenella murmured.

"So your dad said to stay away," Susan said. "That's interesting."

"I can't imagine why," Dorothy replied.

"But you're here now," Brooke said, sounding confused.

"Mr. Gilbert rang me about half an hour ago and asked me to come. He said that the police want to speak with me," she replied. "I don't know why, though, as I wasn't even here during the performance."

"I'm sure the police will explain it all to you," Adam said. "If they ever get around to speaking with you, that is. We've all been waiting for hours."

Fenella glanced at her watch. Although it felt as if the evening had been dragging on for days, the show had finished less than an hour earlier.

"But you were saying something about the play," Dorothy said to Susan. "If you don't like the play, why didn't you say something earlier?"

"I took the part. It's my job to turn up and perform," Susan replied. "I don't have to enjoy the play to do my job."

Dorothy slowly looked around the room. When she looked at Fenella, she stopped her survey. "Ms. Woods, hello," she said. "We've not met, but of course I know who you are."

Fenella nodded. Of course everyone on the island knew who she was. Thanks to the *Isle of Man Times* and their tendency to run photographs of her every time she found another dead body, it seemed as if everyone on the island could recognize her as well.

"Were you in the audience tonight?" Dorothy asked.

Feeling like a deer caught in headlights, Fenella froze. "Um, I mean, yes, I was." she stammered out eventually.

"What did you think of the play?" was the dreaded next question. "Please, be honest. I know it's, well, different. I was trying to capture the uncertainty in our lives, the unique capacity we all have for both love and hate, and the unavoidable horror that is our inescapable destiny."

Fenella stared at her. "That's a lot to try to put into a single play," she said, casting a desperate glance at Breesha.

"But I had to try," Dorothy said earnestly. "I had to pour everything that I had into the story. I'm dying, you understand. This might be my only opportunity to share my talents with the world."

"I'm so sorry," Fenella said.

"You aren't dying," Adam said scornfully.

"I am, though," Dorothy told him.

He shook his head. "Don't feel sorry for her," he told Fenella. "She's not sick or anything, she simply means that she's getting closer to death every day, the same as the rest of us."

"Except my death will extinguish the flame of my creativity," Dorothy said. "Your death will simply be the end of a vain and selfish man."

Adam laughed. "You may be getting the impression that we don't care for one another," he told Fenella.

"I loathe him," Dorothy said flatly.

"Of course, there's a story behind the loathing," Susan said with a sly smile. "Our Dorothy didn't realize that Adam is incapable of being faithful. Maybe it's a trait common to actors. I've never known an actor who's been able to keep his trousers zipped throughout a run."

"I would be faithful to the right woman," Adam countered. "She simply wasn't the right woman."

"I did everything I could to be right for you," Dorothy argued. "You demanded too much."

"I didn't demand anything," he retorted. "And you're making this into a much bigger thing than it actually was, anyway. We went out three times, and we never even slept together."

"We went out four times," Dorothy shot back.

Adam held up a hand. "Dinner after the table read, one. Lunch before the first rehearsal, two. Drinks after some random rehearsal a few days later, three," he said, holding up his fingers as he counted.

Dorothy flushed. "We had dinner again the night after the drinks."

He frowned and then shook his head. "Several of us had dinner together that night. There were a dozen people there. We didn't even sit next to one another."

"Because you sat with Brooke, your next conquest," Dorothy snapped.

Brooke looked surprised and then laughed. "Don't drag me into this. I didn't know you and Adam had had a thing, and I didn't sleep with him that night, either."

"But you did sleep with him," Dorothy said softly.

Brooke shrugged. "It wasn't a big deal. We were supposed to be in love in the play. I find it easier to play love when I've been intimate with my costar. I just consider it method acting."

"I don't think that's what method acting is meant to be about," Susan said.

"If I'd known that you and Adam were together, I never would have slept with him," Brooke told Dorothy.

She shrugged. "You aren't supposed to be in love in the play, anyway. You're supposed to have been in love with him."

"I suppose it's a good thing we only slept together the once," Brooke laughed.

Dorothy sighed. "But, Ms. Woods, you were telling me what you thought of the show."

"It was complicated," Fenella replied. "I think I could see it another dozen times and still see things I hadn't seen before."

"Is that a good thing?" Dorothy asked.

I was hoping you'd think so, Fenella thought. "How long did it take you to write it?" she asked, hoping to change the subject.

"It took thirty-one years of life's most traumatic experiences to get me ready to write it," Dorothy told her. "And then, it took me no more than a few weeks to put the words on the page. Once I'd started writing, I couldn't stop. Words just flowed from my fingers into my laptop. I tried to rest, but I found that I could not. I didn't sleep, and I barely ate until the play was finished."

"That explains a lot," Susan muttered.

"Ah, you must be Ms. Gilbert," Daniel said as he walked up behind Dorothy. "Thank you for coming back to speak to me. If you could come with me, please?"

Dorothy looked around the room. "But everyone else has been waiting for hours," she said. "Surely you should speak to them first."

"I'm talking to people in the order that makes sense to me," he told her. "I'd appreciate it if you'd speak to me next."

"Of course," Dorothy whispered. She glanced at Adam and then turned and followed Daniel out of the room.

"She was in love with you," Brooke said as the pair disappeared.

"We only went out a few times," Adam replied. "It wasn't anything."

"I don't think she'd agree," Brooke said.

Adam shrugged. "It's hardly my fault if she thought we were having a relationship while I thought we were just having some fun."

"That probably happens a lot to you with women, doesn't it?" Susan asked.

"Not really," Adam said. "I rarely go out with a woman more than a few times."

"And then he sleeps with her and she loses interest," Brooke said with a laugh.

A few people chuckled as Adam's cheeks reddened.

"That's probably fair," he said eventually. "I hope you found Josh more to your liking."

Brooke frowned. "I'm not, that is, Josh and I aren't, there's nothing happening there."

"That isn't what Josh said," Adam told her.

"Let's talk about something more pleasant," Eileen suggested. "Ms. Woods, what did you think of the show tonight? Please be honest. We're all dying to know what the audience made of Dorothy's script."

"As I said to Dorothy, there was a lot happening," Fenella told her. "And then there was the disturbance in the box next to mine. I found it almost impossible to concentrate on the show after that."

"If you were in the next box, you must know what happened," Adam said. "Please, tell us what happened."

"I'm afraid I can't say anything," Fenella replied. "I really don't know exactly what happened, anyway."

Adam stared at her. "You're a terrible liar," he said. "You should take some of my acting classes. I could teach you to lie more convincingly."

"Thanks, but I prefer to tell the truth whenever possible," Fenella replied.

"We all know that you're engaged to Daniel Robinson. It looks as if he's in charge of the investigation," Susan said. "Did he send you down here to see what you could learn while he's questioning the others?"

Fenella shook her head. "I came down to congratulate Breesha on her performance tonight. I suspect Daniel would be a good deal happier if I'd done that and then gone straight home. He doesn't like it when I'm involved in his investigations."

"And yet, you continually find dead bodies," Susan said.

"Never intentionally," Fenella replied flatly.

Constable Corlett broke the awkward silence a short while later. "I'm looking for Adam Manning," he said from the doorway.

"Guilty," Adam said, laughing. "I hope that doesn't mean that I've just confessed to anything," he added as he crossed the room.

The constable left with Adam and then reappeared a moment later. This time the woman he wanted was someone Fenella hadn't met.

"She was the angel in act one," Breesha told her.

"There was an angel in act one?"

"In the blue and green dress."

"That was an angel?" Fenella thought for a minute. "I'm not sure if that makes things clearer or more confusing."

Breesha nodded. "That's how I feel about the whole play. I really should have warned you. I'm so sorry."

"I'm not. I'm glad we were here to find the mess in Box A. If we hadn't been here, the play probably would have been stopped after the first act."

"I'm not certain that would have been a bad thing," Breesha sighed.

As the room slowly cleared, Breesha and Fenella moved two chairs together into a quiet corner. They sat down together and watched as the cast and crew were taken in turn to speak to the police. When Brooke left the room, Breesha sighed.

"She can be very sweet, but she can be quite awful as well," she told Fenella.

"Really?"

"Adam is still upset that she ended things with him before he had a chance to end things with her," Breesha explained. "And no one seems to know for certain what's going on between her and Josh, but there's definitely something going on."

"And that makes her awful?"

Breesha shook her head. "I don't care what she's doing in her personal life, but I do care when it causes problems in rehearsals. A few weeks ago, she refused to work with Adam for a few days because of their issues, and last week she wouldn't let Josh work with her on staging because she was mad at him."

"My goodness."

"She always insists that she's an artist and she can't be forced to work when she's feeling unsettled or upset. At the end of the day, though, we have a show to put on, no matter how she's feeling."

"Is she very talented?"

"What did you think?"

Fenella made a face. "I'm not sure this was the best play for me to try to judge anyone's talent, except maybe that of the playwright."

"I'm going to guess that you don't think too highly of the playwright."

"I think the play needed at least a few more rounds of edits," Fenella said slowly. "There were some small sections that caught my attention, and if I could have made sense out of where they were meant to fit into the story, it might have been a brilliant show. As it was, though, it was something of a mess."

Breesha nodded. "As I said before, I kept thinking it was all going to come together once we'd rehearsed it a bit more, but it never did."

"Susan Lucas?" the constable in the doorway called.

"My turn in the spotlight," Susan said, tossing her head and striding to the door.

"Tell me about Susan," Fenella suggested to Breesha.

"She can seem hard, but she has a heart of gold. She simply doesn't want anyone to know it."

"I didn't suspect," Fenella said dryly.

Breesha nodded. "She's getting older and it bothers her to no end, but she's a good person. I've known her for years."

"And what about Eileen?" Fenella asked as a different constable escorted the woman from the room.

"She hasn't been involved with the company for very long. I believe this is only her third or fourth show with us. She's very pleasant, and I've never heard her say anything bad about anyone, but I've never warmed to her."

The room was nearly empty now, aside from a pair of constables at the door and two men who were standing together on the wall opposite from where Fenella and Breesha were sitting.

"Who are they?" Fenella asked, nodding toward the men.

"They work for the theater itself. Harry has a team of five who handle everything from ticket sales to set construction. Those two are part of the construction crew, although they do a number of other jobs as well, including making certain that the theater is ready to open on time each evening."

"And did it open on time tonight?" Fenella asked.

Breesha shrugged. "I believe we were a few minutes late tonight." She looked around the room and then leaned closer to Fenella. "We had a small issue just before we were due to open."

"What happened?"

Breesha sighed. "I told Josh that he should ring the police, but he wouldn't hear of it. I don't think he'd have even mentioned it to me, if I hadn't been there."

"You don't have to tell me anything, but please tell Daniel what you're talking about."

"Oh, I'm going to tell you everything," Breesha said with a laugh. "We received a threatening letter."

"A threatening letter? To the theater or to the company? What did it say?"

"A threatening letter addressed to Josh. It was posted to the theater, and Harry handed it to him when he and I arrived this afternoon."

"You arrived together?"

"Only coincidentally. I walked over from my flat and just happened to reach the building as Josh was parking on the promenade. He shouted 'hello,' so I waited and walked inside with him."

"And then what happened?" Fenella asked as Breesha paused while one of the two theater employees was taken away.

"We stopped by the office to check on ticket sales. Harry had a pile of post for Josh."

"Was that unusual?"

"Not really. Josh gets all sorts of things posted to him. Unsolicited scripts from aspiring playwrights mostly, although he does get the odd bit of fan mail for one of the actors or for the entire company."

"How nice."

"It is nice," Breesha agreed. "But this was different. Josh flipped through the pile of letters and then swore under his breath. When I asked him what was wrong, he said that he'd been getting some rather unpleasant letters lately. Of course, I insisted that he open the letter and show it to me."

"And what did it say?"

"It was incredibly odd. It said something about *Three Gentlewomen from Bologna* being a terrible play, and that the company should be performing plays by the great Forrest Luna instead. Then it said that if we proceeded with our plans to perform Dorothy Gilbert's horrible story, that we would be sorry."

"Someone doesn't like Dorothy or her play."

"That's what Josh and I both assumed. I'm afraid that neither of us took the letter terribly seriously, not even after Josh admitted that he'd had other letters in the past."

"How many other letters?"

"He reckoned he'd had about one a week since we'd started casting the show. Because he doesn't collect the post on any sort of schedule, he couldn't be certain how often the letters actually arrived, but he felt as if they'd been coming weekly."

"And were they all the same?"

"More or less. Basically, they all complained about the current show, and they all mentioned Forrest Luna as a better alternative. He said they were all vaguely threatening as well."

"Who is Forrest Luna?" Fenella had to ask.

Breesha smiled at her. "He's another local playwright, actually. We have performed some of his plays in the past, but it's been a few years since the last one. They're much more traditional than the current show, and they've always done well for us, but Harry wanted us to try something completely different."

"Something his daughter wrote."

"To be fair, Harry has been asking us to do something different for years. He was thrilled when Josh took over. Our previous stage manager would never have considered anything like *Three Gentlewomen from Bologna*."

"How long has Josh been the stage manager for the company, then?"

"He's been here for a few years. When he first took over, he did everything he could to keep things the same while we adjusted to his management style. He isn't just the stage manager during shows, of course, he's also the manager of the entire company. It wasn't until he'd been with us for, I don't know, eighteen months, maybe, that he started talking about doing something different."

"What made him pick *Three Gentlewomen from Bologna* as the first different play?"

"Actually, it wasn't the first. Our last play, *Twinges*, was also quite unlike anything we'd ever done before."

"*Twinges?*"

"It was a series of short plays with an overarching structure around them. We'd never done anything similar, and it was quite a challenge to put together. Adam played five different roles and Brooke had three. Just getting Adam through multiple changes of clothes was a job unto itself."

"So after *Twinges*, Josh decided to do something even more unusual?"

"We were going to do Romeo and Juliet. It had been announced, and we'd put out a casting call and then Josh rang me and said that he'd changed his mind."

"Interesting."

Breesha nodded. "I'm certain that Harry was behind it all. Regardless, I didn't argue. I just love being a part of the theater world. I don't really care what show we do. You know I don't typically take an acting role, anyway. It wasn't until I read the script for *Three Gentlewomen from Bologna* that I started to question Josh's decision."

"And not long after he'd made that change, he started getting threatening letters?"

"That's what he told me tonight, anyway. He told me that he hadn't kept any of them, and he would have thrown away tonight's letter, too, if I'd have let him."

"Do you think that Forrest Luna is behind the threats?"

"I barely know the man, but I doubt it. As I understand it, he's very popular in Australia. Someone told me that at least one of his plays has been performed there every night since some time in the nineteen-sixties. I don't know if that's true, but I believe he's done very well there, regardless. I can't see why he'd care if we did one of his shows or not."

"Presumably, he gets paid when his shows are performed."

"Yes, but it isn't a lot of money. From what I've heard, he's incredibly wealthy. A few of his plays have been made into movies, and I believe he was paid handsomely for those."

"Who else would want to promote his plays?"

Breesha shrugged. "I think that's one of the reasons why Josh and I didn't really take the letters seriously. It's such an odd thing to demand. Neither of us could imagine why anyone would make such a threat."

"Unless someone was simply very unhappy with *Three Gentlewomen from Bologna* and just picked another playwright at random to suggest as an alternate."

"That's possible. I don't think anyone in the company is very happy about *Three Gentlewomen from Bologna*."

"In that case, why are you doing it?"

Breesha sighed. "I asked Josh that months ago, after the first few rehearsals. Believe it or not, it was even worse back then, and I didn't think it was ever going to come together. I suggested to Josh that we should give up on *Three Gentlewomen from Bologna* and start over with something else, but he wouldn't hear of it. He said we'd already put too much time and effort into the show and that we had to keep going."

"Was he right about the time and effort?"

"Yes and no. I made a point of speaking to him when we were only a few weeks into the rehearsal process, long before we'd started working on staging and sets. About ten years ago, under the previous management, we'd switched plays at a similar point, but, as I said, that was under the previous management. Josh listened very politely to my argument and then told me 'no' very firmly."

"Surely he could see what a mess the play was, too."

"He told me that we'd make it work. At the time, I wondered if he and Harry had come to some sort of agreement, seeing that Harry's daughter had written the show."

"What sort of agreement?"

Breesha shrugged. "We're all volunteers, everyone in the company. When we put on a show at the Gaiety, we get a share of the box office takings, and we use that money to pay for sets and costumes and what-not. The Gaiety gets the bulk of the money, of course, but I did wonder if maybe Harry had offered Josh a higher percentage of the box office if we did Dorothy's show."

"And that would have tempted Josh because you needed more money for sets and costumes?"

"That would have temped Josh because he's been trying to convince everyone in the company that his job should be a paid position," Breesha explained. "He does put in a lot of hours, managing the company, but he keeps insisting that he could do a lot more if he could quit his day job and simply manage the company on a full-time basis."

"What does he do for a day job?"

"He works for one of the insurance companies. I forget which one."

"Who gets to decide whether he gets paid or not?"

"Every member of the company would get a vote in that sort of decision. We all have to rejoin every year, but anyone can join, even if they don't plan to take part in our shows."

"I assume it costs something to join?"

"The princely sum of ten pounds per year."

Fenella laughed. "I'm surprised that Josh hasn't persuaded a bunch of his friends to join, just to get them to vote in favor of his being paid."

"Don't say that too loudly or you might give him ideas," Breesha told her with a smile.

"Do you think he should get paid?"

"I don't know," Breesha said with a frown. "The theater world has changed quite a lot since I first started with the company around thirty years ago. Back then, we were strictly amateurs with the idea of putting on a few shows a year and having some fun while doing so. Today, many actors use community theater as a stepping stone to something bigger, and some take breaks from successful careers to step back and do shows with small companies all over the world. Social media has changed the way we operate as well. Josh's job is a good deal more complicated than it used to be, even ten years ago. But, having said all of that, it's important to me that everyone involved in the company is there simply because we all love theater and we want to be a part of it. We're all giving up hours and hours of our time to put on a show, and I can't help but feel as if that should include everyone from Josh down."

A moment later, Daniel walked into the room. "Sorry to keep you waiting, Breesha," he said.

"What about me?" Fenella demanded, smiling at the man to make sure he understood that she was teasing.

He crossed to her and pulled her to her feet. The kiss made her forget everything for a moment. "I'm sorry that you had to wait, too," he whispered in her ear when the kiss was over.

"I suppose I could have left, if I'd wanted to," she replied.

"Indeed. Breesha, I left you for last because I started with Josh. He shared his thoughts on everyone in the company, and now that I've had a chance to meet them all, I'm interested in hearing your thoughts," Daniel said.

Breesha nodded. "I've known some of these people for decades. It's hard for me to imagine why anyone would deliberately attempt to sabotage our show."

"Come back with me and we'll talk," Daniel told her. "Fen, you go home and get some sleep. It's nearly midnight. Katie will be missing you."

She nodded. "Had you ever heard of Forrest Luna before tonight?" she asked Daniel as they all walked toward the door.

"Forrest Luna?" he repeated. "I've never heard of him before right now."

Fenella and Breesha exchanged glances.

"Josh didn't mention the letters?" Breesha asked.

Daniel frowned. "Letters?"

"Josh has been getting threatening letters," Breesha told him. "The letters said that we'd be sorry if we insisted on performing *Three Gentlewomen from Bologna* instead of doing a play by Forrest Luna."

"Tell me about Forrest Luna," Daniel said.

"I can't tell you much," Breesha replied. "He's a local playwright, but he's much more popular in Australia than he is here. I believe he's made quite a lot of money from his work there, but as far as I know, he lives quite modestly somewhere in Castletown."

"But he seems to have at least one devoted fan on the island," Fenella interjected. "One who is prepared to send threatening letters on his behalf."

"And one that Josh failed to mention when he spoke to me," Daniel said with a sigh.

He pulled out his mobile and punched in a number. "Bring Josh Bailey into the station for questioning, please," he said when someone answered. "I'll be at the station within the hour."

Breesha frowned. "I didn't mean to get anyone into any trouble."

"He wouldn't be in any trouble if he'd told me about the threatening letters when I questioned him," Daniel replied.

They walked through the building to the front foyer. "I'm going to have a constable walk you home," Daniel told Fenella. "Technically, I still need your statement, but that can wait for tomorrow, unless you learned anything else in the last few hours that might be important."

She thought for a moment. "I learned a lot about the different men and women involved in the theater company, but I don't have any idea if any of it matters. The threatening letters seem like the most important thing."

He nodded and then pulled her into a quick embrace. "I'll ring you in the morning. I'll probably come to your flat to get your statement."

"I'll look forward to it," she whispered before he turned and walked away with Breesha.

"Ms. Woods?" a uniformed constable said. "Inspector Robinson asked me to walk you home."

She was too tired to argue, so she let the man walk her back to her building. As they walked into the foyer, she stopped. "I'll be fine from here," she told him. "Thank you."

He hesitated and then nodded before turning around and leaving.

Fenella took the elevator to the sixth floor and then dug out her keycard. Katie and Mona were sitting together in front of the windows. Katie jumped down and ran into the bedroom while Mona frowned at her.

"Don't tell me someone was murdered at the show," she said.

4

"**N**o one was murdered," Fenella told her.

Mona looked somewhat disappointed. "There were police cars outside the theater."

"Someone put a dummy or a mannequin in the box next to mine and set it up to look as if he'd been murdered."

"Why would someone do that?"

"That's a great question. I suspect that once the police work that out, they'll find whoever did it."

"You're tired and grumpy," Mona told her.

"It's after midnight, which is late for me. And I've had a very long evening as well. I'm going to bed."

"But how was the show? Knowing Breesha, she was splendid."

Fenella stopped and tried to think of the best way to reply. "The show was rather terrible, but Breesha was very good."

"Terrible? In what way?"

"It was written by the theater manager's daughter, and I think it needs more work."

"What was it about?"

"That's a good question. Ostensibly, it was about three women from Bologna, but it seemed to be about a couple instead, a couple from Birmingham, actually."

"Perhaps '*One Couple from Birmingham*' wasn't as interesting a title."

"And perhaps I'm simply confused as to what the play was about. I'll admit that I didn't follow large sections of it."

"What was Breesha's part?"

"According to the program, she was Carolyn Turner, but her name never came up in the play. She only appeared in the final act, where she walked out, said her line, and then walked back off the stage."

"Was it a good line?"

"She said 'Tuesdays and Thursdays are often best,' and then walked off."

"I suppose I'd understand the line if I'd seen the play."

"I saw the play and I didn't understand the line," Fenella told her. "The couple on the stage were talking about vegetables while the ghost in the corner was whispering something about holidays in the Lake District. There was a man dressed all in black on the other side of the stage. I'm not sure if he was supposed to represent death or not, but he kept leering at the audience and randomly shouting out names."

"Names?"

"Yes, just first names. He'd stare out at the crowd and then shout 'Betty' and then go back to staring."

"I'm confused."

"You're confused? I'm the one who actually sat through the show. I had no idea what was going on the entire time."

"So someone in the company set up a stage dummy to look like a dead man in order to stop the play," Mona suggested.

"Quite possibly, although the theater company has been getting threatening letters, too."

"Threatening letters? Tell me more."

Fenella told her what Breesha had said about the letters.

"Forrest Luna, there's a name I haven't heard in years," Mona said.

"You knew him?"

"Of course I knew him. He was the island's most famous playwright in the sixties. Very few people on the island actually appreciated him, but Max and I thought he was very talented."

Maxwell Martin was the very wealthy man who'd showered Mona with gifts during their long relationship. She'd met him when she'd been only eighteen, and over their decades together he'd given her everything from property to jewelry to cars.

"Tell me all about Forrest, then." Fenella said.

Mona gave her an enigmatic smile. "I never truly looked at another man once I'd fallen in love with Max," she said. "But Forrest was incredibly special. If I had ever been going to cheat on Max, it would have been with him."

"How old is he?"

"Oh, he's probably in his seventies now. He was younger than I was, yes, but he had an old soul. He was wise beyond his years, and we had a very special relationship — one that I cherished until my death."

"And how did he feel about you?"

"He adored me, of course. He pined after me for years, and he wrote a brilliant play about me as well. When I couldn't return his affection, he moved to Australia, which turned out to be a brilliant career move for him, even though he didn't stay for long."

"Breesha said he is very popular in Australia."

"He's huge in Australia. At least one of his plays is being performed every night somewhere in the country. His shows have been performed everywhere, by everything from the best professional companies to tiny community theater groups. Several of his plays were made into movies there as well. He made a fortune several times over in the four or five years he lived there, and he continues to receive huge royalty checks every month, even now."

"Did he ever marry?"

"He did, to an Australian woman. They had three children in five years before he came back to the island."

"What about his wife and the children?"

"They came back with him. She took one look around the island and then got on the next flight back to Sydney."

"Oh dear."

"Forrest didn't mind, really. He missed his children, but not her. At least that's what he told me. He used to visit the children at least twice a year, and once they were old enough, they used to come to visit him here. They're all scattered around the world now. I believe his wife is still alive and still in Sydney."

"Maybe she's here and doing what she can to encourage theater companies to perform Forrest's work."

"Maybe. As far as I know, they're still married. I know Forrest used to send her a huge amount of money each month. Maybe she's doing what she can to help him earn more."

"Do you really think that's possible?"

"My dear, anything is possible, but I think it's unlikely. She was of a similar age to Forrest. I suspect she's very happily settled in Sydney with no interest in traveling here."

Fenella yawned. "I'm too tired to think anymore," she said. "I'm going to bed."

"Perhaps I shall have to visit the Gaiety while you're sleeping," Mona said thoughtfully. "At least one of the ghosts must have seen something, although none of them may be willing to speak to me."

Fenella thought about questioning Mona's words, but she knew that she couldn't trust anything her aunt said about the spirit world. It seemed simpler to just go to bed.

"Have fun," she said, struggling to speak around another yawn.

"I always do," Mona told her before she slowly faded away.

Katie was already curled up in the exact center of the large bed in the master bedroom. Fenella got ready for bed as quickly as she could and crawled under the covers carefully.

"Good night," she whispered to the animal.

Katie replied with a tired "mewww" and then they both slept.

When Katie began to tap on her nose the next morning, Fenella groaned. "It can't be seven," she insisted, squinting at the clock.

It was exactly seven. "I should have asked you to let me sleep until eight," she told Katie as she struggled out of bed.

In the kitchen, she got Katie her breakfast and then started a pot of coffee brewing. While part of her wanted to simply stand and watch the coffee slowly dripping into the pot, she forced herself to take a shower and get dressed before pouring her first cup.

"That was worth the wait," she told Katie after a sip. "Coffee is nothing short of miraculous."

Katie shrugged and went back to chasing a large dust bunny that she'd found somewhere.

"I suppose I do need to clean better," Fenella muttered as the dust bunny floated across the room with Katie in hot pursuit.

"The flat was immaculate when you moved in," Mona said as she appeared behind the kitchen counter.

Fenella jumped, spilling the cereal that she had been pouring into a bowl all over the floor.

Mona sighed. "I really must find a way to warn you that I've arrived," she said. "What's your favorite bird?"

"My favorite bird?" Fenella asked as found the dustpan and broom.

"Yes, your favorite bird, or rather, your favorite birdsong. I'll get a small bird to sing something as a warning that I've arrived."

"I don't know much about birdsong."

"Then I shall select something appropriate," Mona told her. "How are you today? You look exhausted."

"I am exhausted. I should have asked Katie to wait to wake me until eight."

"But then Daniel would have woken you, just about now," Mona told her before she vanished in a puff of smoke. The smoke was still clearing when Fenella heard the knock on her door.

"Good morning," Daniel said, pulling her into his arms. "I hope this isn't too early. I assumed that Katie would wake you on schedule."

"She did, but even if she hadn't, you'd be more than welcome," Fenella replied.

"I wish I could stay, but I need to get your statement and then I need to get into the station. I've piles of paperwork to get through from last night."

"Even though no one died?"

"It was still criminal damage. Harry Gilbert reckons it's going to cost thousands of pounds to replace the carpeting and several of the chairs in that box. Apparently fake blood stains even more badly than real blood."

"Oh dear. It wasn't just a harmless prank, then."

"Not at all, although it may have been meant as one. It seems obvious that someone was trying to get the show stopped, though, and that isn't at all harmless."

"I hope Josh told you everything about the threatening letters," Fenella said, trying not to ask any questions. Daniel wouldn't be able to answer them, and she didn't like putting him in an awkward position.

He shrugged. "Let's get your statement done. I really need to get to the station."

She poured him a cup of coffee and made him some toast while they talked. He took careful notes, even though he'd been with her for most of the evening. When she started talking about the time she'd spent backstage with Breesha, he had her sit down and really focus on what she was telling him.

"And then I came home and went to bed," she concluded, leaving out her conversation with Mona. Although she loved Daniel, she wasn't quite ready to tell him about the ghost in her apartment just yet.

He nodded. "I'll get this typed up and you can sign it later today. Maybe we'll be able to have dinner together, if nothing else happens between now and six o'clock."

"I'd love to have dinner with you. Let's go to that little Italian place," Fenella suggested.

"That sounds good. I'll ring you if I can't make it. Otherwise, I'll be here before six."

She walked him to the door. "Love you," she whispered after the kiss.

"Love you, too," he replied.

As she started to push the door shut, Shelly's door opened.

"Hello," she said to Daniel.

"Hello," he replied. "I'm late for work," he added as he walked down the corridor.

"What happened after Tim and I left last night?" Shelly asked as she watched Daniel board the elevator.

"I talked to Breesha for an hour or two while Daniel questioned everyone about the mess in Box A," Fenella told her. "Then I came home while Daniel went into the station to do some more questioning."

Shelly frowned. "It was a long night for Daniel, then."

"And he was here at seven thirty to take my statement from last night," Fenella sighed. "He works far too hard."

"I was just coming to see if you want to go for a walk. Tim and I had another round of drinks after the show last night, and I feel as if I need to walk for hours to atone."

Fenella laughed. "I'd love to go for a walk. Come in while I find some shoes."

A few minutes later, the pair was walking at a brisk pace along the promenade. There was a single police car parked in front of the Gaiety Theatre.

"I suppose, if someone had been murdered, there would be quite a few more policemen there this morning," Shelly said.

Fenella nodded. "And there would be no chance of me having dinner with Daniel tonight."

"Someone staging a fake murder is odd, though," Shelly said thoughtfully. "Tim and I talked for hours last night, trying to work out why anyone would do such a thing."

Of course, Fenella couldn't say anything to Shelly about the threatening letters. "Everything about last night was odd," she said after a moment.

"Tim did suggest that the whole thing was meant to be part of the show," Shelly told her. "That makes as much sense as anything, really."

"Actually, now that you've mentioned it, it sort of does make sense. Maybe the man who was sobbing in the corner was mourning for the man in Box A."

"Or maybe the woman in the first act who kept shouting 'Stanley' for no obvious reason, was looking for the man in Box A."

Fenella laughed. "I think, if it were meant to be part of the show, that Harry and Josh would have said something last night when we first discovered the, um, mess."

"I wish they would have. Maybe whatever happened in Box A would have tied together the entire plot."

"I doubt it. There were a lot more plot holes than one dead man could explain."

Shelly laughed. "I really want to sit down with the playwright and ask her what she thought she was doing."

"I met her last night. I'm not sure I can remember her exact words, but she told me that she was trying to capture the uncertainty of our lives, the capacity we have for love and hate, and the horror of our destiny or some such thing."

Shelly stared at her for a moment. "That doesn't help," she said eventually.

"I didn't think so, either."

They walked to the end of the promenade and then turned toward home.

"I want to get a local paper," Shelly said as they approached a small row of shops.

"It's far too soon to them to have anything about what happened last night, isn't it?" Fenella asked. "Not that what happened last night is all that newsworthy, anyway."

"I'm going to guess that Dan Ross wouldn't agree with that," Shelly said, nodding toward the board outside the shop door. It had the day's newspaper headline written across it.

"'Terror at the Theater'" Fenella read out. "'Local theater companies threatened by mystery Forrest Luna fan.'"

"What does that mean?" Shelly asked.

"Let's see what the paper has to say," Fenella suggested. She grabbed the local paper and a bar of chocolate and then paid for both. She and Shelly walked as quickly as they could back to Fenella's apartment.

Shelly had purchased her own copy of the paper, so they sat down together to read the headline article.

"Dan Ross is very excited, anyway," Fenella said after she'd skimmed the article.

"I don't blame him. He's managed to break real news, maybe for the first time ever," Shelly replied.

"Only because someone handed him the story on a plate. It isn't as if he did any investigative journalism."

"So, according to the article, someone wants our local theaters to properly appreciate Forrest Luna's plays. He or she has written to Dan, letting him know that every performance of anything other than one of Forrest's masterpieces will be disrupted in some way. I do think whoever it is could have notified the theaters or the performers before last night's attempt to interrupt *Three Gentlewomen from Bologna*."

Fenella shrugged. "Maybe he or she sent letters to the theater company as well," she suggested.

Shelly gave her a suspicious look. "You know something, don't you?"

"Breesha told me that Josh Bailey, the stage manager, received a threatening letter. From what I'm reading here, it was much the same as the letter that Dan received. Josh didn't take the threat serious, but clearly he should have."

"It's been years since I've seen a Forrest Luna play, but they are all excellent stories," Shelly said. She shrugged. "They're all considerably better than *Three Gentlewomen from Bologna*, anyway."

"That isn't saying much," Fenella muttered.

Shelly nodded. "So Forrest Luna's biggest fan sent threatening letters to the theater company and also sent one to Dan Ross. I'm going to guess that he or she was disappointed last night when the show went on in spite of the issues in the box next to ours."

"I would assume so. I wonder when Dan got his letter."

"That's an interesting question. If he got it before last night's curtain went up, he should have been at the theater, waiting to see what was going to happen."

Fenella read through the article more slowly. "Ah, I missed this the first time," she said. "He says that he went to the theater last night when he learned that the police had been called. While he was trying to find out what was happening inside the theater, someone left an envelope on his windshield. The letter inside explained about the campaign to get Forrest Luna's plays performed."

"Dan doesn't say why the letter writer wants to see Forrest's plays."

"He does say that more will be revealed in tomorrow's paper. Let's hope the letter writer said something that will give away his or her identity."

"When is the next performance of *Three Gentlewomen from Bologna*?"

"They're supposed to be performing tonight, but I don't know if the show will go on or not. In light of what Dan's written, I can see Daniel suggesting that they cancel tonight's performance."

"Poor Breesha."

"I'm not sure she'll mind. I don't know that anyone will mind, aside from Dorothy Gilbert. No one else seemed all that impressed with the show."

"Presumably her father enjoyed it, but let's talk about Forrest's fan. I can't imagine deliberately sabotaging a show just because I preferred a different playwright."

"It seems rather odd."

"There must be more to it than just a desire to see Forrest's plays performed."

"Maybe, but what?"

Shelly frowned. "Maybe someone just hated *Three Gentlewomen from Bologna* and wanted to interrupt it. Maybe the Forrest Luna thing is just a made-up excuse."

"It's an odd excuse."

"I should ring Forrest and ask him what he thinks."

Fenella stared at her friend. "You know Forrest Luna?"

Shelly shrugged. "He used to come and talk to my classes about creative writing. We became something like friends over the years. He's charming and kind and very handsome. He's also very clever and very funny. Have you ever seen one of his plays?"

"I'd never even heard of him before last night."

"So he's not big in America, then."

"I guess not, although I didn't go to a lot of community theater shows back home. When I went to the theater, I usually went to see touring Broadway shows. It's entirely possible that some theater group in Buffalo does Forrest Luna plays every single year and I simply never noticed."

"He's huge in Australia. He used to be popular on the island, too, but it's been years since any local theater company did one of his shows. John and I used to go and see his plays whenever we could, mostly to support Forrest. He always went to see his own shows. We used to go with him, sometimes. He'd always have someone else buy the tickets so that no one would know he was in the audience."

"Did he wear a disguise as well?"

"No, but he was rarely photographed, and he was hardly ever recognized. He'd watch the show, and then he'd go home and write a long letter to the director with all of his notes on the performances."

"I'll bet directors just loved that," Fenella said sarcastically.

"They did, actually, because he was always very carefully complimentary. We saw more than one badly done version of his stories, and he still managed to find nice things to say about the actors or about the set or something. He used to let me read the letters before he sent them. I told him once, after one particularly bad performance, that I couldn't believe he'd been able to find so many nice things to say. He laughed and reminded me that he wrote fiction for a living."

Fenella smiled. "When did you see him last?"

Shelly frowned. "It's been years now. He sent flowers and a card when John died, but he didn't come to the funeral. He retired about ten years ago, and he's become something of a recluse since then, I believe."

"It might be interesting to hear what he has to say about all of this. Apparently, Dan got a firm 'no comment' from him."

"That isn't surprising. No one wants to talk to Dan Ross."

"Who would benefit from having Forrest's shows performed?" Fenella asked. "I assume he gets paid when a company does one of his shows."

"He does, but I don't think it's a lot of money. Forrest made his fortune from movie options. A lot of times, he'd sell the option, and then the movie would never get made, and he'd be able to sell the option again a few years later."

"But some of his plays were made into movies?"

"Yes, although I saw a couple of them, and they were nothing like the plays upon which they were supposedly based."

"Were the movies released everywhere?"

Shelly shook her head. "Forrest had private showings on the island for two or three of the movies when they first came out in Australia. I don't think they were ever released anywhere other than Australia, aside from a single showing on the island for Forrest's benefit. I could be wrong, though."

"Maybe someone saw one of his movies and became obsessed," Fenella said thoughtfully.

"Someone is definitely obsessed, unless, as you said, it's all just an excuse to shut down *Three Gentlewomen from Bologna*."

"No one I met last night was Australian."

"Do you think the letter writer is in the show, then?"

"In the show or works for the theater," Fenella replied. "Someone set up the mess in Box A before the theater opened for the evening. I can't imagine them setting all of that up once we were in our box."

Shelly nodded. "I hadn't thought about that. We would have noticed if someone was moving around in the box next to ours. I tried to peek into the boxes on either side of us, actually. Both of the boxes were dark."

"You tried to peek?"

Shelly flushed. "I was just curious who else had booked a box for the show."

"And apparently, no one had."

"Did you specifically book Box B?" Shelly asked.

"Not at all. When I rang, I asked about ticket prices and box prices and then I requested a box. They didn't say anything about which box we would be in until we arrived last night."

"I wonder why they didn't put us in Box A."

"That's a very good question. If they had, we probably would have found the, um, mess before the show even started."

"I wonder if the person who set it all up was expecting it to be found before the show."

"Daniel reckoned that he or she used so much fake blood so that it would drip on someone underneath the box, and that person would raise the alarm," Fenella told her. "But it almost makes more sense that they were hoping the body would be found before the show started."

"If I had a part in *Three Gentlewomen from Bologna*, I'd want the show stopped before it started."

Fenella laughed. "I'd have quit long before opening night."

A knock on the door made both women jump.

"Daniel, hello," Fenella said. "Shelly's here," she added quickly as he pulled her close.

He frowned and then kissed her gently. "Hello," he whispered. "That was going to be a rather more friendly greeting."

She laughed. "Later."

He nodded. "Hello, Shelly," he said as he walked into the living room.

"Hello. Please tell me that you've discovered who's behind the weird letters and the incident at the theater last night."

Daniel shook his head. "I wish we had, but we've only just begun our investigation. Right now, there are a huge number of suspects."

"Everyone in the theater company," Fenella guessed. "And everyone who works for the Gaiety."

Daniel nodded. "The doors were all locked until an hour before the curtain was due to go up. We're fairly certain the scene in Box A was set up before the doors were opened to the general public. While that gives us a long list of suspects, it would be a lot worse if we thought someone from the audience could have been behind it all."

"Surely it can't be that difficult to work out who's obsessed with Forrest Luna," Shelly said.

"Of course, it's entirely possible that whoever was behind what happened has some other motive altogether and is simply trying to divert attention from his or her true motive."

"Do you think that someone just wanted to get *Three Gentlewomen from Bologna* shut down?" Shelly asked.

"That's one possibility," Daniel replied. "If that was the true motive, he or she will be happy tonight. We've asked the Gaiety and the theater company to cancel tonight's performance."

"Why? Fenella asked.

"We're still processing the crime scene," he told her. "And, thanks to the various letters, we've every reason to believe that there could be another incident if tonight's performance is allowed to go ahead. After a lengthy discussion with Josh and Harry, we all agreed that it would be best if tonight's performance was canceled."

"The cast must be disappointed," Shelly said.

Daniel shrugged. "Last night's performance wasn't particularly well received. Josh told me that he felt that the company could use an extra day of rehearsals before they have to perform again. Apparently, ticket sales have been, um, slower than they'd hoped, so they're simply letting people use tonight's tickets for any other performance they would like to attend. They may have to move a few people to different seats, but apparently they have plenty of empty seats."

"That's unfortunate."

"Josh told me that he's really hoping that people use their tickets for other shows and don't request refunds. I gather the play's review in today's paper has led to some requests for refunds for other performances already," Daniel said.

"There's a review in today's paper?" Fenella asked, flipping through the paper she'd left on the table.

"'I should get paid double for having to sit through that nightmare,'" she read out the headline.

"Ouch," Shelly said.

"'*Three Gentlewomen from Bologna* was a lukewarm mess of tropes, tripe, and tired old clichés,'" Fenella read. "'Never have I ever spent a less enjoyable evening at the theater. While I always applaud new playwrights for putting in the hard work necessary to produce a play, in this case, that applause is tempered by the reality that this particular play was unfinished at best.'" She stopped and skimmed the rest of the review.

"Does the critic have anything good to say?" Shelly asked.

Fenella shrugged. "He says that Brooke looked lovely and that Adam managed to be audible, which isn't always the case, apparently."

"Dorothy will be devastated," Shelly said.

"Indeed. I almost feel sorry for her," Fenella replied.

"Only almost?" Shelly asked.

Fenella shrugged. "Even though the review is harsh, I think it's entirely fair and justified. The play was a mess."

Shelly nodded. "I can't imagine that an extra rehearsal tonight will help."

"It may not make any difference, but it will give me a break," Daniel said.

"What do you mean?" Fenella asked.

"When they reopen on Sunday, I'm going to have to go to the show again," he told her. "There's going to be a substantial police presence at every performance of *Three Gentlewomen from Bologna* for the rest of its run."

"I'll come with you, if you want company," Fenella told him.

"That's love," Shelly laughed. "I don't think I love Tim enough to go and see that play again."

Daniel chuckled. "We'll see. I may sit in the foyer during the show for at least some of the performances. For tonight, though, I'm going to see Shakespeare."

"You are?" Fenella asked.

"A theater group in Ramsey is performing *A Midsummer Night's Dream* tonight. The Chief Constable wants me and a few constables in the audience," he told her.

"Do you want company tonight?" Fenella wondered.

"If you'd like to see the show, you're more than welcome to join me," he replied. "We aren't expecting any trouble. We're fairly certain that *Three Gentlewomen from Bologna* is the target of our mystery letter writer."

"No one in Ramsey has been getting threatening letters?" Shelly asked.

"Mark is up in Ramsey right now, asking that very question," Daniel told her. "No one has reported anything to the police there, though. I'd like to think that most people would ring the police if they received a threatening letter."

Mark Hammersmith was another Douglas CID inspector, one who often worked with Daniel.

"Josh didn't," Fenella said.

Daniel frowned. "There are two other theater companies on the island who are preparing shows right now. We've had no reports of threatening letters from either of them, but if anyone has had a letter, we believe the article in today's paper will prompt them to ring us."

"Are we going to have to start going to shows all over the island?" Fenella asked.

"I'm hoping we'll have the case wrapped up before too long, although I don't mind seeing a bit of Shakespeare," he replied.

"I haven't seen *A Midsummer Night's Dream* in years," Fenella said. "I remember the plot being incredibly convoluted."

"It's not as bad as *Three Gentlewomen from Bologna*," Shelly assured her.

Fenella laughed. "If I remember correctly, there are multiple subplots and lots of love potions. It still should be a lot easier to follow than whatever was going on last night."

"This was meant to be my lunch break," Daniel said. "I need to get back to the station. I'll collect you at five for the drive to Ramsey. The curtain goes up at seven, but I need to go through the entire building before the show starts. Have something to eat before five."

"What about you? When will you eat?" she asked as she walked him to the door.

"I'll get a sandwich later," he told her. "Don't worry about me."

He gave her a quick kiss and was gone.

"I will, though," she said after him.

5

Fenella had a light lunch and then put together something like a picnic for Daniel for later. She packed sandwiches, chips, crackers, and fruit and put everything in the refrigerator. Just before five, she ate her share of the food, and then put the bag with Daniel's dinner at the front door.

"Ready?" he asked after he'd kissed her hello.

"I am. I packed you some dinner," she replied, gesturing toward the bag by the door.

He opened it and looked inside. "I didn't get lunch or dinner," he admitted. "But I can't really eat and drive."

"We can take my car to Ramsey," she suggested. She loved the car she'd inherited from Mona and was always looking for an excuse to drive it.

"Which car?"

Fenella laughed. "We can take the sensible one if you want, but I'd much rather take Mona's."

"You'll let me eat in Mona's car?"

"Why not? I'm sure you'll be careful."

He nodded. "I do love that car."

"So do I. And it's fast. We'll be in Ramsey in no time."

A few minutes later they were on their way, cruising along while Daniel ate.

"Thank you for this," he said around a mouthful. "I was starving."

"You need to take better care of yourself. Your brain needs fuel, the same as your body."

"I know. I just couldn't seem to find the time to get anything today. It was my fault for sneaking away to see you on my lunch break."

"I should have fed you while you were at my apartment."

They chatted about nothing much as Fenella drove. Once they'd reached Ramsey, he gave her directions to the building where the show was being performed.

"It looks like a church," she said as she pulled into the nearly empty parking lot.

"It used to be a church, but it's been decommissioned or whatever is the proper word. The town bought it a few years ago and uses it as a community resource. The local theater company performs here, and so do groups from all of the local schools."

"It's a beautiful old building."

"The interior is lovely as well."

They crossed the parking lot, and Daniel pulled on the large wooden door. It was locked. He pulled out his mobile and called someone.

"It's Inspector Robinson. I'm outside," he said when the call was answered.

A minute later, Fenella heard the sound of a key turning in the door.

"Ah, good evening," the man in the doorway said as he pulled the door open. "I'm sorry I wasn't here to greet you. We had a small issue with — ah, but never mind. You aren't interested in our cast dramas. Come inside."

The man appeared to be somewhere in his late sixties, with sparse grey hair and thick glasses.

Daniel gestured for Fenella to enter first. The man shuffled backward to let them both in and then locked the door behind them. They were in a small foyer with three doors in front of them. All of the doors were shut.

"I'm Howard Christian, the caretaker for the building and also the, well, I don't suppose I have a proper title, but I work with the theater company on their productions. Everyone is backstage, getting ready for the show."

"I'm Daniel Robinson, and this is Fenella Woods. She's, um, not here in any official capacity."

Howard looked at Fenella and winked. "We all know who you are," he said. "And we all know that you and the inspector are engaged. Congratulations."

"Thank you," she said, blushing.

"Anyway, you're both more than welcome. We appreciate your concern about our show. What happened last night at the Gaiety was horrible."

"It was, indeed," Daniel agreed.

"I was told you wanted to take a look around the entire building before we open the doors to our audience," Howard continued.

"Yes, that's right. I want to be certain that there aren't any surprises hiding anywhere here," Daniel explained.

"Well, you're more than welcome to look around. It's a small building. I can't imagine it will take you very long," Howard said.

"I'll get started then," Daniel replied.

"Did you want me to walk around with you?" Howard asked.

"If you aren't busy, you'd be more than welcome, but if you have things you need to do, I'm sure Fenella and I can manage on our own," Daniel said.

"I'll just pop backstage to check on everything. If they don't need me, I'll be back out in a minute or two." Howard turned and walked away slowly. "That's the entrance to the church," he added, nodding toward the door on the right. He opened the door on the left and disappeared through it.

"So if that goes backstage and this goes into the church, where does the center door go?" Daniel asked, grabbing the doorknob.

He pulled the door open and he and Fenella looked into the small bathroom. There were two stalls and a single, tiny sink in the space.

"I'd better check that there aren't any surprises in the stalls," Daniel said.

It only took him a few seconds to check behind the swinging doors. "Nothing here," he said as he rejoined Fenella in the foyer. "Let's see what we can find in the church itself."

He opened the door on the right and led Fenella into the dimly lit former church. She stood in the doorway for a moment, studying the space.

They were off to the side of the large room. Whatever seating had been there previously had been replaced by rows of comfortable looking theater seats. There was a wide aisle down the center of the room and smaller aisles on either side of the rows.

"I'm going to guess that used to be the altar," Fenella said, pointing to the small, elevated stage in front of the rows of seats. There were a handful of trees and shrubs in pots scattered across the stage.

"I'm sure it was," Daniel replied.

"And there's a balcony," Fenella said, looking up at the small balcony at the back of the room.

"That's the choir loft," Howard said as he walked out from behind the curtain. "When this was a church, there was an organ up there, but that went years ago."

"There doesn't seem to be too much to inspect," Fenella said to Daniel.

"We need to walk up and down every row," he told her. "We'll do the ground floor first and then take a look at the choir loft."

Ten minutes later, they'd walked through all of the rows.

"I'm assuming you want to look around the stage and backstage as well," Howard said.

Daniel nodded. "I will, but I'll to do the public areas first. You'll want to let the audience in on schedule."

"Oh, aye, we have a number of ticket holders who enjoy getting here a full hour before the show. It's more of a social occasion than anything else for them," Howard replied.

"Ready for the choir loft?" Daniel asked Fenella.

The stairs were at the back of the room. Fenella climbed slowly, breathing in the smell of hundreds of years of history.

"It's bigger than it looked from downstairs," she said when she reached the top. "There must be room for fifty people up here."

She and Daniel walked around the space that was filled with inexpensive wooden folding chairs. When they were done, Fenella stood for a moment at the railing, looking down at the stage.

"Can we watch the show from up here?" she asked Daniel, leaning against the wooden railing.

"If Howard doesn't mind, you can. I'm going to stay on the ground floor, just in case anything happens," he replied.

"I'd rather sit with you. I just like being way up here, tucked away from the crowd."

He nodded. "I need to talk to Howard about who is sitting up here, actually. This would be the perfect place from which to start a disturbance."

Fenella frowned at the widely spaced wooden bars in the railing. "Someone could slip just about anything between these bars," she said. "Maybe Howard shouldn't let anyone sit up here tonight."

They looked around the loft a second time before heading back down to find Howard. He was sitting in a seat in the front row, a worried frown on his face.

"Do you have anyone with tickets for the choir loft tonight?" Daniel asked as he and Fenella joined him.

"Oh, yes, that's Mr. Allen's favorite place to sit. He won't sit anywhere else, actually."

"Mr. Allen?" Daniel repeated.

"Christopher Allen," Howard told him. "He's our most generous supporter for both the building and the theater company."

"What else can you tell me about him?" Daniel asked.

Howard shrugged. "What do you want to know?"

"At this point, everything you can tell me," Daniel replied.

"I don't know much for certain, but I've heard a lot of stories," Howard replied. "He's very wealthy and he loves the theater. He's only been on the island for three or four years, maybe not even that long. As far as I know, he lives alone, except for a single servant who does everything for him."

"Will his servant be coming to the show with him?"

"Oh, yes, Victor goes everywhere with him."

Daniel had his notebook out. "Do you know Victor's surname?"

"He's Victor Miles. He moved to the island with Mr. Allen. I believe he's worked for him for many years."

"Do you know why Mr. Allen moved to the island?" was Daniel's next question.

"He said something once about having grown tired of life in large cities. I believe he'd been in Manchester before he moved here, but I was told he'd lived in London for several years as well," Howard told him.

Daniel made a note. "And those two men are the only people that you expect to be in the choir loft this evening?"

"Yes, unless we suddenly sell several dozen more tickets and have nowhere to put people," Howard replied.

"Is that likely?" Daniel asked.

"It's never happened since I've been here, but you never know," Howard said with a laugh.

"I need to take a look at the stage and the backstage area," Daniel said.

Howard nodded. "There is one thing, though," he said slowly.

"Yes?" Daniel asked after a short pause.

"That article in the local paper today, the one about the threatening letters. Was it true?" Howard asked.

Daniel raised an eyebrow. "The theater company in Douglas did receive some threatening letters, yes."

Howard sighed. "Someone from the police rang earlier and asked me if we'd ever received any threatening letters. I said no almost without thinking about the question."

"But you have been getting letters?" Daniel asked after another pause.

"The show's director got a letter last week," Howard said slowly. "He showed it to me and we both had a good laugh. Neither one of us thought it was anything serious."

Daniel frowned. "Did he keep the letter?"

"No, he threw it away after I'd read it. As I said, we didn't think it was real."

"What did it say?" Daniel asked.

"I can't remember the exact words, but it was something about how Shakespeare was out of date and no longer relevant. The funny part was that it said that we should be doing Forrest Luna's plays," Howard replied.

"Why was that funny?" Fenella asked, flushing as she realized that she wasn't meant to be questioning witnesses.

Daniel winked at her as Howard slowly shook his head.

"It's been years since anyone did any of Forrest's plays. They're all very nice stories, but they aren't exactly what I would consider relevant to modern audiences. Shakespeare's plays are timeless. Forrest's are nice enough, but I wouldn't put them in the same league as Shakespeare. For what it's worth, I'm fairly certain that Forrest would agree with me on that."

"You know Forrest?" Daniel asked.

"Not well, but I've been involved in community theater for years. Back in the sixties, we used to perform his plays on a fairly regular basis. He always came, unannounced, to watch the shows. We all knew who he was, of course, and we'd all do our best on nights when he was in the audience. Over the years, I spoke to him on a number of occasions. He was always kind and complimentary."

"So you believed that the letter was someone's idea of a joke?" Daniel asked.

"It certainly seemed that way," Howard told him "We do get odd letters from members of the public from time to time suggesting that we do this play or that musical. I suppose we both simply thought this was that sort of letter."

"Was there any threat in it?" Daniel wondered.

Howard hesitated and then nodded. "It said something about making us sorry if we didn't cancel our plans and do a Forrest Luna play instead. That was another thing that was almost funny. We were only a week away from opening night. There was no way we could cancel one play and have a different one ready to open in a week."

"So maybe the person sending the letters doesn't truly understand how the theater works," Fenella said thoughtfully.

"Are you quite certain that there weren't any earlier letters?" Daniel asked.

Howard frowned. "The director would have told me if he'd had any others."

"And no one else in the company received any?" was Daniel's next question.

"I don't believe so, but I didn't ask. Maybe you could ask them now," Howard suggested.

"I think that's a good idea," Daniel said. "I need take a look around the backstage areas, anyway."

Howard got to his feet slowly and then began to shuffle toward the stairs that led to the stage. As he climbed them, Fenella turned and looked around the room. If they could keep everyone out of the choir loft, it seemed unlikely that anyone would be able to disrupt the show, unless he or she was willing to stand up in the middle of it and start shouting.

The stage itself was little more than a large, flat platform.

"No traps or anything in the floor?" Daniel checked.

"We aren't anywhere near that sophisticated," Howard told him. "We're lucky we have proper curtains. Mr. Allen paid for those just a few years ago. You should have seen what we had before."

Fenella looked at the thick velvet curtains that were currently open. Presumably, they'd been rather expensive. A second set of the same curtains separated the stage and the backstage areas.

"Knock, knock," Howard called as he led them through the second set of curtains.

A dozen people were sitting in front of a row of mirrors, putting on makeup and fixing their hair. At least a dozen more were pacing or standing around. Some seemed to be muttering to themselves while others appeared to be studying scripts.

"Everyone, this is Inspector Robinson from Douglas. He's here to make sure that we don't have any problems tonight," Howard said in a loud voice. "He's going to take a look around, and then he has a few questions for everyone."

Daniel cleared his throat. "Actually, while I have your attention, I'll ask a few questions now," he said. "I'm sure you've all seen the local paper today. You'll know that last night's performance at the Gaiety was interrupted, and that the company there had been receiving threatening letters. I want to know if any of you have received any anonymous letters in the last month or more, even if they didn't seem threatening."

Several people exchanged glances. A young woman who looked no more than sixteen to Fenella, gasped.

"Letters," she said loudly. "I forgot."

"You forgot what?" Daniel asked.

"I live in a flat next door. It used to be the vicarage for the church, and all of the post for the church still gets stuck through my letterbox. I always forget to bring the letters over to Howard," she explained.

Howard sighed. "I do remind you fairly regularly," he said.

She nodded and flushed. "I'm sorry. I've been so busy with work and rehearsals that it all just went out of my head. It's only one or two letters, and none of them looked to be anything important. I can go and get them now, though, if you need them."

"I'll come with you," Daniel said. "The less they're handled, the better."

The woman flushed and then nodded. As she got up from her seat, Daniel turned to Fenella.

"Take a quick look around in here. I'll be back shortly," he told her.

She nodded and then watched as the pair left the room. The woman seemed to be trying to justify her forgetfulness as they went.

The space was small and tightly packed with people and furniture, so it didn't take long for Fenella to walk through it all. There was a small bathroom in one corner, just big enough for one person at a time.

"What are you looking for?" someone asked as she did another circuit of the room.

"I've no idea," she replied. "Something out of place, I suppose."

"You've never been here before. How will you know if something is out of place?" the man asked.

"I won't," she admitted.

"There's nothing out of place in here, except that box," Howard said, pointing to a large makeup case that had been stacked on top of another case and was leaning crookedly against the wall.

"It's Liza's," a voice called.

Howard nodded. "I'll get it moved before the curtain goes up."

"Why shouldn't it be there?" Fenella asked.

"We never stack cases on top of one another, especially not at that sort of angle," Howard told her. "People forget that these aren't proper dressing rooms, that we're really still on the stage, just behind a curtain. If someone walks past and that case topples to the floor, the noise would interrupt the show."

Fenella nodded, wondering who Liza was and whether she'd stacked her case quite deliberately to cause just such a disturbance.

"Liza is the woman who has been keeping my post," Howard added. "She's incredibly careless about everything."

When Daniel walked back in a moment later, he was frowning.

"I've sent the letters to the station for processing," he told Howard. "There were three of them, all of the same sort as the one we discussed earlier. The first was sent over a month ago, and they seem to have arrived about once a week since, although there wasn't one from this week."

Howard frowned. "I wasn't worried when it was just the one letter, but now I'm concerned about tonight's performance."

"I've requested some backup," Daniel told him. "There should be at least two constables arriving before you're due to open the doors to the public."

He nodded. "And you've been through the entire building. Everything is fine."

"We can't stop anyone from jumping up in the middle of the performance, but we can arrest them for doing so," Daniel replied.

"I really hope it won't come to that," Howard said.

Daniel nodded. "I'm going to take another walk through the theater and then go and wait by the door for the constables."

"I'll join you in a minute," Fenella told him in a whisper. She wanted to see what was going to happen when Liza returned.

The woman walked into the room a moment later. She gave Howard a sheepish grin.

"I'm really sorry," she said. "I didn't know the letters were important."

"You're meant to bring me whatever post arrives, whether you think it's important or not," he told her. "Now move your makeup case before it frightens everyone in the front row by crashing down during the show."

Liza blushed and then grabbed the makeup case. She tucked it under one of the tables in front of the mirrors and then sat down and started playing with her hair.

"So we've been getting threatening letters the same as the people at the Gaiety?" a woman asked Howard.

He frowned and then nodded. "But the police are here. We have nothing to worry about."

"What exactly happened at the Gaiety last night?" a tall man asked. "I mean, I heard the police were everywhere and that someone had blood spilled all over them."

"According to today's paper, someone staged a scene in one of the boxes," a voice replied. "The paper said it was set up to look as if someone had died in the box."

"What about the blood?" the man asked next.

"It was fake blood," Howard said. "No one was actually hurt, and the performance wasn't stopped."

"I heard it probably should have been," Liza said, giggling. "I actually auditioned for that show. I'm ever so grateful now that I didn't get a part."

"Um, Howard, we have an issue," a man said as he stepped between the curtains.

"What now?" Howard snapped.

"There is a group of people here who don't have tickets. They want to buy twenty-five seats, and they want a group discount," the man replied.

"I don't suppose we can just tell them to go away," Howard muttered as he began to walk toward the curtains.

"The thing is, it's the company from Douglas," he was told. "Their performance tonight was canceled, so they came up here to support our show."

Howard muttered something under his breath that Fenella didn't hear. She followed him to the curtain, curious to see what he would do about the problem.

Howard pushed open the curtains and then walked across the stage with Fenella at his heels. "We should go out through the door," he told the other man.

"The foyer is full of people," the other man told him. "George is taking tickets."

Howard frowned. "I thought we'd agreed to find him other jobs to do."

"We did, but Betsy didn't turn up. We didn't have any choice."

Howard sighed and then led Fenella across the stage and through the curtains. There were small groups of people scattered throughout the room now, holding tickets and programs and talking together. Fenella spotted the group from the Douglas company as she and Howard walked down the stairs from the stage. They were all standing together in the back of the room. Fenella smiled at Breesha as she and Howard approached her and the others.

"Ah, Howard, hello," Josh said. "I'm terribly sorry about this. I did try to ring earlier, but my mobile was playing up and I didn't manage it. I'm sure you've heard that our performance tonight was canceled on us."

Howard nodded. "I was sorry to hear about your trouble last night as well."

Josh shrugged. "We're putting it out of our minds and carrying on, or rather we will be carrying on once we're given permission to get back into the building. We were going to have an extra rehearsal this afternoon, and then we moved that to tonight, but the police wouldn't allow us into the building. Rather than just sit around and run lines, we thought it would be a much better use of our time if we came out and supported our other favorite local theater company."

Howard nodded. "That's very kind of you, but we weren't expecting you. It's going to take me some time to find seats for everyone, and you all may not be able to sit together."

"That would be unfortunate," Josh said. "But, obviously, you need to do what you need to do. We'll just stand quietly back here while you work everything out."

Howard nodded and then turned and began to walk away. After a few steps, he turned back to Josh.

"I can put you in the choir loft," he said hesitantly. "We've only sold two tickets in the choir loft for tonight's show."

"We'd love that," Josh said enthusiastically. "That would be wonderful, wouldn't it?" he asked, looking at the others.

A few people nodded.

"Go on up and sit anywhere, then," Howard told him. "Seats 1A and 2A are taken. Otherwise, you can sit anywhere."

"I'm going to sit up in the loft as well," Fenella told Howard.

He nodded. "It's going to be fun up there tonight," he muttered as he began to walk away.

"I told Josh we should have rung first," Breesha whispered to Fenella as she fell into step next to the woman. It seemed to take ages for everyone to climb the stairs into the loft.

"This is lovely," Brooke said, rushing to the front row.

"The view is magnificent," Alfred said loudly. "We can enjoy Shakespeare and ponder his great work. Imagine having one's work performed hundreds of years after one's death. It is something to which all playwrights must aspire, of course, but only a very few will ever actually achieve."

"I can only dream of such a thing," Dorothy said.

Alfred looked at her. For a moment, Fenella thought he was going to say something unkind, but instead, he turned and looked out over the crowd below them. "I hope they are all prepared for a great work by the world's greatest ever playwright," he said dramatically.

"It's very nice, but we're rather high, aren't we?" Adam said, dropping into the seat next to him.

"I didn't know you were bothered by heights," Eileen said to him. "Are you going to be okay up here?"

"I'm fine," he snapped. "I'm not bothered. I just wish we'd had time for a proper rehearsal tonight, that's all. I'm not really in the mood to watch other performers, not when I'm meant to be performing."

"The view from up here is amazing," Brooke said, slowly walking the length of the balcony, her hand on the railing.

Several others joined her at the railing. Fenella was doing her best to keep an eye on everyone as people moved around, talking and laughing together.

"Maybe we should take seats," Breesha suggested. "They're going to fight over the front row, aren't they?" She nodded towards the dozen or more people who were standing at the railing.

"Probably. I just hope they remember to leave Mr. Allen's seats empty."

"Is that who has tickets for up here? I didn't realize," Breesha replied.

"Do you know him?"

"Yes," Breesha replied. The look on her face suggested that she didn't want to discuss it.

At the railing, people were on their hands and knees, crawling around on the floor.

"Do I want to know what's happening up there?" Fenella asked.

"Eileen has lost an earring," Brooke called. "We're going to find it, though. It has to be here somewhere."

"Though we struggle, we all search together, eager to assist our friend in her moment of need," Alfred said.

"I hope it didn't fall over the railing," Eileen said. "It's one of my favorite earrings."

"It will be here somewhere," Dorothy said in a low voice.

"I found it," Harry shouted a moment later, holding up a sparkly earring.

"Hurray," Eileen said as the others slowly began to get to their feet.

"What is going on up here?" an angry voice silenced everyone.

"Mr. Allen," Breesha whispered to Fenella.

She looked at the tall, dark-haired man who was staring at them all. He appeared to be somewhere in his fifties, and he looked horrified by their presence.

"Ah, Mr. Allen, hello," Josh said. He walked forward, rubbing his hands together. Fenella could see dust on his trousers from where he'd been crawling around on the floor. No doubt his hands were dusty as well.

"Mr. Bailey," Mr. Allen replied coldly.

"As our performance tonight had to be canceled, we thought it would helpful if we came to support another island theater troupe," Josh explained.

"How nice," Mr. Allen said faintly.

"Of course, because it was a last minute decision, Howard didn't have enough seats together for all of us. The only place he could put us was up here," Josh went on.

"I'm afraid that simply won't do," Mr. Allen replied. "Victor, sort this."

The forty-something, short, nearly bald man standing next to Mr. Allen frowned. "I'll have to go and find Howard," he said. "Are you going to wait here?"

Mr. Allen took a slow, deep breath and then shook his head. "Out of the question," he snapped. "Where is Howard? He should have known better than to put all of these people up here. What was he thinking? Clearly, he wasn't thinking. That's the only thing that makes any sense. Where is that man?"

He strode through the balcony, glaring at everyone as he marched to the railing. "Howard? Where are you?" he shouted loudly.

Fenella took a few steps forward. From what she could see, everyone on the ground floor was now staring up at Mr. Allen.

"Howard? This is completely unacceptable," Mr. Allen bellowed. He leaned forward and then took a step to the left.

"Mr. Allen, let me go and find Howard," Victor said. "Sit down and relax. I'll be right back."

"Where am I meant to sit?" Mr. Allen demanded. "There are people everywhere."

"You're in seats 1A and 2A," Josh told him. "Howard told us we could sit anywhere else."

Mr. Allen shook his head. "Unacceptable," he said under his breath. "Unacceptable," he shouted loudly. "Howard, where are you?" he asked loudly, leaning over the railing.

Fenella spotted Howard emerging from the behind the stage curtains. He seemed to be hurrying as quickly as he could.

"Howard, there you are," Mr. Allen shouted. "This is unacceptable." He leaned over the railing again, waving a fist in the air.

Everything happened so fast that it was almost a blur. As Mr. Allen leaned forward, part of the railing suddenly seemed to give way. The man shouted something as he fell forward. Fenella rushed to the railing and gasped when she saw the crumpled figure of the man on the floor underneath them. People seemed to be screaming all around her. She looked toward the stage and was relieved to see Daniel running out from behind the curtain.

6

Fenella watched as Daniel took over. Two uniformed constables joined him and they moved the crowd away from the fallen man. Daniel's face was grim as he checked Mr. Allen for a pulse.

"Is there a doctor in the house?" he called after a moment.

"I'm a doctor," a woman replied.

The crowd parted to let the woman through. She said something to Daniel and then knelt down next to the body. After a moment, she spoke to Daniel again and then got to her feet. As she took a few steps away, it seemed obvious that Mr. Allen was dead.

"He'll be okay," Victor said loudly. "He's just knocked himself out from the fall, that's all. I need to get to him. He'll be furious when he wakes up."

He disappeared down the stairs, still muttering "He'll be fine," as he went.

Fenella could hear sirens. As Victor argued with the two constables, several more policemen and women arrived. They were followed by an ambulance crew and a crime scene team. After the screaming had stopped, everyone in the building had fallen silent, but now people began to whisper to one another.

Breesha had her phone out. Fenella gave her a questioning look.

"I was just texting Doncan. Mr. Allen was a client of his."

Fenella nodded.

A uniformed constable appeared at the top of the stairs. "Ladies and gentlemen, if you could come with me, please," he said loudly.

"Come with you? Where?" Josh demanded.

"We need to speak to each of you in turn, and we also need to start processing the crime scene," the man told him. "We need this area cleared of witnesses so that we can begin that work."

"He's dead?" Josh asked.

"That's for the coroner to determine," was the reply.

Several of the women burst into tears. Dorothy threw herself at her father and began sobbing on his shoulder. Brooke pulled Adam out of his seat, put her head on his chest, and began to cry. Eileen wiped away a few tears and then straightened her shoulders and swallowed hard. Susan was staring straight ahead with tears steaming down her face.

"Death is merely a transition from one state to another," Alfred said loudly. "The world has lost someone, but the cosmos has gained a new presence. Tonight, while we mourn, the cosmos will celebrate. Let us all—"

"Down the stairs, please," the constable said, cutting off Alfred's speech. "I'll ask you all to remain at the very back of the theater while we arrange things."

"Come on, then," Josh said. "Let's go."

Fenella stood back and watched as the balcony slowly emptied. While she knew better than to interfere with a crime scene, she was incredibly curious to know what had happened to the railing. As she followed the others to the stairs, she peered at the opening that had suddenly appeared.

"It looks as if a section of the railing simply swung open," Breesha whispered. "But why would it do that?"

"I've no idea," Fenella replied, wishing she'd studied the railings a good deal more carefully when she and Daniel had inspected the balcony earlier.

When they reached the ground floor, they joined the others from the group, standing in a small cluster at the rear of the theater. Fenella watched as people were escorted from their seats, one at a time. No doubt every person in the audience would be questioned about what he or she had seen that evening. While she waited, she watched as several different people went up into the balcony and back down again. She almost waved when Daniel walked past, but he didn't even glance her way.

"Ms. Woods? Inspector Robinson would like to speak with you now," a uniformed constable said to Fenella eventually.

She nodded and then followed him across the room. As she walked past the spot where Mr. Allen had landed, a team of constables was putting up screens around the body. The constable led her onto the stage and then behind the curtain. Daniel was sitting at a table with several chairs around it.

"This is different," she said as she pushed aside some large leaves from the plant next to the table.

He shrugged. "This was the easiest space to use for interviews," he told her. "I have constables speaking with the audience members in corners out front, but I wanted some privacy for the conversations that I'll be having."

She nodded. "I assume the poor man is dead."

"He is."

"I don't understand how that section of the railing simply gave way."

"Do you remember when Howard told us that there used to be an organ in the choir loft?"

"Yes."

"When it came time to remove the organ, they discovered that it wouldn't fit down the stairs. In order to get it out of the loft, they had to cut away a section of the balcony's railing and then lower it from there. Once that was done, they decided to reattach the railing in such a way as to allow it to be easily removed again in the future, in case they needed to do something similar again."

"But it was reattached. I mean, I leaned on it earlier today."

"It was reattached. There are hooks in the floor that lock into the railing and hold it in place. According to Howard, when it was all hooked together properly, you almost couldn't tell that that part of the railing was any different to the rest."

"I certainly didn't notice any difference earlier."

Daniel nodded. "I didn't notice anything, either, but I'm sorry now that I didn't pay more attention to the railing. My concern was that someone might try to throw something over it. I never imagined that anyone would interfere with the railing itself."

"Do you think what happened is tied to the threatening letters?"

"I do. You said yourself that you leaned on the railing when we were in the loft earlier tonight. I'm hoping this will be quite simple, really, as you were with the theater company from Douglas when they were in the loft. Surely you noticed which member of the company spent some time on the floor in front of the railing."

Fenella sighed. "Eileen lost an earring," she told him. "There were over a half dozen people crawling around just behind the railing, looking for it."

Daniel sat back in his seat and tossed his pen onto the table. His lips formed a few words that Fenella thought it was best she not try to lip-read. After a moment, he took a deep breath and then picked up the pen again.

"Which half dozen or more people?" he asked.

"I didn't know all of them, but Brooke, Susan, Josh, Harry, Dorothy, Alfred, and, obviously, Eileen, were all there," she told him. "Breesha should be able to tell you who the other person was."

"So there were eight people crawling around in that rather small space?"

"Yes, and before you ask, they kept bumping into one another and crawling over each other."

"Why?"

Fenella blinked at him. "Why what?"

"Why were they all on the ground? Why didn't just one or two people look for the earring?"

"I've no idea. Breesha and I were standing near the back of the loft. I didn't hear any of the conversation. When I saw all of the people on their hands and knees, I asked what had happened. Someone told me that Eileen had lost an earring," she explained.

"Take me through the conversation as close to word for word as you can," he requested.

She did her best to comply. When she was done, he looked up at her.

"I don't suppose you noticed anyone doing anything on the floor below where the section of railing gave way?"

"No, but from where I was standing, I couldn't actually see the floor. I will say that I was tempted to go up and help look, though. I don't know why, as it was obvious that there were more than enough people searching, but maybe it's human nature to believe that we can find things that others can't."

"And you're certain those eight people were the only ones on the floor at the railing?"

"That's all that I saw up there. I was one of the last to arrive in the loft, though. How complicated is unhooking the railing?"

"Not nearly complicated enough. I went up and had a look just after the accident. The railing fits flat into a channel along the floor. There are three bars that go across the bottom of the railing to keep it in place. The bars are hinged. They're securely fastened on the outside of the railing and simply latched into place on the inside. There's another latch near the top of the rail on both sides, one into the wall and the other into the rest of the railing. As I said, according to Howard, when it's all locked into place, you can't really tell the difference."

"But if all of the latches were undone, surely the whole section would have simply fallen away immediately."

Daniel shook his head. "It fits fairly tightly into place. With the bottom fitted into its channel, it wouldn't have moved at all unless someone put weight on it."

"Which Mr. Allen did," Fenella sighed.

"The three floor bars were unlatched, as was the bar that connected that piece to the rest of the railing. It was only the latch that connected the railing to the wall that kept the entire piece from crashing to the ground."

Fenella tried to picture how that would have worked, but when she closed her eyes, all she could see was Mr. Allen falling forward.

"The railing wasn't broken in any way?"

"Some of the bottom rail, the piece that fit into the channel, has been damaged, but otherwise it seems intact."

"Why would our letter writer tamper with the railing?"

"At this point I can only speculate," Daniel told her. "Perhaps he or she was planning to lean on the railing at some point during the show. It would have taken very little effort to push the piece out of place while pretending to almost fall off the balcony. He or she could then play the victim as the show was disrupted."

"You don't think he or she was hoping someone else would fall through the railing?"

"I don't know. It's entirely possible that whoever unhooked the railing did so in an attempt to injure or kill someone. What happened here tonight might not even have anything to do with the threatening letters or what happened last night in Douglas."

"It's a strange way to murder someone."

"If we hadn't checked the entire building before the performance, including you inadvertently leaning on the railing, we might have thought that the railing hadn't been properly latched for days or weeks or even months. Even if Howard insisted that it was always kept properly latched, I doubt he checks it regularly. I don't believe the space is used all that often."

"Mr. Allen probably wasn't the target," Fenella said as she thought back through the scene on the balcony. "I don't think anyone expected him to lean over the railing looking for Howard so that he could complain about having to share the loft."

"Is that what he was complaining about? Take me through that conversation, please."

Again, Fenella did her best to repeat everything.

"He didn't want to share the loft with all of you."

"Not even for a moment, and he seemed pretty certain that we were the ones who were going to leave as well. I don't think he would have agreed to take seats on the ground floor."

"Since he was a major supporter of the theater, I suspect he may have been correct."

"Maybe. You'll have to ask Howard what he was planning to do with everyone from the Douglas company, though. He'd already said that he didn't have enough seats together to accommodate them."

"Let's start back at the beginning," Daniel said. "Start with when we arrived at the theater tonight, and take me through everything that happened, including the things that happened when I was there."

Fenella swallowed a sigh. "When we first arrived, the doors were locked," she began. "And then I was asked to come and speak to you," she finally concluded some time later.

Daniel had taken extensive notes, but he hadn't interrupted once. Now he looked up at her and sighed. "I'd love to sit and talk through the case with you for hours, but I need to interview the men and women from the Douglas company. I'm going to focus my attention on the ones that you've identified as helping with the earring hunt. As far as I can tell, they were the only ones who had an opportunity to tamper with the hooks in the floor."

"Which rules out Adam," Fenella said thoughtfully.

"You said he sat down almost immediately when you all entered the loft," Daniel recalled, flipping back through his notes.

"Yes, he said something about not caring for heights. I don't think he went anywhere near the railing."

Daniel nodded "Assuming tonight's accident is connected with the threatening letters and what happened last night in Douglas, I suppose I should be happy that we've narrowed the list of suspects to only eight people. Unfortunately, at this point we can't be certain that the two incidents are connected."

"It seems an odd coincidence if they aren't, especially considering that the possible suspects from tonight are also all suspects in last night's incident."

"You're free to go home, if you want to go."

"How will you get home?"

He frowned. "I forgot that you drove us here. I can get a ride with someone, though."

"Or, I could stay," she suggested. "I could go back and hang out with the Douglas company. I might overhear something interesting."

"No one is meant to be talking," he pointed out. "But if you want to stay, you may. Just keep quiet and observe — nothing more."

She nodded. "And then I can drive us both back to Douglas when you're done."

"I may well be here all night. You head back when you get tired. As I said, I'll be able to get a ride with someone."

Daniel had the same constable walk her back to the group. They were all together, some leaning on the walls and others sitting on the floor. As Fenella sat down on the floor near Brooke, the constable asked Breesha to come with him.

"Why her next?" Brooke demanded. "We all want to get out of here."

"I wouldn't count on getting out of here, even after your session with the police," Josh told her. "Ms. Woods just spent half an hour talking to them, and now she's back here."

"She's a plant," someone said. "The police have put her with us so that she can report everything that we say while we're waiting."

"I'm just going to remind all of you that we've asked you not to speak to one another," a uniformed constable said.

"Not much point in the police putting her here, then, is there?" Brooke said as she shifted her legs into a different position.

Fenella looked around at the men and women from the Douglas company. It seemed obvious that one of them was responsible for Mr. Allen's untimely death. *Surely, that person should look guilty,* she thought as she tried to get comfortable on the hard floor. A short while later, everyone watched as the body was removed. There were screens keeping everyone from seeing much of anything, but that didn't stop them all from staring silently at the men as they worked.

"I do hope the police aren't going to keep us here much longer," Josh said several minutes later. "We have rehearsal tomorrow morning at eight and then a matinee performance as well."

"Surely you're going to cancel the rehearsal," Susan said. "We'll all be useless that early in the morning after having such a late night."

"It's not that late," Adam said. "If the show had gone on as scheduled, we wouldn't even be at the interval yet."

Fenella glanced at her watch. Adam was right. It felt much later than it actually was.

"Ladies and gentlemen, you aren't meant to be talking," the constable said loudly.

A short while later, someone Fenella hadn't met was invited to go for questioning. After that, people seemed to be leaving every few minutes. Fenella watched as the group got smaller and smaller until only she and the eight people who'd been searching for the earring were left.

"Mr. Baker?" the constable asked.

The man that Fenella didn't know stood up and followed the constable to the stage. Alfred followed a short while later.

"I don't even know why we all have to talk to the police," Eileen said as Alfred disappeared behind the curtain. "We can't be blamed because the theater failed to properly secure that piece of balcony railing. Mr. Allen's death is a huge tragedy, of course, but it's nothing to do with any of us."

"How did the railing give way like that?" Brooke asked.

"It was simply hooked into place," Josh told her. "They needed to remove that section in order to remove the organ when the church was sold."

"Sir, I'm afraid I'm going to have to ask you to be quiet," the constable said.

Josh nodded. "Sorry," he said, sounding not the least bit sorry.

"Well, clearly the hooks were inadequate," Susan snapped. "I don't understand why we're being treated as if we were all guilty of something as a consequence."

The constable who watching over them sent a text message to someone.

"Ms. Lucas? The inspector would like to speak to you now," a constable told Susan a few minutes later.

Susan rose to her feet and then spent a short while brushing at her trousers and straightening her shirt. Eventually, she sighed dramatically and strode off down the center aisle of the theater toward the stage. The uniformed constable rushed to catch up to her and then escorted her behind the curtain.

After Josh and then Harry were taken away, Dorothy moved away from her space on the wall and sat down next to Fenella.

"I don't understand any of this," she said in a loud whisper.

Fenella glanced at the constable, but he was studying his shoes and didn't say anything.

"It's all very awful," Fenella whispered back.

Dorothy nodded. "This is going to sound terrible, but I'm almost relieved that the same person tried to disrupt tonight's show. I mean, they did disrupt it, of course, but, I'm glad they tried."

Fenella stared at her, trying to work out what she meant.

Blushing, Dorothy shrugged. "That came out all wrong. Of course, I'm horrified that that man died. Watching him fall and not being able to help him was the most traumatic thing that's ever happened to me. I've already started writing a play about it, because that's how I deal with the negative things that happen to me. I write about them, and that makes them less awful."

"I see," Fenella replied when Dorothy fell silent.

"Of course, I don't want to minimize in any way tonight's central tragedy, but it was something of a relief for me to learn that the theater here had also been receiving the same sort of threatening letters."

"Had they?" Fenella asked, feeling as if playing dumb was the best way to handle Dorothy.

"Oh, yes. One of the girls in the company told me all about it. The letters had been addressed to the church, but they were delivered to the vicarage, which has now been made over into flats. One of the girls in the show lives in one of them, and she is meant to give all of the post to Howard. He's the man in charge of the building here. Anyway, she just kept the letters, so the theater never knew that they'd been getting threats."

"And you were relieved to hear that they had been?" Fenella made the statement a question.

"Because it means it isn't personal," Dorothy explained. "Everyone has been saying that the letters were written by someone who hated *Three Gentlewomen from Bologna*, but it's clear now that the person writing the letters is simply determined to get some of Forrest Luna's plays performed. He or she doesn't have anything against *Three Gentlewomen from Bologna* or me and, well, to be honest, I'm flattered to be included in anything that includes a play by Shakespeare."

It wasn't often that Fenella found herself speechless, but the woman's words left her feeling unable to reply.

"Have any of you ever seen a Forrest Luna play?" Dorothy demanded, looking around at the people who remained.

"I saw one, years ago," Josh said. "I was on holiday in Australia, and I did my best to see shows everywhere I went. I actually saw two of his plays, one in Melbourne and one in the middle of the outback where every member of the cast had to play at least three parts because there were so few people."

"Years ago, when I was a young actor, I performed in some of his plays," Harry told them. "The company in Douglas at the time did one of his plays every year in the spring. I believe they did that for six or seven years, although I was only in a few of the shows."

"I was in a few of them as well," Eileen said. "Forrest has a gift for writing parts for young women. He seems to understand them in ways that many other male playwrights do not."

"If he's so wonderful, why isn't he performed more today?" Brooke asked.

"If you want to see his plays performed, move to Australia," Josh suggested. "His plays are everywhere down under."

"But he's here, isn't he?" Brooke asked. "I thought someone said that he lived on the island."

"He does live on the island," Harry replied. "He lived in Australia briefly, years ago, but he was born and raised here, and he moved back to the island after only a few years in Australia."

"Someone told me that he always goes to see his plays when they're performed," Brooke added.

"He certainly used to," Harry said. "He used to think that he was anonymous, sitting in the cheap seats without any fanfare, but we all recognized him, and we all worked to perform at our very best when we knew he was in the house."

"It's been decades since any of his plays were performed on the island, though," Josh added. "I understand he's become something of a recluse in the last few years."

"Mr. Bailey? The inspector is ready for you," the constable interrupted the discussion.

Josh got to his feet and followed the man to the stage.

"I'd love to meet him," Dorothy said softly.

"Forrest Luna?" Brooke asked. "Why?"

"So few people understand what it's like to be a writer, especially a writer of plays," Dorothy told her. "Some days it's a struggle, being inside my own head, with all of the ideas that are running rampant within me. The voices call to me and demand that I tell their story, and there simply aren't enough hours in the day for me to answer all of them. I would love to talk to someone who would truly understand."

"I can ring him and see if he'd be interested in meeting you," Harry offered.

Dorothy flushed. "I don't want people to think that I'm using you to accomplish my dreams. I'm certain there are people who believe that *Three Gentlewomen from Bologna* is being performed at the Gaiety only because of our relationship. No one ever believes me when I tell them that I submitted the script anonymously."

"Because it isn't true," Brooke whispered.

Dorothy flushed. "I want to earn a chance to meet Mr. Luna. I want him to come to see my play and be so struck by what I've written that he has to meet me. Otherwise, I don't want to meet him."

"But Josh just said he's a recluse now," Harry reminded her. "I highly doubt that he's going to come to see your play."

Dorothy sighed dramatically. "If not this one, then perhaps the next. I shall keep working on perfecting my craft, one story at a time, until I've earned his respect and he's ready to meet me."

"Ms. Gilbert? The inspector is ready for you," the constable interrupted again.

As she walked away, Fenella wondered if another inspector had joined Daniel. He seemed to be working his way through the suspects more quickly now, anyway.

"Harry, with all due respect, I do hope this is the last of Dorothy's plays that we perform, for a while, anyway," Eileen said in a low voice.

Harry frowned. "I don't make those decisions," he snapped. "If you have any suggestions for shows you want to do, I suggest you speak to Josh."

Eileen nodded. "I've known you for forty-odd years, Harry. I know you'd do anything for Dorothy, but you do need to consider your own reputation as a theater professional as well. No company on the island wants to be blackmailed in performing your daughter's shows."

Harry face turned bright red. "What are you suggesting?" he demanded.

"I think I've said enough," Eileen told him.

"If you don't like *Three Gentlewomen from Bologna*, then you're welcome to quit the show," Harry told her.

Eileen shrugged. "It's a complicated mess of a show and you know it. There's no real structure. Half the cast looks lost on the stage. No one knows what's happening or why. I won't quit, only because I'm a professional and I'm committed to the show for the duration of the run, but I also won't do any further shows by Dorothy, ever."

"Ms. Harris? Please come with me."

Fenella thought Eileen looked relieved as she followed the constable toward the stage.

Harry scowled at her back as she went.

"Do you have children?" he asked Fenella after a moment.

She shook her head. "Sadly, no," she replied.

"They're wonderful, but they're always your babies, no matter how old they get. You always want them to be happy, even at the cost of your own happiness," he told her.

"I'm sure you did what you thought was best."

"Dorothy wasn't lying when she said that she submitted her script anonymously. I read it and I loved it. It was fresh and different and completely unlike anything that we'd had at the Gaiety since I'd been involved in theater there."

"It's definitely different."

He sighed. "The original script was a bit more linear. The plot was simpler. There were fewer characters. As I said, I enjoyed it a great deal. And then I discovered that Dorothy had written it."

"And that was a problem," Fenella guessed, based on the look on the man's face.

He shrugged. "You've heard what people are saying. I've known Eileen since she played Juliet at sixteen. She actually accused me of blackmailing the company into performing *Three Gentlewomen from Bologna.*"

"Why did the play change so much?"

"When I told Dorothy that I thought maybe someone would be interested in performing her play, she immediately insisted that it wasn't quite ready yet. While she was hard at work, um, improving it, I started talking to Josh and Alfred about them putting it on at the Gaiety. We've been making an effort to showcase more local talent. Dorothy's play seemed a perfect opportunity to do more of that."

Fenella nodded. "And they were happy to agree," she suggested.

He shrugged. "I gave them the original script and they both read it. After some discussion, they agreed to do it as their fall production. By the time they were ready to start casting, Dorothy had finished the revised script."

And that's where all the trouble started, Fenella thought.

Harry stared past Fenella, clearly lost in thought. "I should have stopped her. I should have made her stick to the original scripts. I should have — oh, what's the use? She was happy with the new script, and I insisted that Alfred and Josh accept it, even though I knew it needed some work. I thought, naïvely, that it would all come together in rehearsal. I was so concerned with making Dorothy happy that I stopped worrying about what was right or wrong."

Fenella felt speechless yet again. While she'd hoped she might hear something interesting if she stayed after Daniel had finished questioning her, this wasn't what she'd had in mind.

"Mr. Gilbert? The inspector is ready for you," Harry was told a moment later.

As Harry and the constable walked away, Fenella slowly got to her feet. Her legs ached from sitting on the floor for so long. She walked in a slow circle, waiting for the stiffness to improve.

"Fen?" Daniel's voice called across the nearly empty theater. He crossed to her and pulled her into an embrace.

"Thank you," he whispered when he lifted his head. "Did you learn anything interesting?"

"Maybe, once the constable stopped telling us we couldn't speak to one another."

Daniel grinned. "I texted him and suggested that it might be best if everyone was allowed to talk, as long as I knew I'd be told about the conversations. It's not as if anyone had a chance to come up with a way to alibi one another or anything like that."

"Let me tell you what was said, then." It didn't take long for Fenella to repeat what had been said in the group while people had been waiting for a turn with the police.

"Is there another inspector helping out?" Fenella asked when she was done.

Daniel nodded. "Ramsey sent two inspectors, actually. I've been put in charge of the investigation, though, as we're assuming it's tied to the incident in Douglas last night," he explained.

"Now what?" she asked after he'd asked her a few questions to clarify something.

"Now you need to go home and get some sleep," he told her. "I'm going into the station in Ramsey with the other two inspectors. We'll compare notes and talk through everything before I get one of them to drive me home."

Fenella wanted to argue. She wanted to offer to wait for him, but she knew that his meeting would probably take hours. It had been a long day and a horrible evening. Right now, all she really wanted to do was crawl into bed with Katie and forget all about theaters and threatening letters and poor Mr. Allen.

"I'll walk you to your car," Daniel said.

"Daniel? Did you have any questions for Harry Gilbert?" a voice called.

"Yes," Daniel shouted back. "I'll be there in five minutes."

"You go," Fenella told him. "I can walk myself to my car."

Daniel frowned. "It's late."

"I'll be fine. There are police cars and constables everywhere. The parking lot is probably one of the safest places in the world right now."

Daniel chuckled. "You could be right about that," he said before he gave her another quick kiss. "I'll ring you in the morning," he added.

She nodded and then watched as he walked back to the stage. Sighing, she headed for the door, carefully giving a wide berth to the men and women working in the area where Mr. Allen had fallen.

The parking lot was well lit and Fenella crossed it quickly, her mind still on Mr. Allen and the Douglas company. As she dug out her keys, she heard her name.

"Ms. Woods?" someone hissed. "May I have a word?"

She spun around and looked at the man standing next to the clearly expensive black car that had been parked near hers. "Mr. Miles?" she said in surprise.

"If I could have five minutes of your time, I'd be hugely grateful," he replied.

7

"I know it's very late," Victor Miles said. "I'm sorry."

"Don't be sorry. I'm terribly sorry for your loss," Fenella replied.

The man shut his eyes and took a deep breath before he replied. "Thank you," he said in a low voice. "I'm, well, I still can't quite believe, my brain can't process, I mean, I'm..." He stopped and took another slow breath. "I'm babbling. I am sorry."

"You've no need to be sorry. You've had a huge shock."

"Can we sit down?" he asked. "My car, well, I suppose it isn't my car any longer, but this car, well, it's large and comfortable for our conversation."

"Of course," Fenella said, glancing around nervously. Daniel would never approve of her getting into a car with a stranger.

"We can sit in the back." He unlocked the doors and then pulled open the rear door and gestured to Fenella. After a moment's hesitation, she climbed into the car. He followed her inside and then slammed the door shut behind himself.

Fenella slid across the large bench seat until she was right up against the opposite door. That put her in position to jump out if she didn't feel safe.

"Please, call me Victor," was the first thing that the man said. "No one ever calls me Mr. Miles."

"And I'm Fenella," she replied.

"Thank you. Mr. Allen always wanted me to be as formal as possible."

"Why?"

"He felt that formality between a servant and his employer was appropriate."

"You worked for him for a long time, I understand."

"Twenty-seven years. I went to work for him when I was sixteen."

"My goodness, that's a very long time."

"When I first started working for him, I didn't plan to keep the job for long. I was just out of school with not much in the way of qualifications, so I took the first job that came along. I somehow thought that other, better jobs would be available everywhere, and that I would be able to select a different one whenever I decided that I'd had enough of working for Mr. Allen."

"And those better jobs never materialized?"

"I've had other offers over the years, but always in the same line of work. While I may not have always enjoyed working with Mr. Allen, I always felt that it was best to stay with the devil I knew. Mr. Allen was always satisfied with my work, and he treated me fairly."

Even if he still made you call him Mr. Allen after twenty-seven years, Fenella thought. "You were his personal assistant?"

"I was originally employed as his manservant, but that title has all but disappeared from the world today. More recently, he had been introducing me as his aide. Simply put, I was responsible for making certain that his life ran smoothly. He had a chef to prepare his meals, but I planned them. I booked and kept track of his appointments. I bought his clothes for him and made certain that they were always clean and ready to wear. I accompanied him everywhere and was on duty twenty-four hours a day, seven days a week."

"Surely you were given days off?"

Victor shrugged. "In theory, but not in practice."

"And you put up with that for twenty-seven years?"

"I'd had a rudimentary education and have few qualifications. If I hadn't taken the position with Mr. Allen, I would probably have ended up as a miner or doing some sort of casual labor for a living. Instead, I lived in luxury and traveled the world. Yes, I worked hard, but I also lived very well."

Fenella nodded. "What happens now?" she asked tentatively.

"Mr. Allen once told me that he'd provided for me in his will. I've no idea what he meant, but whatever I've been left, I have sufficient savings to see me through a period of unemployment. I shall, of course, have to move out of Mr. Allen's home, and I imagine that I shall have to purchase my own car, but for tonight the police have said that I can drive myself back to Mr. Allen's house and that I can sleep in my own bed."

"Why did you want to speak with me?"

"I know you've been involved in a number of murder investigations in the past. The police won't answer any of my questions, but I was hoping that you might."

"I'll answer what I can, but that may not be much."

"Of course, you're also engaged to the inspector who is in charge of the investigation. No doubt he tells you things that you can't repeat."

"Actually, frustratingly, he doesn't tell me much of anything."

The man smiled. "That would be frustrating."

"What are your questions, then?" Fenella asked after a short pause.

"Why are the police treating it as a murder investigation? From where I was standing, it seemed to have been a tragic accident."

"I believe all sudden deaths are treated as murder investigations at the start," Fenella told him. "If it's decided that the death was an accident, they can end the investigation. It would be considerably more difficult if they treated it as an accident and then it was ruled murder later."

Victor nodded. "So Mr. Allen's death could still be ruled accidental."

"I believe so."

"I can't see how it could have been murder. No one could have known that Mr. Allen was going to lean on that particular section of the railing. Someone must simply have forgotten to reattach it properly after it was last opened."

"Unless someone was trying to cause a disturbance and deliberately unhooked the railing to do so," Fenella suggested, trying to be careful with what she said.

He stared at her for a moment. "The police think what happened tonight is tied to the threatening letters that were received at the Gaiety, do they?"

"That's one possibility."

"I don't understand any of this," Victor said as he sat back against the seat and shut his eyes. "No one wanted to kill Mr. Allen. His death was just a horrible accident. Even if someone was trying to cause a disturbance, that someone wasn't targeting Mr. Allen."

"I'm inclined to agree with you, but it's really up to the police to work out what happened."

He opened his eyes and stared at her for a moment. "I'm afraid I'm going to get blamed," he said in a whisper.

"Why would you get blamed?" she asked, surprised. "You weren't anywhere near the railing. There's no way you could have tampered with it."

"But if it was murder, I had a motive."

"Did you?"

"I don't know what's in Mr. Allen's will, but he always told me that he'd left me something. It could even be a significant amount. He said once that I'd never need to work again, but, as I said earlier, I never knew what to believe."

"Even if you had a motive, you didn't have the means or the opportunity," Fenella told him. "You followed Mr. Allen up the stairs. There wasn't any way you could have tampered with the railing."

"I was here yesterday. I came to collect the tickets for tonight's show, and I sat in the choir loft for a short while, watching the rehearsal. That gave me plenty of opportunity to tamper with the railing."

"Except the police walked through the entire building before tonight's show. The railing was fine just before the doors opened."

Victor stared at her and then slowly shook his head. "I'm afraid to believe you," he said. "I was certain that the police were about to arrest me. I knew Howard would tell them that I'd been in the choir loft yesterday and that they'd decide that I'd deliberately unhooked the railing. It would have been easy, really, to get Mr. Allen to lean against it, if I'd known it was unhooked."

"And if you'd wanted to kill him."

Victor chuckled. "Yes, of course, and I didn't want to kill him, in spite of everything."

"What do you mean?"

He sighed. "We were having difficulties," he said slowly. "I never wanted to move to the Isle of Man. When Mr. Allen hired me, he had a flat in London and another in Paris. He also had a home in the countryside near Devon. We moved between those three properties fairly regularly, but also traveled just about everywhere in the world. For a few years, he had a flat in New York City as well. I loved New York."

"It's a great city to visit, but I wouldn't want to live there."

Victor shook his head. "I'd love to live there. I've been, well, I've been trying to find a job there, actually. I was trying to be very discreet about it, but Mr. Allen found out, and he was very upset. He thought I was being disloyal."

"But if you were unhappy on the island, you had every right to look for a new job."

"That's what I told him, but he didn't agree. He rang the man who was considering hiring me and told him a number of horrific lies about me. Obviously, that ended my chances of getting that particular position."

"I'm sorry."

"Mr. Allen told me that he would never provide me with any sort of reference. As he's the only employer I've ever had, that was a real problem."

"How dreadful for you."

"I didn't know what to do." He sighed and then looked down at his hands. "Mr. Allen was fond of reminding me that he took a chance on me when most people wouldn't have," he said softly. "I'd managed to get myself into some trouble, you see, when I was a good deal younger."

"Trouble with the police?"

Victor nodded. "I got arrested a few times when I was in my teens.

The head teacher at my school knew Mr. Allen from somewhere, and he suggested that I go and talk to him about a job. I think the head teacher thought that Mr. Allen would put me to work in one of his businesses. He had several back then. We were both surprised when Mr. Allen offered me the job as his manservant."

"You were sixteen?"

"I was. Mr. Allen had a manservant already, a man called John Stuart. John was getting ready to retire, though, so Mr. Allen brought me in as a sort of apprentice. I thought I'd work for him for a few months or a year and then find a much better job elsewhere, but it didn't work out that way."

"What happened to John Stuart?"

"He retired about a year after I'd started working for Mr. Allen. Sadly, he passed away less than a year after that. Mr. Allen was very upset when he died. John had formerly worked for Mr. Allen's father, and he'd known Mr. Allen for his entire life. I believe Mr. Allen was closer to John than he was to anyone else in the world."

"Were you and Mr. Allen close?"

Victor shrugged. "That's a difficult question to answer. When I first went to work for him, I was terribly intimidated by him and by just about everything. Over time, I came to understand the world into which I had moved, but that isn't to say that I enjoyed living there. Mr. Allen was my employer. We were not friends, but I'm certain that I knew him better than anyone else in the world, and in a strange way, he knew me better than anyone else as well."

"You're going to miss him."

"Yes, of course, but I'm also looking forward to having some freedom. I was at his beck and call for twenty-seven years. Tonight, for the first night since I was sixteen, I can go to bed and not worry that Mr. Allen will need something in the night."

"Did he often need something in the night?" Fenella had to ask.

"Not often, but often enough that I never felt as if I slept particularly soundly," Victor replied with a sigh. "I was never able to simply forget about my responsibilities, you see. Wherever we were and whatever we were doing, I was responsible for keeping Mr. Allen happy."

"Except *you* weren't happy."

"Not in the last year, no. The Isle of Man is a beautiful place, full of stunning scenery and wonderful people. Mr. Allen and I were made to feel very welcome here, and I'm not sorry that we came, but I was ready for another change. For the first twenty-two or twenty-three years that I was working for Mr. Allen, we never stayed anywhere for more than three months. He enjoyed moving from place to place, and I came to love that lifestyle. After a while, I came to miss that lifestyle."

"And now you have many additional options."

"I do, but I have also lost someone who was very dear to me. I'm not certain how I feel, really. We were not friends, but we lived with an intimacy that I've never shared with anyone else. I knew everything about Mr. Allen, and he knew a good deal about me, as I mentioned — more than anyone else in the world knows."

"He never married?"

"He found women difficult to understand. Because of his wealth, he had no trouble in attracting them, but his relationships rarely lasted for more than a fortnight. I've also had various women in and out of my life over the years, but because we never stayed in one place for any length of time, none of the relationships ever became serious. There was one woman in New York who could have become important to me, but, well, we left New York, and when we returned some nine months later, she'd found someone else."

Fenella wondered if the man would try to contact her now that he was free to go where he chose, but she didn't ask. Instead, she yawned and then checked her watch. "It's getting late," she said. "Was there anything else?"

"I would like to talk to you all night," he replied. "I simply don't have anyone with whom to talk, and I'm afraid I don't really know what to do with myself. I've spent my entire adult life taking care of another person, and now that person is gone." He stopped and then stared at her for a moment. "He's really gone, isn't he?"

Tears began to pour down his cheeks as he began to weep. Fenella instinctively put her arms around him and began to mutter soothing words as he sobbed on her shoulder. For several minutes the man cried, soaking Fenella's shirt with his tears. When he finally got his emotions back under control and lifted his head, he looked horrified.

"I'm so terribly sorry," he said. "That sort of behavior is unacceptable. I can't apologize enough."

"You've had a huge shock, and you've lost someone close to you. There's no need for you to apologize. Do you have anyone you could get to stay with you for a few days?"

"Stay with me? I don't, I mean, there's no one. I don't have friends. Mr. Allen was my entire life."

"I don't think you should be alone right now."

"But I am alone. For the first time in twenty-seven years, I'm alone." Victor took a deep breath and shook his head. "I have to stop thinking about it. Mr. Allen would be appalled if he saw how I was behaving. He never approved of emotional outbursts. I simply must bring myself back under control."

He breathed in and out several times and then straightened his back and shoulders. "Again, I do apologize for my behavior."

"You've no need to apologize."

"As you said, it's getting late. Thank you for giving up so much of your valuable time to speak with me. I feel a good deal better for having spoken with you."

"Are you going to be okay?"

"Of course. I'll feel better in the morning, after some sleep. Tomorrow my new life begins. I'm not certain what that will mean, but I suppose I'll start working that out tomorrow."

"I have a spare bedroom in my apartment. You're welcome to stay there tonight if you want company," Fenella said, knowing that Daniel would be furious with her for making the impulsive offer.

"That's very kind of you, but I want to sleep in my own bed tonight. I've a great many things to do tomorrow, to start putting Mr. Allen's affairs in order. I shall need an early start, I believe. There are many people who will have to be informed of Mr. Allen's untimely demise and there are a number of business concerns that will have to be dealt with. I expect I shall have to spend most of tomorrow with Mr. Allen's local advocate and his solicitor in the UK, sorting so very many things."

Now that the man was focused on the jobs that needed doing, he appeared to be in complete control of his emotions. Fenella patted his arm and then reached for her handbag.

"Please call me if you need a friend," she said, digging out a small notebook. She wrote her name and her mobile number on a sheet and then tore it out and handed it to him. "I really mean it," she said.

"Thank you. I appreciate it. Please don't worry if I don't ring, though, as I expect to be very busy for the foreseeable future."

"You're welcome to ring anytime, even if it's six months from now and you've suddenly found yourself a good deal less busy."

He nodded. "I don't suppose you need a personal assistant?"

She laughed. "I don't, and I don't believe I know anyone who does, either."

"Thank you again," he said, opening the car door and climbing out.

She followed him out of the car and gave him a quick hug before heading back toward her car. "Good night," she called over her shoulder.

"Good night," he replied as he got behind the steering wheel of the luxury car.

Fenella sat and watched as he drove away. When his headlights disappeared around a corner, she started her car. She needed to tell Daniel about the conversation, but she wanted to do that from the comfort of her own apartment. She'd had more than enough of sitting in cars for one night.

While she was tired, Mona's car was still fun to drive. She seemed to get back to Douglas in record time. Katie was asleep in front of the windows when Fenella opened her door. The small animal jumped up and looked around before rushing away, heading straight for the master bedroom.

"I'll be there as quickly as I can," Fenella told her as she walked toward the kitchen. She felt as if she needed coffee, but she knew better than to drink any this late at night. After a short debate, she poured herself a glass of apple juice and sipped it while she texted Daniel.

I had an interesting conversation with Victor Miles after I left the building. He thought he was going to be a suspect.

She pressed send and then dug a box of custard creams out of the cupboard. While they didn't necessarily go well with apple juice, she felt as if she needed some sugar.

Her phone rang a moment later.

"Tell me everything," Daniel said in a tired voice.

As Fenella began to speak, Mona appeared in the living room. She walked over and took a seat at the counter.

"And then I drove home," Fenella finally concluded, yawning over the last word.

"We aren't telling anyone that the building was inspected just before the show," Daniel said.

"I'm sorry. I didn't think it would hurt to tell him. He was so worried about being a suspect in a murder investigation."

"All things considered, it's probably a manslaughter investigation, rather than murder, but at this point he hasn't been ruled out as a suspect."

"But he wasn't anywhere near the railing tonight."

"We didn't specifically check that the railing was secure," Daniel told her. "I know you leaned against it, but what if you simply didn't put enough weight in just the right place to push that section of railing out of place?"

"Even if he had tampered with the railing, he had nothing to do with Mr. Allen leaning against it. He told him to sit down and that he would go and get Howard."

"Except he knew Mr. Allen better than anyone else did. Perhaps he said that knowing that Mr. Allen would ignore him and try to find Howard himself by looking over the railing."

"It sounds very much as if you think Victor killed Mr. Allen."

"Not at all. I think Mr. Allen's death was a tragic accident caused by the man or woman who is sending threatening letters to theaters across the island. I'm simply pointing out that there are other possibilities and that I don't want you to do anything that might put you in danger, including inviting a suspect in a murder investigation to stay in your spare bedroom."

"You said yourself that it was probably a manslaughter investigation," Fenella muttered.

Daniel chuckled. "I love you. I want to keep you safe. I never should have taken you along tonight, but I wanted to spend some time with you. Maybe you should stay home tomorrow."

"What's happening tomorrow?"

"The matinee performance of *Three Gentlewomen from Bologna*," he reminded her. "I'll be going over to inspect the Gaiety before the show, and then I'll be at the performance."

"Seeing *Three Gentlewomen from Bologna* is dedication above and beyond the call of duty."

He laughed. "I don't intend to watch the show. I'll be watching the audience."

"That sounds a good deal better than watching the show again."

"According to Josh, they've made some important improvements to the show. They'll be rehearsing them tomorrow morning."

"Maybe it will be worth going to see what's different, although I can't imagine they'll be able to make many changes with only a single morning of rehearsals."

"He told me he was confident that the company would be able to make the necessary adjustments and perform better than ever tomorrow."

"Okay, I'll come with you."

Daniel chuckled again. "I just said maybe you should stay home tomorrow."

"But then you promised me an improved show. I want to see what they've managed to improve."

"I'll collect you at one o'clock, then. There's an entire team of people coming to help me search the theater. The company is going to be kept elsewhere while we're working, and then they're going to be carefully watched once they return to the building."

"Maybe, since someone has died, the letter writer will stop."

"But he or she isn't any closer to getting any of Forrest Luna's plays performed. I believe our letter writer is desperate enough to keep going. My job is to make that increasingly difficult."

"I thought your job was to catch him or her."

"Yes, of course, but in the meantime, I want to make it impossible for any more shows to be disturbed, not just at the Gaiety, but everywhere on the island."

"What will happen with the show in Ramsey?"

"They've canceled the rest of the performances. The building is going to be a crime scene for several days, and the show was only meant to be happening over two weekends, anyway. Howard said something about trying it again in a few months, once everything has settled."

"Are there any other shows going on around the island at the moment?"

"There's a theater company in Port St. Mary in rehearsals for a new show. The first performances are in November. The group in Douglas that does the annual Christmas pantomime is also in rehearsal, but those shows don't start until late December. There's also a group in Castletown, but they don't have any shows scheduled until March. They haven't even cast their next show yet."

"And how many of the groups have been getting threatening letters?"

"I can't answer that, in part because I can't discuss the case, but mostly because I simply don't know. Someone will be questioning the people associated with each of the different companies tomorrow morning."

"I'm going to guess that someone is going to speak to Forrest Luna as well."

"I'm planning to do that myself."

"Shelly knows him."

Daniel sighed. "After you speak to him, because no doubt you will, please ring me immediately."

"You know I always do. I'll use any excuse to call you."

He laughed. "I'll see you tomorrow. I hope to talk to Mr. Luna myself before I head to the theater tomorrow afternoon."

"Don't forget to pick me up along the way," she reminded him.

"I won't."

"Make sure you get some sleep, too."

"That's going to be a good deal more difficult than remembering to collect you. I expect to still be here for at least a few more hours."

"You won't be any good to anyone if you're exhausted."

"I know, but I want to be certain we've done everything we can here before I leave. Mr. Allen deserves my best efforts."

Fenella thought about arguing further, but she knew Daniel wouldn't listen. "I love you," she said instead.

"And I love you. Maybe we should start talking about setting a date for the wedding, or maybe we should think about living together. I'd love to know that I was coming home to you tonight."

"Sure, we can talk about both those things. It might be better to wait until the case is solved, though."

"I know you're right. This case is going to consume all of my mental energy for the next few days. I'll see you around one tomorrow. Love you."

"Love you, too," she replied before she put the phone down.

"I'm not ready to get married," she told Mona. "And I'm not ready to live with him yet, either."

"Will you ever be?"

"Yes, of course. I just need some time to get used to the idea."

"He won't be patient forever, and he won't always be caught up in murder investigations, either."

"I wish I shared your optimism about that," Fenella replied. "I feel as if we've lurched from one murder to another ever since I arrived on the island."

"And yet Daniel still loves you," Mona said thoughtfully.

Fenella made a face at her and then headed for the bedroom. It was late and she was tired.

"But you haven't told me what happened tonight," Mona said as she followed Fenella. "I gather that someone is dead."

"Mr. Allen fell from the balcony. It was horrible."

"Mr. Allen? Not Christopher?"

"I think that was his first name. I don't really remember. Everyone always referred to him as Mr. Allen, even his assistant, Victor."

"Victor Miles? The poor man will be devastated. He devoted his life to Christopher — not that Christopher truly appreciated him."

"So you knew them both?"

"Yes, of course. Not terribly well, because they only moved to the island a few years ago, but we were often at the same charity events. Christopher and I had mutual friends in London and elsewhere. He was, well, eccentric, but I enjoyed his company."

Fenella yawned. "Can we talk about this in the morning? I'm exhausted."

"Just tell me exactly what happened to him, and then I'll go and let you sleep."

"I already told you what happened. He fell from the balcony."

"You're going to have to do better than that," Mona insisted.

Sighing, Fenella turned and walked back into the living room. "Sit down," she told Mona. "I'll tell you the whole story."

8

A n hour later, Fenella was yawning in between sentences, but she'd told Mona everything.

"The poor man," Mona said when Fenella had finished. "He would have been terribly upset to have found such a large crowd in the choir loft when he arrived."

"Why? I mean, he'd only purchased two seats. Surely he didn't expect the theater to leave the rest of the loft empty?"

"I suspect that very few people ever bought seats in the loft. He'd probably sat up there all by himself for dozens of shows. Had he known that the Douglas company was going to show up without tickets, he probably would have purchased every seat in the loft himself, just to keep them out."

"That isn't very nice."

"I told you that he was eccentric. He didn't care for people, especially crowds of people. He would come to parties and find a quiet space somewhere and just stay there all evening. He used to buy boxes at the theater and reserve private dining rooms when he went out for a meal. In spite of his considerable wealth, he only ever had a single servant who did everything for him."

"Victor told me that he had a chef as well."

"I very much doubt that Christopher ever spoke to the person," Mona told her. "Victor will have planned the menus and served the food. The chef probably stayed in the kitchen when he or she was in the house."

"Can you think of any reason why anyone would want to kill him?"

"Christopher? No, not at all. He was a bit odd, but he was harmless enough, and he kept to himself."

"He was wealthy."

"Yes, of course. I wonder who will inherit his wealth. That's an interesting question."

"Victor said he'd never married."

"No, Christopher found people too difficult, especially women. He was the only child of two only children. He always told me that was why he didn't care for crowds. He'd grown up alone, with only a single nanny for company. The nanny was replaced by a tutor when he was six, and that man stayed with him until he went to university."

"He must have found university difficult."

"Actually, he told me that he'd rather enjoyed it. He had his own little house, and he admitted that he didn't go to many lectures, but he found another young man who was doing the same course of study, and that man was happy to tutor him through all of his coursework in exchange for a small sum — or what Christopher considered a small sum, anyway. It may have been a lot for a struggling university student."

"And after university?"

"His father bought him a flat in London. Christopher hired a man who'd formerly worked for his father as his assistant, and he began traveling and enjoying life."

"He never worked?"

"He never needed to work. His parents had both inherited considerable fortunes. His father inherited several businesses from his own father, but I believe he left only a few to Christopher. He'd simply sold the businesses, one at a time, whenever he'd needed more money. He had no interest in actually working, and Christopher felt much the same."

"I mean, who really wants to work?" Fenella asked.

Mona nodded. "No doubt there are people who love what they do, but I suspect most of them would happily live off of a large inheritance, given the opportunity."

"Daniel loves his job."

"Yes, and it's going to take you some time to persuade him to quit and simply enjoy life with you."

"Do you think I'll manage it one day?"

"Maybe, one day."

Fenella sighed. "That's what happened tonight, anyway. I'm going to bed now."

Mona nodded. "I'm actually quite sad about Christopher's untimely death. I considered him a friend, although he may not have felt the same way about me. Victor must be very upset."

"He'd been trying to find another job."

"I wasn't really listening when you were telling Daniel about your conversation with Victor. At that point, I didn't realize you were talking about anyone I knew, of course. Tell me again what Victor said to you."

Fenella repeated the conversation as quickly as she could. As soon as she was finished, she got to her feet. "And now I'm going to bed," she said, walking toward her bedroom.

Mona stood up and followed. "I find it odd that Victor was looking for another job. When I knew them, he was devoted to Christopher."

"But he didn't want to stay on the island all the time."

"I'm struggling to believe that Christopher would have refused to give him a reference as well. If Victor wanted to leave, I can't imagine Christopher forcing him to remain here."

"We have only Victor's side of the story, of course," Fenella said as she walked into her bathroom. She started brushing her teeth as Mona followed, stopping in the doorway.

"He wouldn't have lied about such a thing," Mona said thoughtfully. "Not when what he said gives him a motive for killing Christopher. I wonder why he told you, actually. He'd have been better off pretending to have loved his job and the island."

"Maybe there are other people who know he was job hunting,

people who he knew would be talking to the police," Fenella said as she rinsed her toothbrush.

"Perhaps."

"Anyway, tomorrow I'm going back to the Gaiety to see *Three Gentlewomen from Bologna* again. I think I'd prefer it if someone interrupted the show again."

Mona chuckled. "But I heard Daniel tell you that the show has been improved. Surely you want to see what they've done to it."

"Maybe? I can't help but feel as if it's beyond saving, really," Fenella said as she washed her face.

"But you'll go again anyway, mostly because you don't want to miss the next disturbance, whatever it is."

"I'm going because Daniel invited me. I don't actually expect the letter writer to do anything else. A man has died. Surely that's enough to stop him or her from doing anything further."

"I hope you're right, but I worry that our letter writer is too focused on the goal to stop, even after tonight. For whatever reason, he or she wants to see one of Forrest's plays performed. Perhaps it would be best for everyone if some company announced plans to cast one of his shows."

"Do you think the letter writer wants to be in one of the shows? Could that be the motive?"

"I think anything is possible."

Fenella walked back in the bedroom and changed into her pajamas. "I don't know what to think anymore. None of this makes any sense, but that may be because I'm so tired."

"Good night," Mona said. She faded slowly and then, as Fenella switched off the light, Mona disappeared in a shower of bright lights.

"That was lovely," Fenella said as she pulled the covers up. "If you could let me sleep until eight, I'll give you an extra treat tomorrow," she whispered to Katie, who was fast asleep.

"This is unacceptable," Mr. Allen said crossly. He frowned at Fenella and then leaped over the edge of the railing.

She ran forward and stared into the abyss below her.

"You'll have to go after him," Victor told her. "It's the only way."

"The only way for what?" she asked.

"The only way to find out who killed him, of course. You need to jump," he replied.

"I'm not jumping. I can't even see the bottom. I'd just die, too."

"Death isn't so bad. That's what Mona told me, anyway," Victor said.

Fenella frowned. "But I'm the only one who can see Mona."

"But you forget that all the time," Victor countered. "Even when you're dreaming."

"I'm dreaming? That makes more sense."

"And since you're dreaming, you can jump," he told her.

"I'm still not jumping."

"I'll go then," Victor said with a sigh. "But when I find out what's really going on, I'm not going to tell you."

Fenella opened her mouth to argue, but Victor ran past her and jumped over the railing. He screamed something as he disappeared from sight.

"Hello?" Fenella said after a moment. "Is anyone there?"

"I'm here," a voice called. "We're all here, actually, everyone from the show. You should join us."

"Everyone from the show?"

"Everyone from *Three Gentlewomen from Bologna*. We're all here, having a lovely time with Mr. Allen and Victor. Jump down and join us," the voice said.

"I can't see you."

"It's a long way down, but it's safe enough. Jump."

Fenella hesitated at the railing. Multiple voices began to chant "jump" at her as she stared into the darkness below her.

"It's just a dream," a voice reminded her.

"More like a nightmare," she muttered as she reached for the railing.

"Merowww," a voice said in her ear.

Fenella opened her eyes. Katie was standing on her pillow, staring at her. When she looked at the clock, she was surprised to see that it was five minutes to eight.

"You were waiting until eight to wake me," she said to Katie. "Thank you. Too bad my nightmare woke me before you did."

Katie made a noise and then jumped off the bed and disappeared through the door. *No doubt she's in the kitchen, complaining about her lack of breakfast,* Fenella thought as she slowly climbed out of bed.

The dream had been upsetting, but Fenella often had disturbing nightmares, especially when she was caught up in a police investigation. As she walked to the kitchen, she shook her head, hoping to clear away her memories of the dream.

After she gave Katie her breakfast, including the promised extra treat, Fenella took a shower and got dressed. There was very little in the kitchen in the way of people food, so after sighing deeply, Fenella made a shopping list and the headed to the grocery store.

"I still bought more for you than for me," she told Katie a short while later as she carried shopping bags into the apartment. After an early lunch, she got ready for another trip to the theater.

"I'm not looking forward to this," she muttered as she touched up her makeup. "But at least I'll get to see Daniel again."

He knocked on her door just before one.

"Hello," he said, pulling her into a kiss.

"Did you get lunch?" she asked when the kiss finally ended.

"No, but we're already going to be late," he replied. "Maybe I'll be able to get something before the show starts."

"Or you could eat this sandwich while we walk to the Gaiety," she suggested, handing him the bag with the sandwich she'd made for him earlier.

"This is why I love you so much," he said. "You worry about me and you take care of me."

The walk to the Gaiety only took a few minutes, but it was enough time for Daniel to eat his sandwich and the banana that Fenella had included in the bag.

"I feel much better," he told her. "Now to inspect every inch of the Gaiety."

There were half a dozen uniformed constables waiting for him in the foyer. Harry was there with a large map of the building's interior. It didn't take long for Daniel to divide the building into sections and to assign each section to a constable.

"What are we going to do?" Fenella asked as the men and women scattered.

"We're going to check the boxes. They aren't being used today, but I want to be certain that they're all empty anyway."

Fenella followed Daniel to the corridor outside the boxes. Harry had given him the keys, so Daniel unlocked each of them in turn. They were all empty.

The box where the dummy had been found on Friday night still had police tape across the door. Daniel removed the tape and opened the door. There were still pools of fake blood on the floor, and the dummy had been moved to the center of the box. Fenella looked at it and shuddered.

"I don't know why I thought you would have removed the body by now," she said in a low voice.

"We're leaving it here until we're ready to remove the police tape. It's a fairly low priority for the crime lab to process, but they will go over it eventually to see if they can learn anything from it."

"Is it more important now that Mr. Allen's death might be connected to it?"

"Yes and no. We dusted it, and the entire room, for prints and couldn't get anything useful. The clothes on the dummy came from the costume department here and so did the wig he was wearing. Everyone involved in the current show has been all over the theater in the past few weeks. Even if the lab finds hair on the mannequin that can be matched to one of our suspects, it won't prove anything."

Fenella sighed. "So the body may as well stay here, safely tucked away under lock and key."

"Exactly. For today's performance, it's also going to be guarded by a pair of constables. I'm leaving one at each end of this corridor to block access to the boxes. In fact, they should already be in place."

As they walked out of Box A, Fenella nodded and smiled at the uniformed constable who was standing a few feet away. He frowned as he studied her.

"No one has any reason to be up here today," Daniel told him. "Politely turn them all away. They can talk to Howard if they have any questions."

"Yes, sir," the man replied smartly.

Daniel walked down the hall and had a short conversation with the constable at that end before rejoining Fenella.

"Time to help with the search backstage," he told her.

Half an hour later, he looked at her and shrugged.

"I think we've done all that we can," he said. "There will be three constables back here during the show. They'll keep an eye on everyone."

"And we'll be out front, watching the audience," she guessed.

"I'll be watching the audience. You can sit back and enjoy the show."

"I'd rather watch the audience."

He chuckled. "There will be two additional constables keeping an eye on the audience. There are four of us, so hopefully we'll spot anything out of the ordinary."

"I'm really hoping that the letter writer has given up," Fenella admitted as she and Daniel walked back into the building's foyer.

"I suppose that will depend on how determined he or she is to achieve the goal."

"Did you get to talk to Forrest Luna today?" she asked.

He nodded. "He seemed as bewildered as we are as to why anyone would cause problems in an attempt to get one of his shows produced. He was very upset about Mr. Allen's death, especially because it could be tied to the letter writing campaign."

"Did he know Mr. Allen?"

"He didn't think they'd ever met, but he wasn't certain. After we spoke, he gave a statement to Dan Ross. In it, he appealed to the letter writer to stop. He told Dan that he won't allow any of his shows to be performed until the letter writer is caught."

"Oh dear. That's going to upset the letter writer, isn't it?"

"Probably, but it also might put an end to the matter. If Mr. Luna won't allow anyone to perform his plays, the letters won't make any difference."

"What if the writer decides to target Mr. Luna next?"

"He's thinking of hiring a bodyguard just to be on the safe side," Daniel told her. "The entire thing is making him understandably nervous.

"It will be interesting, when you find the letter writer, to find out what his or her motive was."

Daniel nodded. As he opened his mouth to reply, he was interrupted.

"Inspector Robinson, the company is here and eager to get inside to start on makeup and hair," Harry said.

"They can all come in through the stage door," Daniel told him. "There are three constables backstage who will be keeping an eye on everything."

"Some people aren't going to be happy about that," Harry muttered as he walked away.

"What do we need to do now?" Fenella asked Daniel.

He shrugged. "In another thirty minutes or so they'll be opening the doors to the audience. I want to watch everyone coming in. We're especially concerned about anyone bringing in backpacks or large bags."

"I thought you were pretty sure that the letter writer was someone involved in *Three Gentlewomen from Bologna*."

"We believe so, but that doesn't preclude them having an accomplice, maybe a good friend who would be happy to, I don't know, release a handful of balloons during the show. Or maybe an animal of some kind. Or maybe one of a dozen other things that would cause a small disturbance."

Fenella sighed. "They should just cancel the rest of the shows."

"And let that damned letter writer win? Never," Harry snarled as he walked back into the room. "Dorothy has worked too hard to have her dreams destroyed by some cowardly person hiding behind anonymous threats. If the letter writer has complaints about the show, he or she should have come and talked to me about them."

"And now poor Mr. Allen is dead," Josh added as he walked into the foyer. "I'm afraid everyone is struggling with concentration this afternoon."

"How did the rehearsal go?" Daniel asked.

Josh made a face. "It was a bit ambitious of us to try to make any changes at this late stage, no pun intended. Last night was horrible to witness, and I doubt anyone got enough sleep once we were permitted to leave Ramsey. Everyone made valiant efforts to incorporate the changes, but it is all a bit overwhelming."

Harry frowned. "Dorothy told me that things were much improved after this morning's rehearsal."

"I think people better understand their role in the play now," Josh told him. "Some of the rewritten scenes helped clarify things for the actors, but I'm not certain they were able to learn all of their new lines — not today, not after everything that has happened over the past few days."

A loud buzzer startled Fenella. She looked at Daniel, who shrugged.

"It's time to start admitting the audience," Harry told them. "The buzzer is a warning to the actors to let them know that they need to be quiet, and that they have only thirty minutes before the curtain goes up."

Daniel and Fenella stood back and watched as he walked to the main doors and unlocked them. As he pushed them open, he shouted into the small crowd.

"Please have your tickets ready for inspection. The bar is open in the foyer. The show starts in exactly thirty minutes."

A moment later, several dozen people filled the foyer. Fenella did her best to look out for large handbags or backpacks, but it was difficult to see much of anything through the crowd.

"I'm going to go and stand at the back of the theater," Daniel told her. "I'll watch people as they take their seats."

"I'm going to stay out here for a few more minutes," she replied. "Where are we sitting?"

"Harry said we can sit anywhere in the back three rows. None of those tickets have been sold."

"I'll look for you there just before show time," she told him.

As he walked away, a handsome man in a red polo shirt walked into the foyer. He looked to be in his late twenties, and he was carrying a huge backpack.

"Did you want to leave that with us in the foyer?" Harry asked him.

The man shook his head vigorously. "No, thank you. I'll keep it with me," he said firmly.

Wondering what he could possibly have brought to the theater in such a large bag, Fenella began to walk toward him.

"Where's the bar?" the man asked Harry.

Harry gestured toward the small table that had been set up in the corner of the room. There were two men behind it, serving drinks to a handful of customers. Fenella turned and walked to the bar, arriving just before the man in the red shirt.

"After you," he said, nodding toward Fenella.

"A glass of white wine, please," she said even though she didn't normally drink alcohol in the afternoon.

"I'll get her drink if you add a lager to the order," the man said from behind her.

"That isn't necessary," Fenella told him.

"But I don't mind, and I should get my drink a bit faster," he laughed.

"Are you looking forward to the show?" Fenella asked as they waited for their drinks.

"Eh, I've been seeing a girl who's in it for a few weeks now. She gave me a ticket and asked me to come. I don't even know what the show is about, though."

And you won't know any more after the performance, Fenella thought.

The bartender handed them their drinks. Fenella's companion gave him a twenty-pound note. "Keep the change, mate," he said with a wave.

"I've met some of the cast," Fenella said as the man started to walk away. "Who is it you're dating?"

"Her name is Brooke Blake. I'm not even certain who she is in the play, though. Maybe she's one of the gentlewomen? She did say she had a fairly large role."

"I've met Brooke. She seems very nice."

"She's beautiful, too, which matters more to me than nice," he replied. He laughed loudly and then shook his head. "I'm kidding, of course. But I'm not really looking to settle down — not yet, anyway. I'm too young."

Fenella nodded. "And Brooke is very young as well."

"She is, aye, but she's more ready to settle down than I am. She's already talking about getting married and having children. I'll be ready for that in about twenty more years, I reckon."

That doesn't sound like the Brooke I know, Fenella thought. "Did she tell you anything about the show?"

He shook his head. "She said it was different and that she loved being able to bring someone's unique vision to life. I've no idea what that means."

Fenella laughed. That did sound like Brooke. "Did you bring your own snacks?" she asked in a teasing tone, nodding toward the large backpack.

"I wish I had," the man laughed. "I've been staying with a friend, sleeping on his couch. He and I had a bit of a disagreement earlier and he asked me to leave. Brooke is going to be thrilled when I tell her that I'm moving in with her."

I'm not so sure about that, Fenella though. "You're moving in with her?"

"Yep, today, right after the show, actually. As I said, she's been talking about marriage and babies, so she should be delighted that I want to live with her. We'll try it for a few weeks anyway. I can always move out. I have lots of other friends who'll let me sleep on their couches for a few days."

"Or you could get your own apartment," she suggested.

He laughed again. "I could, but that costs money, and I'm nearly always skint. I need to find a new job, really, but looking for work isn't any fun."

Fenella swallowed a dozen different replies. "What do you do?" she asked eventually.

"Oh, this and that," he told her. "It's hard to get jobs when you have a record, though. I never did nothing really bad, and I've learned my lesson now, but the record doesn't go away, not if you got caught after you were eighteen, anyway."

"Well, good luck to you," she said as a chime warned them that the curtain would be going up in five minutes.

"I know who you are," he said in low voice. "I don't suppose you're looking for, I don't know, someone to do handy work around your flat?"

"I'm sorry, but I'm not."

"Yeah, I didn't think so. Everyone tells me to get a job, but no one actually wants to hire me."

"What do you want to do? I mean, if you could do anything?" she asked.

"I've always wanted to work on cars and motorbikes — mostly motorbikes, but I don't have the qualifications."

"Can you learn how to do that locally?"

"There's a course at the college, but I don't have the qualifications to take it. Even if I did, I don't have the money for the course."

In spite of everything he'd said, Fenella found herself taking to the man. She pulled her notebook and a pen out of her bag and wrote down Doncan's phone number. "Call my advocate's office and tell them that I told you to call. If you truly want to go to school and learn to fix cars and motorbikes, I'll help, but you're going to have to do the work."

He stared at her for a moment and then nodded slowly. "I can work hard, when I'm motivated," he said. "I'll need some GCSEs before I can do anything else."

"So get them. If that costs money, I'll pay for it, but the offer is good only if you stay out of trouble. If you know who I am, you'll know that I'm engaged to a police inspector. If you get arrested, I'll hear about it."

"You don't even know my name."

She laughed. "I suppose you'd better tell me that."

"I'm Eric Christian and I'm, well, I think I'm speechless, really."

"I'll tell Breesha to expect your call," she said. "Now, you'd better find your seat."

The foyer had been slowly emptying. Eric dug his ticket out of his pocket and headed for the door to the theater. Fenella followed more slowly, wondering if she'd done the right thing or something very stupid. Daniel was waiting for her at the back of the theater.

"He's a worry," he murmured as Eric found his seat near the front.

"His name is Eric Christian," she told him. "He's dating Brooke, and I've just offered to pay his way through college."

Daniel stared at her for a minute. As he opened his mouth, the lights began to flicker.

"We'd better sit down," Fenella suggested.

Sighing, Daniel walked to the back row and gestured for her to go in first. She sat in the second seat from the end of the row and Daniel took the aisle seat.

"Here we go again," she muttered as the lights went down.

As the curtains opened, it quickly became obvious that the actors were having trouble focusing. Adam seemed to be mumbling his lines, so much so that a member of the audience shouted "Louder" during one of his speeches. Brooke looked as if she'd been crying as she made her entrance, and as she crossed the stage, she managed to trip over the edge of a couch and fall to the ground.

"This is a mess," Fenella whispered to Daniel.

"It's not going well," he agreed. "It seems that the letter writer is disturbing the show without doing a thing."

A short while later, Susan wandered onto the stage, looking as if she had no idea where she was or why she was there. She walked from one side to the other and then stopped and turned back around. "Tuesdays or Wednesdays," she announced to Adam who nodded.

As Susan left the stage, Daniel looked at Fenella. "This is quite different to what we saw on Friday."

"I thought Josh said they'd decided not to change anything."

"I did as well," he replied.

By the time they stopped for the intermission, Fenella was ready to go home. "That was horrible. Maybe an unexpected interruption would be a good thing."

Daniel frowned. "I don't even know how to reply to that. It was quite dreadful, really, but I don't want our letter writer to have the satisfaction of interrupting the show, either."

"No, of course not, especially not after causing Mr. Allen's death last night."

"I'm going to take a walk through the lobby and then go backstage to check on everything. Can you stay here and keep an eye on the crowd, please?"

Fenella nodded. "Am I watching for anything in particular?"

He shrugged. "Anything out of the ordinary, really."

As he walked away, Fenella stood up and began a slow stroll through the room. She walked down the center aisle, nodding and smiling to people as she went. Everything she overheard suggested that the play was not going over well.

"...lost, just completely lost. I think we should leave," one woman said.

"I'm sorry we came," her companion replied.

"...thirty odd years and I've never seen anything so dreadful," a man was saying loudly.

"...the theater manager's daughter wrote it, of course. I suppose, when your father is in charge of the theater, you can get any nonsense you want performed," another woman said.

Fenella walked to the very front row and then turned and walked along the edge of the stage. People were still grumbling, and it appeared that a great many of them were gathering their things and heading for the exits. As Fenella scanned the crowd, she spotted Dorothy sitting near the center of the room. She was frowning and there were tears streaming down her face.

Feeling as if she ought to say something to the woman, Fenella began to walk back up the center aisle. She'd only taken a few steps when someone began to scream.

9

enella spun around. The sound was coming from backstage. Without stopping to think, she ran up the stairs and onto the stage. Ducking behind the curtain, she kept following the screams, which were getting increasingly shrill. As she pushed aside the second set of curtains, a police constable rushed past her.

Just inside the backstage area, Fenella stopped and looked around. Everyone seemed to be staring at Brooke who was standing near the center of the space. She was pointing at something in the shadows off to the side and screaming.

"Brooke, stop," Josh said loudly, stepping between her and whatever she'd seen in the wings.

After one additional loud scream, Brooke took a shaky breath and then burst into tears.

"That's quite enough," Josh told her. "You're chasing away the audience."

"The play already did that," Susan said.

Josh frowned at her and then looked back at Brooke. "What is wrong with you?" he demanded.

"There was a mouse," she told him. "It was huge."

"Maybe it was a longtail," Adam suggested.

Fenella knew that, according to Manx folklore, it was bad luck to use the word rat, but she was sure she'd been told that the superstition only applied on boats.

"It was neither," Harry snapped as he strode into the room. "We've never had a mouse or a rat in the theater. I don't know what you saw, young lady, but it wasn't either of those."

Brooke shook her head. "I'm so sorry," she sobbed. "I haven't slept properly since our show was interrupted on Friday and, I'm afraid my imagination got away from me. I swear I saw something moving. Something small and furry with horrible pointy teeth."

One of the uniformed constables walked in the direction that Brooke had been pointing. "Where did you see it?" he asked.

"Right against the wall," she told him. "At the edge of the curtain."

The man used the flashlight on his phone to illuminate the area. There was clearly nothing there but a bit of dust. He moved the curtain sideways and then let it fall back into place. "Nothing here now," he said.

Brooke sighed. "I didn't mean to scream. I was trying to find my focus again, to get back into character. I had my eyes closed and I was rerunning the first act in my head when I heard a strange noise. When I opened my eyes, all I could see was this large furry creature running along the wall. I, well, I shouldn't have screamed. I'm really sorry."

"And now you've ruined the show," Dorothy said flatly. She'd walked up behind Fenella at some point. Now she strode into the center of the room. "You've driven away all of the audience," she told Brooke angrily. "There's no one left to watch the second act."

"That's just as well, as the second act is even more of a mess than the first," Adam said.

Dorothy turned toward him. "If you'd done your part the way it was written, instead of changing things, the first act would have been a good deal better."

"I did my best. You were the one who changed nearly everything at today's rehearsal," he shot back.

"I only made the changes that were needed," Dorothy replied. "If you truly understood your character, if you'd truly inhabited your character, the changes would have made complete sense and would have felt totally natural."

"I'm sorry that I failed to understand the ridiculous drivel that you wrote and then rewrote and then rewrote again," Adam said. "I should have had a bottle of wine before the show today. Maybe that would have made your script clear to me."

"I think everyone needs to calm down," Daniel said. He'd been standing quietly in the back of the room. Now he stepped forward. "Brooke, are you okay?" he asked.

She gave him a watery smile and then slowly shook her head. "I'm afraid I need to lie down," she said. "I'm feeling completely overwhelmed."

"I can have a constable escort you home," Daniel said. "That's assuming the second half of the show isn't happening?" he added, looking questioningly at Josh.

Josh sighed. "Has the entire audience actually left?" he asked.

"I'll check," Harry said. He pushed past Fenella and the curtains. When he came back a minute later, he was swearing softly under his breath.

"There are about a dozen people left in the theater. I'm going to tell them that the show won't be continuing and offer them tickets to another show. There's no way Brooke can perform right now."

Brooke nodded. "Dorothy, I'm terribly, terribly sorry. I'm just too upset to perform right now. It's entirely my fault. I'm simply not a good enough actor. I can't pull myself together enough to go back out there. I simply wouldn't do your story justice in my current state."

Dorothy shrugged. "I don't know that anyone can do my story justice," she said with a dramatic sigh. "I'm beginning to think that no one here truly understands my vision. No one understands the story I was trying to tell. No one understands me." She turned her back on the room and began to cry.

"Could today get any worse?" Josh asked. He looked at Harry, who sighed and then crossed to Dorothy.

"Come on, you need to get home," Harry said, putting his arm around her. "We'll go up to my office and I'll ring your mother. She can take you home and look after you."

"I don't want to go home. I want to stay here and watch them rehearse. I want to watch them repair the damage they've done and see that they get everything right before the next show," Dorothy replied.

"There isn't another show until Friday," Josh said. "We'll start rehearsing again tomorrow night. That's soon enough."

"It is not," Dorothy shouted. "You didn't rehearse enough before the first show, and you didn't rehearse enough today. I've half a mind to make my father cancel the rest of the run."

"Go ahead," Adam said. "It isn't as if this show is doing any of us any good. I'm not going to be putting this show on my CV, that's for certain."

"That's enough," Josh said before Dorothy could reply. "We're all upset about having to cancel the rest of today's show. Let's not take it out on one another. What happened was disappointing, but let's face it, things weren't going well out there. No one was properly focused. I think last night upset everyone."

"We watched a man die," Brooke said. "Of course it upset all of us."

"We'll feel better when the police work out who's been sending the threatening letters," Josh said, glancing at Daniel. "That person had to have been responsible for Mr. Allen's death, and he or she needs to be behind bars."

"It would help if our cast didn't help the letter writer with his or her evil plans," Adam said. "Brooke shut us down today. The letter writer didn't have to do a thing."

"I wouldn't have been so on edge if it wasn't for the letter writer, though," Brooke countered. "He or she upset our show on Friday and may have caused last night's accident. It's very hard to go out on stage knowing that I might be the next target."

"The significant police presence must have interfered with today's plans," Josh said.

"And that was another distraction," Susan said. "All those handsome men in uniform everywhere made it very difficult for me to focus on anything."

"Do they remind you of your son?" Eileen asked with a nasty smile.

Susan frowned. "You're in a lovely mood," she snapped back.

"It's been a difficult day after a terrible evening. I'm in the mood to be horrible to everyone," Eileen replied.

"That makes two of us," Susan told her.

"We're all upset," Josh said quickly. "I think everyone needs to go home and rest. We'll meet here tomorrow night at seven for a rehearsal."

"What play will we be rehearsing?" Susan asked. "The original one or the rewritten one?"

"It wasn't rewritten," Dorothy said tightly. "It was improved in several small ways. No one should have any trouble with the tiny number of changes."

"You gave me twenty-six new lines," Susan said.

"And you gave me fifteen fewer," Adam complained.

"And I'm in three more scenes than I used to be," Brooke said. "I'm not complaining, of course, but it's a lot more entrances and exits to remember."

Dorothy took a deep breath. "We can go back to the original script," she said. "I was simply trying to make things better. Clearly, I was alone in seeing that as desirable. If you're all happy with the original script, we'll use that for the rest of the run."

"Dorothy, honey, ain't no one happy with either script," Adam told her. "But at least we know our lines and our staging from the original script, and we can do the show. Assuming the letter writer doesn't interfere, of course."

"Which is where Inspector Robinson comes in," Harry said. "Can you guarantee that the letter writer won't interfere with the rest of our run?"

"Of course not," Daniel said. "I can only promise that we'll do our best to monitor the theater during performances. I think things on that front were going well today, right up until the disturbance that may or may not have been caused by our letter writer."

"Wait," Brooke exclaimed. "Are you suggesting that I may have actually seen a mouse? That maybe the letter writer set one free in the room?"

"At this point, I'm reserving judgment," Daniel told her. "There are a number of possible explanations for what you thought you saw."

Including that you're the letter writer, causing your own disturbance, Fenella thought.

"I'm going to go and announce that the show won't be continuing," Harry said.

"No," Brooke said. "I'm feeling better. I think we should continue."

"There's no point," Dorothy said. "There's no one left to watch."

"There are about a dozen people," Harry told her. "They deserve a show if you think you can give them one."

Brooke looked around at the others. "I'm willing to try if you are," she said. "I'm not in the first five minutes of the second act. I'll redo my makeup while you start."

Adam sighed. "I think this is a complete and utter waste of time," he said.

"Those people paid good money for their tickets," Josh argued. "We owe them a show."

Brooke walked over the row of mirrors and pulled a makeup case up from the floor. As she opened it, Josh looked around the room.

"Are we doing this?" he asked.

"If we can go back to the original script for the second act," Adam said.

"That will confuse things," Dorothy said.

"Things are already confused," he countered. "It can't be any worse than trying to do the changed show that we don't really know yet."

"I'm going to agree with Adam, just this once," Josh said. "We'll do act two from the original script. Everyone has two minutes to get ready."

"Make it five," Daniel said. "I want to do another quick check of the theater before you start. Anything could have happened while we've all been back here." He motioned to the uniformed constables to follow him and then left through the door to the foyer.

Fenella hesitated and then slowly followed him, feeling as if there was no way she could simply walk back across the stage. When she reached the foyer, she walked back to the theater door and looked inside.

Harry seemed to have slightly underestimated the crowd. By her reckoning, there were probably twenty people sitting in their seats, staring at the dark stage. As she walked toward the back row to take her seat, Fenella noted that Eric was one of the people who'd stayed. He gave her a small wave as their eyes met.

A moment later, Josh walked out onto the stage. "Ladies and gentlemen, we appreciate your patience. There was a small incident backstage, but everything has been sorted now. Without further ado, may I present the second act of *Three Gentlewomen from Bologna*." He stepped sideways as the curtains opened and the play began again.

Daniel slid into the seat next to Fenella a few seconds later.

"Everything look okay?" she asked as he leaned his head back against the seat.

"I hope so. If anything else interrupts the show, it's over for today."

"That was quite the fight backstage. I can't believe they all agreed to come back and do the second act. I really thought Brooke was going to go home and Dorothy was going to fire Adam."

"It certainly wasn't pleasant. Tensions are high, of course."

"Do you really think someone set a mouse loose backstage?"

"It's certainly possible. There's a great deal of clutter in the wings. If someone brought in a small cage and left it there, I doubt anyone would notice."

"But how would they get the mouse to run out while everyone was backstage?"

"I don't know, and I don't really think that's what happened. I'm just saying it's possible."

"What do you think happened, then?"

"I think Brooke saw something out of the corner of her eye and overreacted very badly."

"Or she's the letter writer and she was causing her own disturbance."

"Also possible."

"But she seems to love Dorothy and the play. Why would she want to disrupt it?"

"Perhaps, whatever she thinks of *Three Gentlewomen from Bologna*, she'd still rather be in a Forrest Luna play," Daniel said.

Someone a dozen rows in front of them turned around and frowned at them. Daniel and Fenella exchanged glances.

Knowing she'd been rude didn't stop Fenella from wanting to talk to Daniel. He reached over and took her hand and gave it a squeeze. Sighing, she sat back in her seat and tried to watch the show.

When Brooke made her entrance, she looked miserable. She spoke her lines in a dull monotone while staring out at the audience. Adam suddenly seemed energized, though, and he began shouting out his lines, putting emphasis on seemingly random words.

Susan walked through her scenes, seemingly in a hurry to get back off the stage as quickly as possible. When Eileen made her entrance, she took two steps forward and then tripped over something and tumbled to the ground. Without missing a beat, Adam pulled her to her feet and they carried on with the scene.

"Brooke tripped in the same place in the first act," Fenella whispered. "Someone must have moved the couch."

Daniel nodded. On stage, someone Fenella didn't know began to wander around in circles. Adam said something to him that was completely inaudible. The man jumped and then ran off the stage.

Twenty minutes later, the show lurched to its end. Fenella felt even more confused about the story than she had been after the first show, but she hadn't expected anything else. As the audience slowly filtered out, Daniel leaned over and whispered in her ear.

"Go backstage. I'm going to follow the audience out. I'll see you back there in a few minutes."

Fenella headed for the stage. She hadn't gone far when she realized that she was following Eric. He walked across the stage and pushed back the curtain.

"Hello?" he called.

"Darling," Brooke said as she rushed out from behind the second curtain. "Was it very awful?"

Eric shrugged. "I've never been to a proper play before, aside from when I was dragged to things when I was in school. I didn't understand it, but that's probably my fault."

Brooke shook her head. "It's a terribly confusing show. I'm in it and I don't fully understand it. I've had long talks with the playwright, and

I think I understand her vision, but I don't think we came anywhere close to that vision today. We were all distracted."

"You were brilliant," Eric said. "That's all that mattered to me." He took a few steps forward, letting the curtain fall behind him.

When Fenella pushed it aside a moment later, Eric and Brooke were in an embrace. She thought about coughing or clearing her throat. Before she could move, Brooke pulled back.

"Could you tell how upset I was?" she asked Eric. "I saw a mouse during the interval."

"Was that you screaming?" he asked. "I heard someone screaming, but I didn't want to rush backstage and upset everyone. I would have done, if I'd known it was you, though."

"It was me, but you were right to stay in your seat. Once I'd calmed down, we continued with the show."

"Without much audience. I was shocked when so many people left. There was a lot of grumbling about how difficult the plot was to follow."

"Don't say that too loudly," Brooke warned him, glancing over her shoulder. "Dorothy gets very upset when she hears that people didn't like the show."

"Dorothy?"

"The playwright," Brooke explained. "She's an artist, so she's very sensitive."

Eric nodded. "Anyway, I thought maybe we could go and get a drink and talk. I, er, I mean, Pete sort of threw me out."

Brooke stared at him for a moment. "Pete threw you out?"

"He wanted me to start paying half the rent and I don't have the money. He told me I had to come up with two hundred pounds by the end of the day or leave. I decided to leave."

Brooke nodded slowly. "But where will you go?"

"I thought maybe I could sleep on your couch for a few nights while I work things out with Pete."

"You need to find a job."

"I'm going to go back to school. I was talking to this woman earlier, and she said she can help me get funding so I can go back to school."

Brooke sighed. "You know if you go back to school that you're going to have to study and work really hard, don't you? You can't quit after a week because you get bored."

"I'm going to work hard. I just need a place to stay for a week or so until I get my plans sorted."

"You can stay with me for a few days," Brooke told him. "But that's all. I'm not ready to live with anyone."

He nodded. "Just a few days," he promised. "It'll be fun."

She didn't look convinced, but she shrugged and then gestured at the curtain behind her. "I need to get back there. Josh wants to talk to all of us before we leave."

"Can I come with you?"

"Sorry, but it's cast only," she replied. "Why don't you sit on the promenade and wait for me? It's a lovely night."

"It's a bit chilly, but sure, why not?" he replied. "I'll be right outside."

As he turned around, Fenella took a step backwards and then stepped forward and pushed open the curtain again, trying to look as if she'd only just walked up to the stage.

"Ah, hello," Eric said brightly. "I was just talking about you."

"Were you?" Fenella replied.

He nodded. "Brooke, this is the woman who was telling me about funding for me to go back to school. If she's right, I'll be making good money doing what I love in a few years."

"Ms. Woods? My goodness, how kind," Brooke said.

Fenella shrugged. "I was just trying to help."

"Eric, you'd better go," Brooke said. "They'll be locking all the doors soon."

He nodded and then rushed past Fenella and through the curtain. Brooke sighed deeply and then looked at Fenella.

"He's never going to actually go back to school, you know. He'll look into it and apply for funding and whatever, but when it actually comes time for him to do the work, he'll drop out and go back to living on someone else's couch."

Fenella shrugged. "I hope you're wrong. He seems like a nice young man."

"He's nice enough, but he's lazy as, er, heck. But I'm supposed to be backstage."

Brooke turned around and headed for the second curtain. Fenella stayed a few steps behind her. Brooke held the curtain for her, though, once she'd gone through it.

"Ah, there you are," Josh said. "I just need five minutes of everyone's time, please."

Brooke nodded. She walked across the room and dropped into a chair in front of the mirrors. After a moment, she turned the chair around so that she was facing into the room.

Fenella looked around, and when her eyes met Daniel's, she smiled.

"I think the second act went better than the first," Josh said.

"Someone moved the couch," Eileen said.

"I thought that, in the first act," Brooke said. "I was going to check during the interval, but then, well, everything went wrong."

"I'll check it when we're done here," Josh said. "It will be in the right place for the next performance, I assure you."

"It was probably our letter writer," Susan said. "That would be a really easy way to disrupt most shows. When the police went through the whole theater, they probably didn't even think to check that everything was in the right place on stage."

"They wouldn't know what they were looking for anyway," Brooke said. "Not unless they do theater themselves."

"I'll take responsibility for checking the stage position for the furniture for the rest of the run," Josh said. "I usually do it before every show, but I left it this afternoon because I wanted to stay out of the way of the police."

"Adam missed half of his cues," Susan said.

Adam raised an eyebrow. "Half of my cues were rewritten, and some people were following the old script and some were following the new one. I was endlessly confused for both the first and second acts."

"We were doing the old script after the interval," Josh said.

"Except Brooke kept doing lines from the new scripts," Adam said.

"I may have done a few of the new lines," Brooke admitted. "I couldn't remember what was new and what was old."

"We're going to rehearse tomorrow night," Josh said. "We'll iron all of this out at that time. I don't want anyone to worry about any of this for the next twenty-four hours. Go home and forget all about *Three Gentlewomen from Bologna.* Spend some time with your loved ones, get yourself a treat, just relax and enjoy life. I want you to come back fresh and ready to work hard tomorrow night."

"I'm going to rework the script," Dorothy said.

Everyone groaned.

"You must be kidding," Susan snapped. "We're already completely muddled up. You can't make any more changes."

"Nearly everyone left this afternoon," Dorothy said. "They didn't understand the first act. They didn't feel my vision."

"That's mostly our fault," Brooke said. "We mixed up the two different versions."

"No, it's my fault," Dorothy countered. "As I watched, I could see exactly where things went wrong. When you confront Adam about his behavior, we need more angels and fewer cats."

Fenella glanced at Daniel. *There were cats?* She looked around the room, trying to figure out which cast members were meant to be cats.

"Fewer cats makes sense," Brooke said. "But I still think you need to give us a chance to work on the second version of the script. We just didn't have enough time to learn all the changes before today's performance."

"I'm done," Adam said. "I want an agreement right now as to which script we're going to be using going forward. If I can have that, fine. I'll do my best to learn whatever my part is in whichever script that is, but that's all I'm prepared to do. If we can't reach an agreement right now, I'm out."

"You can't quit now," Josh told him. "You're the star of the show."

"Not hardly," a voice muttered.

"He can go," Dorothy said. "I can write him out while I'm doing the rewrite. He's completely expendable."

Adam chuckled. "I imagine you were hoping that you could change my mind with that, but I'm actually delighted. You do your rewrite and write me out of the play. I'll go home and forget this nightmare ever happened. I wish you all good luck with whatever emerges from Dorothy's pen. Good night."

He headed for the door. Daniel stopped him and the pair had a short exchange before Adam left. As the door swung shut behind him, several people began to speak at once.

"He can't just..."

"We needed him..."

"No one will miss..."

Josh held up a hand. "Dorothy, I hope you're right about not needing him, because I don't think we can get him back."

Dorothy shrugged. "It will be fine," she said as a tear slid down her cheek. "I'm sure it will be fine."

"I'll talk to him," Harry said. "I'm sure I can persuade him to come back. Let's not worry about that for now."

"We do have plenty of other things to worry about," Susan said grimly. "How many people have requested refunds on their tickets for future shows?" she asked Harry.

"That isn't your concern," he said. "It's my job to worry about the box office. You worry about your acting."

"Are you suggesting that I didn't perform well this afternoon?" Susan asked, clearly angry.

Harry shook his head. "I thought you all did very well today," he said loudly. "The circumstances were difficult, and you all rose to the occasion. Well done."

"What did you think?" Dorothy asked, looking at Fenella.

"Me?" Fenella replied as everyone in the room turned to look at her.

"You were in the audience," Dorothy said. "What did you think of the show? Was it better than last time?"

"I wasn't really watching," Fenella said apologetically. "I wasn't here to enjoy the show. I was here to help keep an eye out for any potential disturbances."

"No doubt you heard what other people were saying during the interval," Dorothy continued. "What did you hear?"

"I didn't hear much of anything," Fenella told her. "I had only just started walking around the room when Brooke started screaming."

Dorothy nodded. "Yes, of course. We still don't have a believable explanation for that, do we? I can't help but wonder if Brooke knows more about the threatening letters than she's admitting to."

Brooke gasped. "I can't believe you just said that."

"But everyone is thinking it," Dorothy told her. "With the heavy police presence today, you didn't have much of a chance to do anything more than move a bit of furniture around on the stage. When that didn't shut down the entire production, you had to improvise."

"I don't have to sit here and listen to this," Brooke said. "I've been doing my absolute best for this show, learning and relearning lines every time you changed things; learning how to cry on demand, only to have you take that part of the story out of the script; and defending you and your insane, disjointed, sorry excuse for a story to anyone and everyone. Adam was right to quit, and now I'm doing the same. Good night."

She got up and stormed to the door. Just before she reached it, she stopped and turned back around. No one spoke as she flounced back through the room, grabbed her large makeup case, and then walked to the door again. Daniel said something to her just before she left.

"And then there were none," Susan said in a low voice.

"We don't need her, either," Dorothy shouted. "We can do the show without her and without Adam. It will be even better, actually. I can rewrite it and give everyone else more lines and better parts. It's going to be amazing. I'll go home and get started on the revisions now. I'll have them for you tomorrow night."

Dorothy rushed toward the door. As Daniel stopped her, Josh clapped his hands together.

"I want you all to go home and get some rest. You all need to be here at six tomorrow night. We'll worry about what happens next from there."

"But what about..." Susan began.

Josh held up a hand. "I don't want to talk about anything right now. The more we talk, the more people quit the show. If this continues, *Three Gentlewomen from Bologna* is going to end up being a one-woman or one-man show."

A few people muttered comments, but Fenella didn't hear any of them clearly. As the cast slowly trickled out, Daniel spoke to each person. Fenella stood near the curtain, just watching. When Josh and Harry were the only two people remaining, Daniel joined them near the center of the room.

"I want to see this couch," he told Josh.

Josh nodded. "I don't know that there's anything to see, but we can take a look."

Fenella followed as they all walked through the curtains and onto the stage. She'd paid little attention to the couch and chairs that were set up on one side of it.

"The tape shows where the furniture is supposed to go," Josh explained. "As I said earlier, I usually check everything just before the curtain goes up, but I didn't today."

There were clear markings on the floor, and from where Fenella was standing, it looked as if the couch was about six inches out of place.

"I should have checked in during the interval," Harry said. "I saw Brooke trip over it during the first act, but then, with all the screaming, I got distracted."

Daniel slid the couch back into place and shrugged. "It's very light. Anyone could have bumped it accidentally and moved it slightly out of place. There's no way we can get fingerprints off of it, and I'm certain everyone from the cast has touched the couch at some point over the past week or so, anyway. Now that I know what to look for, I'll be certain to check the furniture while I'm going through the theater, though."

Harry nodded. "We'll all keep a better eye on things," he said. "But for right now, I need to go home and talk to Dorothy. I'm going to do everything in my power to get Adam and Brooke back on board before tomorrow, even if that means convincing Dorothy not to make any additional changes."

"Good luck," Josh said grimly.

"If you're done here, I need to lock up," Harry told them.

Daniel had the team of constables walk through the building, checking that nothing had been disturbed during the show. A few minutes later, Daniel and Fenella were walking down the promenade together.

"I'm starving," Fenella said.

"Let's get takeaway from somewhere and go back to my flat," Daniel suggested. "I need to hear about your conversation with Eric."

Fenella nodded. "And the one I overheard between Eric and Brooke."

He nodded. "That, too."

❧ 10 ❦

In Daniel's lovely apartment that overlooked the promenade, Daniel and Fenella ate Chinese food as she told him everything that Eric had said, and then repeated the conversation between him and Brooke. When she was done, Daniel sighed.

"I can't believe you actually offered to pay for his education. Brooke is probably right about him."

"She may be, but I thought he deserved a chance. Maybe he's actually trying to change."

"Maybe," Daniel said, sounding skeptical.

"I can afford to help him," she said quietly.

He nodded. "I know, and I know you mean well, but I don't want you to be disappointed when he drops out halfway through his GCSEs."

"Let's talk about something else," Fenella suggested. "Anything else."

He laughed. "I just want to ask you one question about your talk with Eric. You said he'd just been thrown out of the flat where he was saying and that he told you he was skint, didn't you?"

"He did. I assume that meant broke."

"It does. But you also told me that he paid for the drinks and that he gave the bartender a twenty-pound note and told him to keep the change. That seems quite extravagant for someone who's skint."

Fenella stared at him. "I didn't even think about that."

"That's why I'm the police inspector," he told her with a laugh.

"He was really casual about paying, too. He had the money out, ready to pay, as I was ordering. Maybe he was just showing off."

"Maybe, but why?"

"Maybe he knew who I was, and he wanted to strike up a conversation with me. Maybe he thought he could buy a few minutes of my time and, I don't know, talk me into paying for his education. Maybe the education thing is all a big scam and he's hoping to take me for a fortune."

Daniel shrugged. "I'm not ready to accuse him of planning a serious scam, but I do want you to be careful of him."

"I did give him Doncan's number, not mine. I trust Doncan to look after my interests, even if I do something dumb, like telling him to pay for Eric's education."

"And now, let's talk about something more pleasant," he suggested as he pulled her into his arms.

It was quite late when Fenella finally got home. Daniel insisted on walking her back to her apartment.

"Good night," she whispered in her doorway.

"Good night," he told her. "I'll ring you sometime tomorrow. I'm probably going to have to go to the rehearsal tomorrow night."

"Good luck with that."

He chuckled. "Maybe, if I see a week's worth of rehearsals, I'll start to understand the show."

"No chance," Fenella told him.

She shut the door behind him and then leaned against it.

"You could just live together," Mona suggested.

Fenella jumped and somehow managed to bang both her head and her elbow on the door. "Ouch, ouch, ouch," she shouted, trying to rub her head with the arm with the sore elbow while she rubbed the elbow with her other hand.

"Are you quite all right?" Mona asked.

"I hit my funny bone. I have pins and needles in my arm and my head hurts. No, I'm not all right."

"How was the show?"

Fenella sighed. "You want to hear it all, don't you?"

"Of course I do. You and Daniel should have come back here after it finished."

"Daniel's apartment was closer," Fenella told her. *And a good deal more private*, she added to herself.

"I would have only stayed long enough to hear about the show," Mona told her. "Then I would have made a gracious exit."

"Of course."

"So tell me everything," Mona insisted as Fenella headed for the bedroom.

As Fenella got ready for bed, she gave Mona an abbreviated account of everything that had happened that afternoon.

"Eric Christian is going to be trouble," Mona predicted. "He bought you a drink, even though he's broke. He's going to do something to try to get money from you."

"Maybe, but Doncan can deal with him," Fenella replied.

"I think Brooke is behind the letter writing campaign," Mona continued. "It's even possible that Eric is helping her. Perhaps he had a mouse in his backpack and he released it during the interval."

"And it made its way backstage in time to surprise Brooke?"

"Of course not. It probably found somewhere warm and quiet and went to sleep. What matters is that in the next day or two it will leave evidence of its existence around the theater, thus proving that Brooke was telling the truth."

Fenella thought for a minute. "That's actually very clever."

"Yes, it is. I suspect Brooke is quite intelligent. She's doing stupid things, though."

"What do you mean?"

"Setting up the fake murder scene on opening night was probably the smartest thing she's done in working towards her goal. I'm certain she didn't mean to kill Mr. Allen, but once she's caught, she's going to have to deal with a manslaughter charge at the very least. And causing today's scene herself will surely move her up the list of suspects, if she isn't already at the top of the list."

"I'm still not clear on why she wants someone to do one of Forrest Luna's plays."

Mona shrugged. "Perhaps one of them has what she thinks will be the perfect part for her."

"Then why not name that play as part of her demands?"

"Maybe you should ask Forrest Luna that question," Mona said as Fenella changed into her pajamas.

"Sure, I can do that. I'll just have to try to stumble across the man somewhere. He's a recluse, as I understand it, but I'm sure he'll be out and about the next time I take a walk or something," Fenella replied sarcastically.

"Perhaps you should listen to your answering machine more often," Mona suggested. "Good night." She disappeared in a huge cloud of smoke.

Fenella stared at the cloud and then slowly shook her head. "I should listen to my answering machine, shouldn't I?" she muttered as she walked back into the living room.

The machine was on the table near the kitchen, and it showed three messages. The first was a man who did his best to convince her that she needed new windows. She deleted it before the second message began to play. It was her dentist's office, reminding her that she was due for an appointment. After jotting down the phone number, she deleted that message, too. The third was the interesting one.

Fenella, it's Shelly. I've been talking with Forrest Luna, and he'd like to meet you. He's spoken to Daniel and to Dan Ross, and now he wants to speak to someone who understands how criminal investigations work. He knows you've been through a fair few, and he knows that we're friends. Anyway, he'd like to talk to you tomorrow, if possible. He's offered to buy us lunch at the Seaview at midday. If that doesn't work for you, please ring me back.

Lunch at noon at the Seaview sounds perfect, Fenella thought. She didn't have any other plans for the next day, and the food at the Seaview was always excellent. It would be nice to see Jasper, the owner and manager, again as well. Shelly was having her wedding reception there, and it had been a while since Fenella had heard anything about the plans. No doubt Jasper would have an update for them.

With her mind on Forrest and food, Fenella crawled into bed and shut her eyes. Katie made a noise and then rolled over as Fenella tried to get comfortable. Convinced that she'd toss and turn all night, Fenella shut her eyes and breathed out slowly.

❧

What felt like a moment later, Katie began to tap on her nose.

"Breakfast time already?" Fenella asked, glancing at the clock. "I dreamt about food all night," she told Katie. "American food. Piles of pancakes with stacks of bacon. Fried chicken and hamburgers and apple pie. Waffles with maple syrup. Barbequed ribs with coleslaw and potato salad."

Her mouth watering, she went into the kitchen and got Katie's breakfast for her. "I want pancakes," she said as Katie began to eat.

"Porridge is better for you," Mona told her.

Fenella jumped and then landed on the side of her foot. "Ouch," she shouted, hopping up and down on the other foot.

Mona sighed. "I must try to remember to announce myself," she said.

"I'm going to get a shower," Fenella told her. "Breakfast can wait."

After her shower, Fenella made herself some toast and ate an apple. "It wasn't what I wanted," she told Katie. "But I don't have the ingredients for pancakes."

Someone knocked. Fenella headed for the door and then stopped. The knocking didn't sound as if it had come from the front door. As she stood in the middle of the room, the sound came again, and then Mona appeared in front of her.

"How was that?" Mona asked.

"I didn't jump."

"So, an improvement. Good. You need to get today's paper." She vanished before Fenella could reply.

"Why don't you bring one with you next time?" Fenella shouted after her. It took her only a few minutes to get ready to go out. When she opened her door, she surprised Shelly, who was standing just outside of it.

"I was just about to knock," Shelly told her. "Do you want to go for a walk?"

"I was just going to get the local paper. I'm certain there's something about the threatening letters in it today."

Shelly nodded. "No doubt Dan is having a wonderful time with all of this. But I haven't seen you in a few days. Was what happened to Mr. Allen truly awful?"

"It was fairly awful. I'll tell you the whole story while we walk to the shop," Fenella offered.

"Before I forget, are you willing to have lunch with Forrest today?" Shelly asked as they made their way toward the elevators. "I promised him that I would ring him this morning if you couldn't make it for any reason."

"I'm looking forward to meeting him," Fenella replied.

"Good. He's very upset about everything that's happened."

"I can't imagine that I'll be able to help."

"He's read about you in the local papers. He knows you've been involved in several police investigations. I think he just wants to talk to someone who might understand but who isn't actually with the police."

"I'm going to repeat everything he says to Daniel. I'll have to warn him."

"He already knows that. I told him that, and he said he expected as much. He knows you and Daniel are engaged, but I think he believes that you'll be sympathetic towards him."

"Of course I will. I can't imagine how he's feeling. If he truly doesn't know anything about the person behind this, then he must be confused and angry."

"He's definitely angry that someone got killed. He's also badly shaken by the whole thing. What's happening is, well, odd, and possibly crazy."

Fenella nodded. "And now this," she sighed as she pointed to the headline being heralded on the sign outside the small shop.

"'Theater Threat Writer Contacts Us Directly,'" Shelly read. "What a mess," she sighed.

Fenella bought the paper and a bar of chocolate. Shelly bought her own copy, and the pair made their way back to Fenella's apartment.

As soon as they were inside, both women sat down and began to read the headline article.

"What does it say?" Mona asked as she appeared on the couch next to Fenella.

It took a great deal of effort on Fenella's part not to react to the woman's sudden appearance. She looked up and glared at Mona before returning to the article.

"But where's the letter?" Shelly asked, flipping pages. "I don't want to read what Dan Ross thought about it. I want to read the actual letter."

"It's on page six," Fenella told her. "It starts with 'While I'm devastated that someone suffered a tragic accident as a result of my efforts, those efforts will continue until I accomplish my goal.'"

"Surely it would have been smarter to say that Mr. Allen's accident was nothing to do with him or her?" Shelly said.

Fenella shrugged. "I don't think our letter writer is thinking clearly. The rest of the letter is all about how brilliant Forrest Luna is and how his plays are significantly better than Shakespeare's."

Shelly sighed. "It sounds as if someone has lost touch with reality."

"Or someone wants us to believe that he or she has lost touch with reality," Mona said thoughtfully.

Fenella frowned at her and then went back to reading. "According to this, the letter writer has warned every single theater group on the island, but none of them are taking the threats seriously. That's why he or she is now writing to the papers."

"After Mr. Allen's death, I suspect some of them will be taking the threats very seriously indeed," Shelly said.

"But no one has announced casting for a Forrest Luna play yet," Fenella replied.

"They can't, even if they want to. Forrest has said that he won't permit it," Shelly told her.

"I wonder if the letter writer has heard that yet," Fenella said.

"Maybe Daniel should announce that at the rehearsal tonight," Mona suggested.

"Daniel is going to the *Three Gentlewomen from Bologna* rehearsal tonight. He should probably announce it," Fenella said. "Of course, Adam and Brooke have both quit the show, so they won't be there to hear the announcement."

"Do you think one of them is the letter writer?" Shelly asked.

Fenella shrugged. "I've not really given it much thought. When it was just a stupid prank the first night, I didn't think it much mattered. Now that Mr. Allen has died, though, it's a lot more serious."

Shelly nodded. "Can you tell me what happened in Ramsey?"

Fenella gave her a quick version of events and then added a rundown of everything that had happened at the Sunday matinee of *Three Gentlewomen from Bologna* as well. When she was done, Shelly shook her head.

"It has to be someone from the cast or crew of *Three Gentlewomen from Bologna*, doesn't it? I mean, they had the best opportunity to set up the mannequin on Friday. They were in the balcony on Saturday, and they were all backstage on Sunday. If someone did set a mouse loose, they're the prime suspects," Shelly said.

"But was there a mouse?" Fenella asked. "Or did Brooke just start screaming to cause a disturbance?"

"I don't understand what the letter writer is even trying to do. Does he or she want to get shows canceled? Or just upset everyone? Or what?" Shelly replied.

"I think if we knew the answer to that, we'd be a lot closer to working out who's behind all of this. Whatever the intention, Friday's show at the Gaiety went on as scheduled, but their Saturday performance was canceled. Saturday's show in Ramsey was canceled before the curtain went up, and the company has now canceled the entire run. Yesterday's matinee, though, did finish, albeit with a much smaller audience than the one that was there when the show started," Fenella said.

"I think Brooke is behind everything," Mona said. "She gave herself away when she started screaming yesterday."

Fenella opened her mouth to reply, only stopping herself just in time. "Brooke seems the most likely, really, after yesterday," she said to Shelly.

"But how did she manage to get Eileen to lose an earring?" Shelly asked. "I was thinking that Eileen was the most likely, as she was the one who lost her earring, which was what made everyone crawl around on the balcony floor."

"Maybe that wasn't the plan, but when the earring was lost, our letter writer took advantage of the opportunity to unhook the railing," Fenella said.

"I suppose that's possible," Shelly admitted.

"Daniel did say that it was possible that the balcony railing was unhooked when we checked it, and we simply didn't notice," Fenella added.

"But the letter writer admits to having done it," Shelly said.

"If he or she is telling the truth, then that rules out Adam," Fenella told her. "He didn't go anywhere near the railing on Saturday night."

Shelly nodded. "Is that the only person who can be ruled out?"

"No, there are others. If we assume that the person who unhooked the railing was one of the people searching for the missing earring, then there are only eight suspects," Fenella replied.

Shelly picked up a pen and looked at Fenella. "Who are they?" she asked.

Fenella sighed. "Eileen, obviously, Brooke, Susan, Josh, Dorothy, Harry, Alfred, and some man named Mr. Baker. I don't know his first name."

Shelly quickly wrote down the names. "Let's talk about each of them in turn," she said.

"Where shall we start?" Fenella asked.

"With a cuppa," Shelly laughed. "Should we move this over to my flat? I feel the need for a cuppa."

"I'm more than happy to make tea," Fenella told her. "Let's move into the kitchen and I'll see if I can find something sweet to go with our tea."

Mona glided across the room and sat at one of the stools at the counter. Shelly took the one next to her as Fenella filled the kettle with water. Then she found some cookies and put them on a plate.

"We don't want to eat too much," Shelly reminded her. "Lunch is going to be good."

Fenella nodded. "I've never had a bad meal at the Seaview."

"Okay, let's talk about the eight suspects," Shelly said once they were both sitting down with tea. "Do any of them seem less likely than any of the others?"

"I don't know Mr. Baker at all," Fenella replied. "He may be the most likely. I've never even spoken to him. He's probably around thirty-five. He's tall and slender and he has a small goatee."

"I think for now I'll put him at the bottom of the list," Shelly said. "What part does he play in *Three Gentlewomen from Bologna?*"

"Do you remember the man in the pink jacket who shouts at Brooke about cheese in the first act?"

Shelly nodded. "Was he saying 'cheese'? I don't know why I thought he was saying 'tease.'"

"Maybe that makes more sense. Maybe he's meant to be accusing her of teasing him in some way," Fenella said thoughtfully.

"But he did say 'cheddar' and 'edam,'" Shelly recalled.

Mona made a noise. Fenella looked over at her.

"Edam? What did that have to do with the play?" Mona asked.

Fenella shook her head. "He's in the second act as well. Remember when the older woman comes out and starts hanging up her laundry?"

Shelly nodded. "And it's all socks? Yes, I remember that."

"Mr. Baker is the man who comes through and starts taking everything down behind her," Fenella explained.

"If I were him, I'd be doing just about anything to get out of the show," Mona said.

"I can see why he'd want to shut down *Three Gentlewomen from Bologna*, but I don't know why he'd want to do one of Forrest's plays," Shelly said.

"We really need to work out why our letter writer is so obsessed with Forrest Luna," Fenella said. "I think that's the key to solving the whole thing."

"Maybe he or she is just a big fan," Shelly suggested.

"Maybe. I'm told it's been years since any of his plays were performed on the island. Maybe someone just really wants to see one of shows again, or, more likely, be in one of his shows," Fenella replied.

"But there must be ways to make that happen that don't include setting up fake death scenes and killing innocent people," Shelly added.

Fenella nodded. "What the letter writer is doing does seem quite extreme. I don't know how theater companies work, but I would have thought that anyone in the company could suggest a play for a future production."

"You should ask Breesha," Mona suggested.

"I wonder if Breesha is home and could answer that for me," Fenella added.

"Why don't you ring her?" Shelly asked.

Fenella dug out her mobile phone and found Breesha's number. She put the phone on speaker mode and set it on the counter.

"Hello?"

"Breesha? It's Fenella. Shelly and I were just talking about the letter writer, and we were wondering how the company decides which play to perform next."

"Because couldn't someone just suggest one of Forrest's plays without having to write threatening letters and whatnot?" Shelly interjected.

"It's not quite that simple," Breesha told them. "Anyone can suggest plays or musicals, but the decision-making process is a complicated one. It isn't just about what the company wants to produce, it's also about working with the venue to find shows that they want."

"I'm not sure I understand," Shelly said.

"We perform all of our shows at the Gaiety, and so do two or three other theater companies on the island. If three other companies want to do Shakespeare or maybe musicals, then the Gaiety is less likely to agree to our company doing those things. They want as much variety as possible in their schedule," Breesha explained.

"So they get final say in what you do?" Fenella asked.

"I wouldn't put it quite that way, but they definitely get input. Typically, Josh goes to Harry in January with a list of shows that we're interested in performing, and he and Harry work together to select the three that we eventually do. Last year, they chose two and then left the third, the end-of-the-year show, open, because they couldn't agree. Harry came to Josh in June with the script for *Three Gentlewomen from Bologna*."

"I can't believe Josh approved it," Fenella said frankly.

Breesha sighed. "The initial script was quite different to what you've seen on stage. This is the first time we've ever done a show with the playwright having a hand in the production, and Josh insists it's never going to happen again. Dorothy has made changes to the script at every single rehearsal since we started."

"What would happen if one of the actors wanted to do one of Forrest Luna's plays?" Fenella asked.

"We have regular company meetings every few months, including one in December that doubles as the Christmas party. At that party, Josh always asks for suggestions from everyone for what they'd like to do the next year. We always get suggestions, but I don't know that we've ever actually done any of the shows the cast has suggested," was the reply.

"And has anyone ever suggested a Forrest Luna show?" was Fenella's next question.

"Not that I recall. I'm certain we did at least one over the years, but not recently. I think, if anyone had suggested it, Josh would have said that the plays are outdated now, though."

Fenella looked at Shelly. "Do you have any other questions?" she asked her.

"I didn't have any questions to begin with," Breesha laughed.

After a brief exchange, Fenella ended the call.

"So that explains that," Shelly said. "Someone could have suggested a Forrest Luna play, but it still probably wouldn't have been done."

"Let's get back to the suspects," Mona said.

Fenella looked over at her and had to hide a smile. Mona had her own small notebook in front of her, with her own neatly printed list of suspects.

"I didn't meet any of the suspects," Shelly said after a sip of tea. "You'll have to tell me about each of them."

"Eileen is the older woman who was hanging up the socks," Fenella told her.

"She seemed quite sweet in the play," Shelly replied.

"She seems quite sweet outside of the play, too, although she was in a bad mood yesterday," Fenella said. "But she is the one who lost the earring, which is what gave everyone the excuse to crawl around on the floor in the balcony."

"Which makes her one of the top suspects," Shelly said, circling her name.

"Brooke is the young woman who is the star of the show," Fenella continued.

"She's beautiful," Shelly replied. "I thought she looked as if she'd go through men quite quickly."

"I believe you're right about that, but I can't see that that has anything to do with the letters," Fenella replied.

"But she did cause the disturbance yesterday," Mona pointed out.

"She did," Fenella replied.

"She did what?" Shelly asked.

Fenella flushed. "She did cause the disturbance yesterday," Fenella said quickly. "I started the sentence and then lost my train of thought."

Shelly nodded. "So she has to be one of the main suspects, too." Shelly circled her name as well.

"Then there's Susan," Fenella told her. "She's in her forties, and she was the woman who sat on the couch for ten minutes in the second act without saying a word."

"I thought she looked grumpy," Shelly said. "But maybe she was acting."

"She can be a bit, well, grumpy is a good word," Fenella told her. "I can't see why that would make her more likely as the letter writer, though."

Shelly shrugged. "She can go under Brooke and Eileen, then."

"Josh is the stage manager, but he's also the one who helps choose the plays each year. Surely, if he wanted to do a Forrest Luna show, he'd just ask Harry to let them do one," Fenella said thoughtfully.

"Maybe Harry turned him down," Shelly suggested.

"I'm sure Daniel has asked Harry about that," Fenella replied.

"Harry was there, too," Shelly said. "Tell me about him."

"I keep changing my mind about him," Fenella told her. "Part of me thinks that he wouldn't do anything to deliberately interfere with his daughter's show, and part of me thinks that he's doing everything he can to stop the show from continuing. It is something of a disaster, but he's the one who suggested it in the first place."

"I'm going to put him and Josh with Susan," Shelly told her. "What about Dorothy?"

"Same answer, really. I can't imagine her sabotaging her own show, but we know she isn't happy with it. I can't see why she or her father would target shows elsewhere on the island, though, or why they'd want to promote Forrest Luna. I would expect, with Harry being in charge of the Gaiety, that he could find a company that would be willing to do one of Forrest Luna's plays without too much difficulty."

"Who's left?" Shelly asked. "I don't know who Alfred is."

"He's the director, and he has to know that *Three Gentlewomen from Bologna* is a mess. Having said that, I can't see why he'd want to cause trouble elsewhere, even if I can imagine him sabotaging his own show in an attempt to save his reputation."

"Maybe that's the goal, and the threats to the other theaters are just window dressing," Shelly said. "Maybe the letter writer picked Forrest at random, just to have something to demand."

"At this point, I think anything is possible," Fenella said with a sigh.

"It's also possible that we're going to be late for lunch," Shelly said, glancing at her watch. "I need to go home and change."

Fenella let her out and then put the dishes and plates into the dishwasher. "What should I wear?" she asked Mona who'd followed her into the bedroom.

"The grey dress," Mona told her.

Fenella opened the wardrobe and pulled out the grey dress that was right in front of her. She was fairly certain she'd never seen it before. It only took her a minute to pull it on.

"It's stunning," she said as she twirled in front of the mirror.

"I do wonder if Forrest will remember it," Mona said. "I wore it one evening to a party. That night, Forrest and I danced for hours."

Fenella raised an eyebrow. "Maybe I should wear something else."

"No, that dress is perfect for lunch at the Seaview. I was almost underdressed for the party, but it was outdoors in the summer."

Fenella found the matching shoes and handbag and then fixed her hair and makeup. She was moving what she needed from one handbag to the other when Shelly knocked.

"Ready?" she asked when Fenella opened the door.

"I just need my keys," Fenella told her. "We can take Mona's car, if you want."

"Oh, yes, please," Shelly replied.

Fenella gave Katie her lunch and then followed Shelly into the corridor. After checking that her door was locked, they walked to the elevators and rode down to the large garage under the building.

"Does it use a lot of petrol?" Shelly asked as Fenella drove slowly to the exit.

"Surprisingly little," Fenella said. She thought back over the past year. It wasn't possible, but she couldn't remember putting gas in the car even once. When she looked at the fuel gauge, it showed a full tank, though. That suggested that the gauge was broken, which was worrying. She'd have to have that checked as quickly as possible. The last thing she wanted to do was run out of gas halfway across the island.

The women chatted about the weather and local news as they made their way to Ramsey. Fenella found a spot in the Seaview's large parking lot, and they walked together to the entrance.

"Forrest is here," Shelly said, gesturing toward a large antique car that was parked near the doors.

❦ 11 ❧

"I should have parked near the restaurant entrance," Fenella said as they walked into the hotel's enormous lobby.

"But then we would have missed out on walking through here," Shelly replied. "I love walking through this lobby. It's just so gorgeous."

"Thank you kindly," a voice said from their left.

"Jasper," Fenella said as the man rushed toward them.

Jasper Coventry was one of the owners of the hotel and also its manager. He gave each of them a hug and then stepped back and smiled at them. "The wedding plans are moving along nicely," he reported. "I've been speaking with your florist. She has some exciting ideas. I think you'll be pleased."

"Nothing too expensive," Shelly said worriedly, glancing at Fenella.

"Money is no object," Fenella countered. "I want my dearest friend to have the most wonderful wedding possible."

Shelly looked as if she wanted to argue, but Jasper held up a hand.

"We're being mindful of the budget," he told Shelly. "But we're working on doing something truly spectacular as well," he said to Fenella. "The florist has been wanting to try a few super creative things that she saw in a magazine, and I've agreed to try to help her. I worked in a florist shop in London for a few years when I was much younger. I think, between us, we're going to wow everyone."

"I'm certain of it," Fenella replied.

"And now, you're meeting Mr. Luna for lunch," Jasper said. "It's lovely to have him here. I'm a huge fan of his work."

"Have you ever done any acting?" Shelly asked.

Jasper blushed. "I did a bit at university, and I was part of a small community theater company for a few years after that, but it's been decades since I performed."

"There are a number of very good local companies," Shelly told him. "Maybe you should audition for something."

"I wish I had the time, but this business takes up just about all of my waking hours. I'm not certain why Stuart and I thought it would be fun to have our own hotel. It's a good deal more work than either of us ever imagined it would be."

"It's such a beautiful place," Fenella said.

He nodded. "And we've loved being able to live here, but we're both getting older." He took a step closer to her and lowered his voice. "Stuart and I have been talking about retiring," he whispered. "At the moment, we're just turning the idea over in our minds, but we aren't getting any younger. Having said that, we deliberately booked ourselves a long holiday this winter, and now we're coming back for a fortnight right in the middle of it all. Neither of us is any good at not working."

"I hope you aren't coming back just for me," Shelly said quickly.

"Not at all. I'm delighted that we're able to fit your wedding into our plans, actually. It's going to be the highlight of our fortnight back on the island."

Fenella wondered why they were coming back to the island at all, although she was grateful that they were, because Shelly had really had her heart set on using their ballroom for her wedding reception.

"And now I must escort you to Forrest," Jasper said. "I should never have kept you for so long."

He offered them each an arm and then led them through the lobby and down a long corridor. When they reached the restaurant, he escorted them to one of the private dining rooms at the back of the room.

When he opened the door, the grey-haired man who was sitting at the table slowly got to his feet. He smiled broadly. "Shelly," he said softly. "It's so good to see you again."

Shelly crossed to his side and pulled him into a hug.

"Enjoy your lunch," Jasper said as he shut the door behind himself.

"I've missed you," Forrest said as he sat back down. "I'm terribly sorry that I didn't attend your husband's funeral. I've had a long battle with ill health, and it's only in the last couple of months that I've begun to feel like myself again. I'm sorry for your loss."

Shelly blushed. "Thank you. It's good to see you, too. I didn't realize that you'd been ill. I should have stayed in touch more."

He shrugged. "I've always been a fairly private person, in spite of my becoming well known for a short while. Over the last few years, I've become known as a recluse, and I've found that it suits me."

"I don't believe I told you, when we talked on the phone, that I'm getting married again," Shelly said after a moment. "You'll be getting an invitation to the wedding soon."

Forrest looked surprised and then smiled. "What wonderful news. I assume the man in question must be someone very special."

"He is," Shelly replied. "But where are my manners? This is Fenella. Fenella, this is Forrest."

Fenella took a few steps forward and held out a hand.

He stared at her. "But that was Mona's dress," he said after a moment. "I remember it so very clearly."

She nodded. "In addition to inheriting her estate, I also inherited her wardrobe," she explained.

He shook his head and then took her hand. "I do apologize. I almost feel as if I've seen a ghost."

Fenella forced herself to laugh as she quickly glanced around the room to see if Mona had made an unexpected appearance. There was no sign of her aunt anywhere. "It's very nice to meet you," she said.

"Likewise," he replied. "Your aunt was a very special person. I'd like to believe that we had a unique connection. I could have fallen in love with her so very easily, if she hadn't been so devoted to Max. Of course, after a while I was married, which was another complication, but I do believe, if I could do my entire life over again, I would have done more to try to convince Mona to leave Max and run away with me. In my dreams, she always says yes."

Fenella smiled. "I'm glad you have fond memories of her."

"But we aren't here to talk about Mona," Forrest said with a sigh. "I feel as if I should apologize for wanting to speak with you, but I thought you might be the one person who could help. I know you've been caught up in a number of murder investigations, and I know that you're marrying a police inspector. Who better to discuss my concerns with than you?"

"I don't know what I can to do to help, but I'm happy to listen," Fenella replied.

"Let's order lunch," Forrest suggested. "I'm starving, although I don't actually eat much these days."

They looked over the menus, including a separate sheet that listed the day's specials, and then Fenella pushed the button to summon the waiter. Once they'd ordered, she sat down next to Forrest, with Shelly on his other side, and smiled at him.

"What did you want to discuss?" she asked him.

"I can't help but feel as if I should know who is behind this letter writing campaign," he said. "I can't imagine anyone becoming obsessed with me. It simply doesn't make sense."

Fenella nodded. "As you say, I've been involved in a number of murder investigations. Many times, the killer's motive hasn't made sense to me."

Forrest sighed. "Would it be terribly rude of me to tell you my life story? I gave Inspector Robinson an abbreviated version, but there must be something I've missed. There has to be something, some-where in my past, that is causing what's happening today."

"I'm more than happy to hear your life story," Fenella replied. "But you should know that it's also possible that the letter writer wants a play, or more than one play, shut down for reasons that have nothing to do with you. He or she may have selected you at random, just to have something to demand, if you see what I mean."

"As odd as that sounds, it's almost more believable than anything else," Forrest said. "None of this makes any sense to me. And I can't help but feel responsible for that poor man's death as well."

"You are in no way responsible for Mr. Allen's death," Fenella said firmly. "You mustn't feel that way."

The waiter pushed the door open and entered, carrying their drinks on a tray. "Your lunch will be here shortly," he said after he'd given out the drinks.

"Thanks," Fenella said.

As the door shut behind him, Fenella turned to Forrest. "So, tell me your story," she said.

He frowned. "This could be a complete waste of time."

"We could talk about the weather or the royal family," Fenella replied. "But I'd really like to hear your life story. I'm sure it's fascinating."

He chuckled. "I wish it were considerably more interesting than it actually is," he told her. "I'm afraid I shall bore you completely."

"If I get bored, I'll let you know," Fenella teased.

"I don't even know where to begin," he protested.

"Were you born on the island?" Fenella asked.

"I was, indeed," he told her. "Seventy-um, well, seventy-plus years ago. I haven't counted exactly how many lately. The Second World War still had a year or two to go, but I didn't pay that any attention while I was busy learning to walk and talk." He stopped to take a sip of his drink.

"Do you have any brothers or sisters?" Fenella asked after a moment.

"Sadly, or maybe fortunately, I was an only child. My mother had fallen pregnant while my father was home on leave from the army, or at least that's the story I was always told. The dates didn't quite work, and my mother never fell pregnant again, so I've always wondered if my father was someone other than the man to whom my mother was married, but such things were never discussed in those days," he told her.

He fell silent again. After a minute, Fenella asked another question. "Did you get along well with your parents?"

"My mother's husband, I find it painful to call him my father, was a difficult man with whom to live. I suppose today he would be diagnosed with post-traumatic stress disorder and probably several other mental health issues, but in those days he was simply regarded as angry and short-tempered. I spent the bulk of my childhood hiding from him."

"I'm sorry," Fenella said.

"He worked only intermittently. It's difficult to hold down a job when you drink for eight or ten hours a day. When he wasn't working, he sat at home and shouted at my mother. In his defense, he never abused her physically, but he was always so angry. Inexplicably so to a small child."

"How awful for you," Fenella murmured.

Forrest shrugged. "I learned to live inside my head. We didn't have much money, but I read every book I could get my hands on, from children's books to my mother's romance novels, to whatever happened to be lying around anywhere that I went. When I had nothing to read, I made up my own stories. I really should be more grateful for my miserable upbringing, as it fed my imagination. Perhaps if I'd had a happy childhood, I would have become an accountant, or found some other job that requires less in terms of creativity."

"Some accountants are very creative," Shelly laughed.

"Did you have close friends in childhood?" Fenella asked after a moment.

He shook his head. "I struggled to make friends. I've never been very good at it. I can write about relationships more successfully than I can negotiate through them in the real world."

"Can you remember anyone from your childhood who might still remember you and, I don't know, want to see another of your shows?" Fenella wondered.

"There was a girl called Helen who went to school with me. She was the closest thing I had to a friend. I don't remember her surname, but she and her family moved across when we were around nine or ten. I haven't seen or heard from her since, though."

Fenella sighed. "No one else?"

He shook his head. "I could give you a list of names of some of the boys and girls who were in my class at school, but none of them were a part of my life outside of school. I went to class, and then I went home and kept to myself. I went away to university at eighteen, eager to get off the island and reinvent myself elsewhere."

"Where did you go?" Fenella asked.

"Cambridge," he told her. "For one term. I found the experience overwhelming. Being surrounded by people all the time was difficult for me after my solitary childhood. I left for the winter break and never went back."

"Here we are," the waiter said brightly as he walked in with their food. It took him only a moment to deliver their plates. "Do you need anything else?" he asked when he was done.

"I think we're good," Fenella told him. She waited until he'd gone before she turned to Forrest. "What did you do after you left Cambridge?"

"I decided I didn't want to come back to the island, so I took myself off to London. I had no idea what I was going to do with my life, but I thought I had a better chance of accomplishing something in London than anywhere else."

"If Cambridge was overwhelming, London must have been just as bad," Fenella suggested.

He chuckled. "Of course it was. It was hideous, but I made up my mind to stay there for at least a year. I counted down the days, though, from three hundred and sixty-five to one. I promised myself that if I could make it for the entire year, I could go anywhere else in the world."

"This is delicious," Shelly said.

Fenella nodded. "It's very good," she said, feeling impatient. Forrest didn't seem to mind talking about his past, but she felt as if she was having to drag information out of him, a tiny bit at a time. "So you left London after a year?" she asked after another pause.

"Yes, and I came back to the island," he told her. "I'd started writing plays by that time — plays, stories, novels, a bit of everything. The first thing I sold was actually a short story. I sold it to a magazine in London just a few days before I moved back here. They encouraged me to send them more stories, and I started to think that maybe I could make a living from writing, something that hadn't seemed possible in London."

"What did you do in London?" Fenella wondered.

Forrest stared at her for a moment and then laughed. "Anything and everything to make ends meet," he told her. "I probably held half a dozen different jobs over the course of that year. I worked in a pub. I worked in the mailroom of one of the national newspapers. I waited tables. I worked as an assistant gardener at a stately home. I'm sure there were other jobs that I've forgotten as well. I didn't enjoy any of them, but they all gave me a chance to watch people. I was quickly discovering that watching people was what I enjoyed most of all."

"But you moved back to the island just after you sold your first story?" Fenella checked.

He nodded. "London was expensive, even back then. I knew I could live on the island much more cheaply. I also knew that I had enough ideas to write a thousand stories. I decided that I could always move back to London again when I ran out of ideas."

Fenella swallowed her last bite. "When did you start writing plays?"

"Once I'd realized that I love writing, I started writing a bit of everything. Not just stories, plays, and novels, but across genres as well. I wanted to try it all. I just kept hoping that something might succeed. Writing for a living was the ultimate dream. I envisioned having a little cottage somewhere remote and simply writing all the time."

Fenella looked over at Shelly. Her friend smiled sympathetically. "What happened once you were back on the island, then?" Shelly asked.

"I rented a tiny flat in Port St. Mary, and I wrote and wrote and wrote," he told her. "I sold stories to a dozen different magazines, all under different pen names. I don't remember how many stories I sold or all of the names that I used. I also worked on the docks around the island, helping the fishermen with their daily catches. I get too seasick to do the fishing myself, but I could make a bit of money helping them when they went out in the morning and when they got back at night."

"Pudding?" the waiter asked as he cleared their plates.

"Yes, please," Fenella said, feeling as if she deserved something sweet.

He handed around dessert menus. After they'd ordered and the man left, Forrest sighed.

"I'm making this into an ordeal for you," he said. "I've never been good at talking about myself. I'm going to try to speed things along. Otherwise, we'll still be here when it's time for dinner."

"I'd happily eat here again," Shelly told him.

He nodded. "I'd forgotten how good the food is here, but where was I? I was working on the docks and writing stories for everyone. I had a few plays drafted, but then I wrote one that I thought had a real chance at success. I polished it as best I could and sent it to a few contacts I'd made in London. To cut a long story short, that play was my first big success. It was performed on the West End, and for a short while it looked as if I was going to be quite famous."

"Was that something you wanted?" Fenella asked.

He sighed. "There were aspects that I enjoyed, but I wasn't interested in going back to London, and that was necessary if I wanted to truly capitalize on my initial success. What did happen, though, was that I was suddenly a good deal more popular on the island. I moved into a new social circle, one that included Mona and Max, and that changed my life."

"Pudding," the waiter announced as he walked back into the room.

After he'd passed around their plates and left the room, Fenella took a bite of her chocolate cake and smiled. "Delicious," she sighed. "But you were saying something about Max and Mona," she said.

"They were incredible. I fell in love with Mona, but I think most men did. I had too much respect for Max to try to take her away from him, but as I said earlier, I would do things differently if I had another chance. There were rumors and stories about Mona, but I never believed any of them. She was devoted to Max, and I don't think she truly ever looked at another man, whatever people said about her."

Fenella nodded. "I believe you're right about that."

"I wrote a play about them — well, it's really about Mona. It became a huge success. I'd already decided that I needed a change. I needed to get away from the island. I felt as if I needed new experiences, that my plays needed to be filled with new sights and new adventures. I selected Australia as the perfect destination."

"I've heard it's a wonderful country, except for the spiders," Shelly said.

"Spiders, crocodiles, snakes, Australia is full of things that want to kill you. But if you stick to the cities, you're as safe there as you are in London," he replied. "Of course, I had to spend some time in the Outback, hiking and looking for trouble. While it had taken me years to find success, in some ways it came too easily for me. I didn't feel as if I deserved the accolades. If I'm honest, I still don't believe that I deserve the success that I've had."

"Your plays are brilliant," Shelly told him.

He shrugged. "There are plenty of brilliant writers out there. I was also lucky."

"What happened next?" Fenella asked as she scraped up the last of her icing.

"I fell in love," he said with a sigh. "Or rather, I fell in lust or infatuation or something. Jane looked a good deal like Mona, which was what caught my eye initially. We met on a Tuesday and I proposed on the Friday. We were married a week later."

"My goodness," Fenella said.

He chuckled. "We both thought we were madly in love. Maybe we were. I don't know. Although I write love stories, I don't truly understand the emotion."

"Does anyone?" Shelly asked.

He shrugged. "Perhaps it's best that we don't. The confusion allows writers to make fortunes telling stories about it, at least. But we've had lunch and pudding and I'm still over thirty years behind the present. Jane and I got married. We honeymooned in New Zealand and then started our life together in Sydney. Our first child arrived ten months later, and the next two followed in quick succession. I adored them. Anything I do actually know about love comes from having had my children. They were the best things that ever happened to me."

"Boys or girls?" Fenella asked after a moment.

He smiled at her. "One boy, the oldest, who is, of course, a man now. And two daughters. Please don't get me started talking about my children. We'll be here until the weekend, and we won't get any closer to working out who is writing those horrible letters."

"Just tell us a little bit about each one," Shelly suggested. "You used to tell me about them, years ago. In fact, I believe I met one of your daughters once."

He thought for a moment and then nodded. "Rosalind, my youngest, visited frequently through her teen years. She and her mother had a difficult relationship. She didn't want to live here, but she used to spend months at a time visiting when she got breaks from school. Now she's a teacher in Wyoming, of all places."

"How did she end up in Wyoming?" Fenella asked.

"She went to Cambridge for university, following in my footsteps, although that's something of a joke, seeing that I dropped out after a single semester. I do have an honorary degree from them, though. Anyway, her first year there she met an American student on some sort of exchange program. They fell in love, and once they were both finished with school, they got married, and she moved to Wyoming to be with him."

"And your other two children?" Shelly wanted to know.

"My son, Antony, lives in Switzerland. He loves to ski, so he started working for a ski resort there while he was at university. He's now the manager and part-owner of one of the largest ski resorts in the country."

"Is he married?" Fenella asked.

"No, I don't believe his lifestyle is conducive to long-term relationships. Every time I visit him, he has a different woman in his life. My other daughter, Portia, lives in New Zealand. She's a mechanical engineer, and she's single at the moment. She was married for a year to a man she'd met through work, but obviously it didn't work out."

"How often do you see your children?" Fenella wondered.

"Fairly regularly. I should go back in time a bit and tell you about my marriage, though. We were happy together for about three years and stayed together for five. At that point, I realized that I wanted to come back here. It took some effort, but Jane eventually agreed. Sadly, we arrived back on the island on a rainy day in February. By March, she was on a plane back to Sydney."

"With the children?" Shelly checked.

"Yes, with the children. They were still very young and we both agreed that they needed their mother more than they needed me. I considered going back with them, but once I'd returned to the island, I found that I had no interest in going back to Australia. It had been a pleasant enough interlude, but it wasn't home."

"I can understand that," Fenella said. "The island has very quickly come to feel very much like home to me."

He nodded. "So, Jane and the children left, and I settled back into life on the island. I'd written quite a few plays while I'd been in Australia and they were proving very successful there. Some of them had even been made into movies. To put it bluntly, I didn't need to work any longer. I bought a large house, and I stopped doing much of anything other than enjoying myself. That lasted about a month. Then I started writing again."

"Can I get anyone anything else?" the waiter asked as he cleared away the dessert dishes.

"I don't think so, but we may be here for a bit longer," Fenella told him.

"Stay as long as you like," he told them. "The lunch crowd has gone, and we won't have people coming in for dinner for hours yet."

"I need to talk faster," Forrest said. "Where was I? Oh, yes, I couldn't seem to stop myself from writing. In between plays, I traveled back to Australia to see the children. They used to come here as well, for weeks at a time, sometimes all together and other times each on his or her own. Jane and I used to try to divide their time between us as much as possible, but, of course, school was also a consideration."

"And you and Jane remained married?" Fenella asked.

"We're still married," he told her. "We often speak of trying again, now that we're both older and wiser. I think, if we'd done so a few years ago, we might have made it work, but now Jane's health isn't good and she can't travel here. I could go there, if I truly wanted to see her, but, sadly, I don't want it badly enough. I'm too settled in my ways now, I fear."

"And the children are all adults," Fenella said.

"Yes, indeed, and they all try to see me at least once or twice a year.

We take it in turns to do the traveling, although they all visit their mother in Sydney at Christmas. I've spent months at a time in Wyoming, and I've been on ski holidays to Switzerland most winters as well. I don't believe I've ever gone more than six months without seeing any of them."

"And, aside from some traveling, you've been on the island ever since?" Fenella asked.

He nodded. "I've never wanted to be anywhere else. I've kept writing as well. I retired from actively putting my work out there years ago, but I never stopped writing. My children will inherit a stack of unpublished scripts. What they choose to do with them is entirely up to them."

"I wonder if the letter writer knows about your unpublished work," Fenella said thoughtfully. "Maybe he or she is hoping to drag you out of retirement."

"No one knows about the unpublished work, aside from you and Shelly," he told her, winking at Shelly.

"What about other women in your life?" Fenella asked.

"Since Jane and I are still married, I haven't looked at another woman since I said my vows. I know that's an old-fashioned notion, but I'm an old-fashioned man."

"You must have made some friends over the years," Fenella said as she tried to think.

He shook his head. "As I said earlier, I've always been happiest on my own. I was close to my agent for many years, but Don passed away about fifteen years ago now."

"Was he married? Did he have children? Maybe one of them is trying to restart your career. If that happens, would the children be entitled to anything?" Fenella asked.

Forrest chuckled. "It's a brilliant idea, but Don never married. He had a longtime companion named Robert, but they never had children."

Fenella sighed. "Maybe the letter writer is simply a fan," she said. "Do you get a great deal of mail from fans?"

"Years ago, I used to get letters. I still have several boxes of them tucked away somewhere. I used to read through them whenever I started to feel as if I couldn't write, which used to happen fairly frequently," he told her. "These days, I get a handful every month, and nearly all of them come from Australia."

"I wonder if it would be worth going through the letters, looking for anyone who might have a connection to *Three Gentlewomen from Bologna*," Fenella said thoughtfully. "Maybe Adam's mother wrote to you every week in the seventies, or some such thing. Maybe someone was raised to be obsessed with you."

Forrest frowned. "I could try to find the old boxes and take a look through them, but they aren't complete. I only kept the most complimentary of letters. They all went to my agent, and Don used to reply on my behalf before he'd send them on to me. Once in a while, he'd ask me to write a short note to someone who had a particularly compelling story. I'm sorry to say that I didn't always comply."

"Do you know if you still have the letters that he asked you to reply to?" Fenella asked. "There could be something there, although it's a real long shot."

"I can look," Forrest said. "I'll do that this afternoon. I can get my assistant to get the boxes out for me, and then I can go through them before and after dinner. I'll ring you if I find anything of interest."

"Do you have the names of the people who are involved in *Three Gentlewomen from Bologna*?" Fenella asked.

"You'd better make me a list," he replied.

Fenella dug through her handbag. She'd had the program from the show in her other bag, but she'd probably not bothered to move it to this bag. "Ah, ha," she exclaimed when she found it buried under her wallet.

"You can keep this," she told Forrest. "I have others."

He took the program and sighed. "It's been far too long since I've seen a show," he told her, slowly turning the pages.

"You should come and see *Three Gentlewomen from Bologna* with me," Fenella said impulsively.

"There's a thought," Forrest replied.

❧ 12 ❧

"Were you serious about taking Forrest to see the show?" Shelly asked Fenella as they made their way home a short time later.

"Yes and no," she replied. "Daniel may not think it's a good idea. Until we know more about the letter writer, it's possible that Forrest is in danger."

"I hadn't thought of that," Shelly said. "Now I'm going to worry about him even more than I already was."

"He's a lovely man."

"He is, and he's very upset by what's happening."

"I don't blame him. I can't imagine what he's feeling."

"This has to be the strangest thing ever. Why would someone want one of his plays performed? I don't understand it."

"You and Josh both mentioned that Forrest used to go to see his own shows," Fenella said as the idea popped into her head. "What if someone wants to meet him and can't figure out any other way to accomplish it?"

"Surely, he or she could just ring him up and ask him out to lunch or something," Shelly argued.

"He said he was a recluse. Maybe he doesn't accept invitations."

Shelly frowned. "You could be right. When I rang him the other day, I actually had to speak to his assistant for several minutes before the man would even agree to tell Forrest that I'd rung. I had to convince him that I truly did know Forrest and that Forrest really would want to speak with me."

"So there you are. Maybe someone rang Forrest's home and the assistant wouldn't let him or her talk to Forrest. Maybe that someone is now causing all sorts of problems, simply because he or she wants to meet the man."

"It's the most plausible theory I've heard yet," Shelly told her. "That isn't saying much, though," she added.

Fenella laughed. "I'll call Daniel when we get home and see what he thinks of my theory."

The drive back was uneventful.

"Do you want to come in?" Fenella asked Shelly at her door.

"I'd really like to hear what Daniel thinks of your theory," Shelly admitted.

"Why don't you go and get Smokey?" Fenella suggested. "The cats haven't had a chance to play together lately."

The two cats chased each other around the apartment for a minute or two and then settled down together in a sunny spot near the windows. Fenella made tea and then reached for the phone.

"Three messages," she said as she looked at the answering machine. "Should I listen first and then call Daniel, or call Daniel first?"

"I'd listen first, just in case Daniel is one of the people who rang," Shelly said.

"Good point," Fenella laughed.

She pressed the play button on the machine.

Ah, Maggie, hello, a familiar voice said. *I was just calling to say hello, really. Um, Linda says hello, too. We're doing well, and we've been discussing coming over to see you one day soon. I'll call back later today or tomorrow.*

Fenella deleted the message and looked over at Shelly. "Jack and his wife might be coming for a visit," she said.

"Is that good news?"

"I guess so," Fenella replied. "I mean, I like Linda, and I was happy to go to the wedding and celebrate with her and Jack, but I'm not sure I want them coming here."

"And he's still calling you Maggie," Shelly laughed.

"I actually started to tell him not to and then decided that I didn't really mind all that much," Fenella told her. "It would be odd now, after all these years, for him to call me anything else."

She leaned forward and pressed play on the answering machine again.

Fen, it's Daniel. Just wanted you to know that I was thinking of you.

She smiled and pushed the button to save the message.

Fenella, it's Breesha. Dorothy asked me to ring you. She wants me to invite you to tonight's rehearsal. She wants your opinion on some of the changes she'd like to make to the show. I told her that I would invite you, but that you may be busy. You don't have to ring me back. Rehearsal starts at seven. The stage door will be open, but I believe there will be a constable stationed there. You may need to get permission from Daniel to be allowed inside the theater.

"I suppose I'd better call Daniel," Fenella said.

"Do you want to go to the rehearsal?" Shelly asked.

"I'm not sure I want to sit through *Three Gentlewomen from Bologna* again, but I'm curious what changes Dorothy is planning to make. I also wonder if Adam and/or Brooke will even turn up. I think my nosiness is stronger than my dislike for the show, but only slightly."

Shelly laughed. "Now you've made me want to come to the rehearsal, too," she complained.

"I can call Breesha and ask her if anyone would mind if I brought a friend."

"I don't want to be in the way."

"Let me see what Daniel has to say first." Fenella dialed the number for his office.

"Daniel Robinson."

"Hello," she said. "I had lunch with Forrest Luna. I thought you might like to hear what we talked about."

He chuckled. "Why am I not surprised?"

"I have a theory as to why the letter writer is writing the letters, too," she told him.

"That's one possibility," Daniel said after Fenella had told him everything that happened over lunch and then shared her theory with him.

"Do you think I should bring Forrest to a show, then?" she asked.

"Let me give that idea some thought," he replied.

"When I got home, I had a message from Breesha," she added. "Dorothy asked her to call me and invite me to tonight's rehearsal. Apparently, Dorothy wants to see what I think of some of the changes she's planning to make."

"Why you?"

"I've no idea."

He sighed. "Do you want to go to the rehearsal tonight?"

"I was just telling Shelly that part of me wants to go, and part of me doesn't ever want to see *Three Gentlewomen from Bologna* ever again."

Daniel laughed. "Yes, well, I have to go to the rehearsal tonight, whether I want to or not. I'd love to sit with you and watch the show together, but I'll be backstage, keeping an eye on our, um, witnesses."

"I don't want to upset you or do anything stupid. Do you think I'd be in any danger if I came?"

"It won't upset me if you come, as long as you're sensible about it. There will be several constables there and more than one inspector as well. Maybe you could bring Shelly with you as well. The important thing is to not find yourself alone with anyone."

"Do you have plans for dinner?" she asked.

"I'm going to be working straight through dinner, I'm afraid. I'll probably be here until half five, and I have to be at the theater not long after six. I'll grab a sandwich somewhere along the way."

"I could bring you something."

"I promise that I'll eat," he told her. "Take Shelly out for a nice meal as an apology for dragging her to see *Three Gentlewomen from Bologna* again."

Fenella laughed. "There is that."

They chatted for a few minutes longer about nothing much. When Fenella put the phone down, she sighed.

"What's wrong?" Shelly asked.

"I knew it wasn't going to be easy, being involved with a police inspector, but it would be nice to have dinner with him once in a while."

"My fiancé isn't a police inspector, and I haven't seen him since Saturday," Shelly replied.

"Where's Tim?"

"He had to go across on Sunday for some big meeting. He'll be back tomorrow."

"So we can have dinner together and then go to the theater and watch the rehearsal."

"We can?"

"Daniel suggested that I bring you along," Fenella told her. "I suppose I should ring Breesha and see if she thinks anyone at the theater will mind, though."

"Doncan Quayle's office," Breesha's voice came down the line.

"Hi, Breesha, it's Fenella. I'm happy — well, maybe not happy, but I'm willing to come to the rehearsal tonight. Willing doesn't sound quite right, either, though."

Breesha laughed. "I understand what you mean, though. I think we're all quite tired of *Three Gentlewomen from Bologna*. Dorothy will be thrilled to hear that you're coming. She said that you've given her the best advice of anyone after each performance."

"I don't remember giving her any advice."

"Maybe that's what she meant. Maybe she wants you there because you don't make any suggestions about things to change."

Fenella sighed. "I wouldn't know how to help her change things, anyway. The play is such a mess as it is."

"So I'll see you tonight around seven."

"One more thing," Fenella said quickly. "Will anyone mind if I bring Shelly with me?"

"No one will even notice, and if they do, they won't mind," Breesha assured her. "Rehearsals are always full of people coming and going. People invite friends or family members and all sorts. The only difference tonight will be a significant police presence. No one at the theater will mind, but Daniel might."

"It was his idea," Fenella told her. "He doesn't want there to be any chance of me ending up alone with any of the suspects."

"I don't blame him for that. I don't want to be alone with any of them either, even though I don't really think anyone is in any real danger. In spite of Mr. Allen's tragic death, I don't think the letter writer wants to hurt anyone."

"I hope you're right. Regardless, I think we'll all sleep better after he or she has been arrested."

"Indeed."

Fenella put the phone down and looked at Shelly. "Where would you like to get dinner?" she asked.

Shelly laughed. "I feel as if we just had lunch, but it's already getting close to dinner time. We talked to Forrest for a long time."

"He's led an interesting life. I enjoyed talking with him."

"I just wish we'd found some hint in his past as to who is writing the letters," Shelly sighed.

"Maybe he'll find something when he goes through his fan mail. I think the threatening letters have all been typed, so the police won't be able to compare handwriting, sadly."

"What about the envelopes?" Shelly asked. "I was just reading a murder mystery where they identified the killer because he had hand-written the envelope when he sent the ransom demand. He printed the letter on his printer, but he didn't know how to print envelopes."

Fenella smiled. "I know how to print envelopes, but I very rarely bother. It's usually easier to just write them out. Remind me to ask Daniel about the envelopes tonight."

"Of course, Forrest might not find anything interesting in his letters."

"And if he does, those might be typed as well. I doubt he'll have kept the envelopes."

Shelly sighed. "Let's talk about something else," she suggested.

"Wedding plans?"

She made a face. "Things are coming along, and I'm really trying not to think about the wedding. I'm looking forward to it, obviously, and to being married to Tim, but I'm also quite terrified of both the wedding and the marriage. I do best when I pretend it isn't happening."

"Are you okay?"

Shelly looked at her and then slowly nodded. "It's mostly cold feet, and Tim and I have discussed it several times. He's absolutely certain that we're doing the right thing and that we're going to live happily ever after. When I'm with him, I feel much the same way, but when I haven't seen him for a few days, the doubts start creeping back into my head. I'm making myself crazy, which is why I'm trying not to think about it at all."

"I won't bring it up again, but if you find that you need someone to talk to, I'm more than willing to listen," Fenella told her. "For what it's worth, I'm happy to be engaged to Daniel, but I'm not ready to plan our wedding yet. He said something the other day about setting a date, and my heart skipped a beat."

Shelly chuckled. "We're a mess, both of us."

"So, what should we talk about?"

They chatted about favorite books until time for a quick dinner at a nearby restaurant. They were at the theater a few minutes before seven.

"Ms. Woods," Constable Corlett said as they approached the stage door. "Inspector Robinson told me to expect you and Ms. Quirk." He opened the door for them.

"Thanks," Fenella said as they walked inside.

"Where are we?" Shelly asked, looking around the dark space.

"Behind the stage and behind another set of curtains," Fenella told her. "We can go backstage or out into the theater. Which sounds better?"

"The theater," Shelly replied.

Fenella nodded. "I think you're right."

As they walked along the narrow passage next to the stage, Fenella could hear voices.

"...five or six times," someone was saying. "You can't just shout out your lines as if you don't know what they mean. You need to tell the story."

"Dorothy, darling, if I knew the story, I'd try to tell it," was the reply.

"Do you recognize the voices?" Shelly whispered.

"I think Dorothy was talking to Adam," she replied. "Which means he may not have quit the show after all."

A moment later, they emerged into the brightly lit theater. Daniel was sitting in the front row with a constable on either side of him. As Fenella glanced around, she spotted a constable in one of the boxes and another near the back of the room. Another familiar face was standing near the stage.

"Good evening," Mark Hammersmith said.

Fenella nodded and forced herself to smile at the man, who worked with Daniel. Some time back, while Daniel had been in Milton Keynes for several weeks, Mark had been put in charge of several murder investigations in which Fenella had been involved. At the time, she'd felt as if he hadn't cared for her, and nothing had happened since to change her mind on the subject. "Good evening," she replied.

"Let's try that again," Dorothy said as she walked down the steps from the stage. She smiled brightly when she saw Fenella. "Ms. Woods, you came," she exclaimed. "We've only just started. We can start over again, actually. I want you to see it all."

"I don't want to cause difficulties," Fenella protested.

"It's fine. I'm so happy you're here. And you brought your friend. That's even better," Dorothy replied.

Fenella introduced Shelly to the woman, and then she and Shelly took seats in the front row. Dorothy went back up the steps and said a few words to the actors on the stage. When she was done, the actors all left while Dorothy walked back down to sit next to Fenella.

"The new opening is very powerful," Dorothy told her in a loud whisper. "And curtain," she shouted.

The curtains slid shut and then opened again. As they opened, Brooke and Adam walked out onto the stage.

"Seven times seven times seven," Adam said flatly.

"Three hundred and forty-three, if it matters," Brooke replied.

"Everything matters. Nothing matters. The world is a simulation wrapped in an enigma," Adam replied.

"Or maybe three hundred and forty-three of them," Brooke suggested.

"Two times two times a million and three," a voice shouted.

Fenella slid down in her seat, regretting her decision to come. Beside her, Shelly seemed to be suppressing laughter as Dorothy stopped the show.

"You got the line wrong," she told Susan who'd just walked onto the stage. "The correct line is three thousand, seven hundred, and six."

"But that's not the right answer to the math problem that Adam just said," Susan argued.

"It's meant to be wrong," Dorothy told her. "Your character gets such things wrong."

Susan shrugged. "Whatever," she muttered as she walked back across the stage. "Three thousand, six hundred and ninety-one," she said.

"That isn't the line either," Dorothy interrupted again.

"You said I was supposed to get it wrong. That's definitely wrong," Susan said crossly.

"But it isn't the line," Dorothy argued. "Please do it exactly the way I wrote it."

Susan sighed and then started again.

Half an hour later, Fenella needed something for a headache.

"I need a drink," Shelly whispered in her ear as Dorothy stopped the rehearsal yet again.

"This is worse than the actual play," Fenella replied. "At least they didn't keep stopping during the show. I've no idea where we are in the play, but I don't think we're anywhere near the end."

"Dorothy, I think we all need a break," Harry said a short while later. He'd been sitting at the very back of the theater. Now he walked down the center aisle and looked at his daughter. "Everyone is getting muddled up because of all of the changes. Maybe you should try doing a table read first, just to take everyone through the new script."

"We could do that," Dorothy said, frowning.

"Everyone take a five minute break," Harry announced. "When we come back, we'll sit around the stage and read through the new script. People can ask questions, if they have any, and Dorothy can hear how it all sounds."

Dorothy sank down in her seat and put her head in her hands. "It just isn't working," she said softly.

"Are you okay?" Fenella asked after a moment.

"Not at all," Dorothy said. She looked up with tears streaming down her cheeks. "They won't listen to me and then, when they can't make sense of the story, they blame me. It's complex and layered with meaning, but it works only if everyone knows his or her lines and says them perfectly. As soon as one person makes a mistake, the whole script becomes incomprehensible."

As Fenella tried to think of a way to reply, Dorothy got to her feet. "I need some fresh air," she said before walking quickly out of the room.

Fenella blew out a breath. "Do you want to leave?" she asked Shelly.

"I want to know who the eight suspects are," Shelly told her in a whisper.

"Why don't you go backstage and introduce Shelly to everyone?" Daniel suggested.

Fenella hadn't seen him move, and she jumped when he spoke near her ear.

"Are you coming with us?" Fenella asked as she and Shelly stood up.

He nodded. "I thought it might be interesting if you told the cast and crew about the man you had lunch with today," he said.

"Oh? Should I try to get him an invitation to come and see the show?" Fenella asked.

"It might be better if he comes to a rehearsal," Daniel replied. "So far, no one has tried to sabotage the rehearsals."

"I don't know. I feel as if Dorothy is coming close," Fenella muttered.

Daniel sighed. "I can't imagine why anyone is still willing to do the show. If it were me, I'd have quit a long time ago."

The trio walked up the steps to the stage, and then Daniel led Shelly and Fenella through the curtains to the backstage area. It was oddly quiet as they stepped through the second set of curtains.

"Ah, please tell me that you've come to arrest me for something," Adam said. "I'll even confess to something if you can get me out of here."

Daniel shook his head. "Unless you're ready to confess to having written the threatening letters, I'm not going to arrest you."

"Yes, well, the problem with that is that the letter writer has also confessed to causing Mr. Allen's death. I certainly don't want to be associated with that," Adam replied.

"Surely, no one does," Susan said.

"The letter writer clearly does," Adam argued. "Instead of confessing, he or she could have insisted that the railing must have been unhooked before we arrived at the theater."

"But the police checked the theater before they opened that night," Brooke said. "The railing had to have been tampered with by someone in the audience."

"Brooke, darling, you're accusing all of us of murder," Adam said.

She flushed. "It wasn't murder, and anyone from the audience could have sneaked up into the balcony and unhooked the railing before we even arrived at the theater."

"Except the door to the balcony was locked," Josh said. "Howard unlocked it for us, remember?"

Brooke shrugged. "There were people going in and out all over the place that night. Anyone could have done it."

Fenella looked at Shelly as an awkward silence descended. "This is my friend, Shelly Quirk," she said after a moment. "Shelly, I can't introduce you to everyone, but I can do my best."

She went around the room, naming each person she knew, and apologizing to those she'd not met before. When she was done, she'd learned that Mr. Baker's first name was Herbert, which didn't seem at all important.

"It's very nice to meet you all," Shelly said. "I was here on opening night, and I was happy to have a chance to be at the rehearsal tonight."

"I do believe that opening night might have been our very best performance," Adam told her. "I only understood about half of the play on opening night, but now that Dorothy has rewritten it twice, I only understand about ten percent of it."

"It isn't that bad," Eileen said. "I think I understand what Dorothy is trying to do, anyway."

"We don't have to understand," Brooke interjected. "It isn't our place to even try to understand. It's our job to perform the words the playwright has written. It's the audience who must attempt to make sense of the beautiful chaos."

That wasn't what you said on Sunday afternoon, Fenella thought.

"You were in the audience," Susan said to Shelly. "Did you understand the, um, beautiful chaos?"

Shelly shrugged. "I very much enjoyed the show. You're all very talented. The story was complicated, and I can't say that I understood all of it, but I admire the playwright for what she was trying to convey."

"Thank you," Dorothy said quietly from behind them.

Fenella turned around and smiled at the woman. "We were talking about you over lunch today," she told her.

"Me? Why?"

Fenella took a deep breath and then glanced around the room. There was no way she could watch everyone's faces at the same time. Trying to rearrange the eight suspects so that they would be standing together when she spoke was impossible, of course.

"Shelly and I had lunch with another playwright," she said. "We were telling him about *Three Gentlewomen from Bologna*."

"Another playwright?" Dorothy repeated. "Who?"

"Actually, it was Forrest Luna," Fenella replied. She quickly looked from suspect to suspect. Everyone looked slightly surprised, but that was probably to be expected.

"I didn't know you knew Forrest Luna," Dorothy said.

"I don't, or rather, I didn't before today. He and Shelly are old friends, though," Fenella replied.

"I thought he was a recluse," Adam said.

"He doesn't go out much, but I was able to persuade him to have lunch with us," Shelly told him. "We've been friends for decades."

"What did you tell him about my show?" Dorothy asked.

"Not a lot," Fenella replied. "But enough to raise his interest in seeing the show."

A few people gasped. Fenella looked around, but she couldn't tell where the sounds had come from.

"There is no way we want Forrest Luna at this show," Adam said.

"I'd love to have him here," Dorothy countered excitedly. "I'd love to hear what he thinks of *Three Gentlewomen from Bologna.*"

"He's going to hate it," Susan said. "He won't understand it any more than we do."

"He should understand it," Dorothy countered. "He's a genius."

"You're implying that we're all stupid," Susan snapped.

Dorothy seemed to think for a moment. "Not at all," she said eventually.

"It might be best if Mr. Luna comes to a rehearsal, rather than an actual public performance," Harry suggested. "I'm told he doesn't enjoy crowds."

"As if the show is going to get a crowd," Adam laughed.

"We've sold a fair few tickets for the next shows," Harry replied.

"People can't believe it's as bad as they've been told," Adam said. "They want to see for themselves. Or maybe they want to be here when the letter writer strikes again. Maybe they're hoping to get drenched in fake blood like the woman on opening night."

"She wasn't drenched in anything," Harry snapped. "A few drops of fake blood landed on her arm. She overreacted."

"She had blood in her hair," Josh countered. "And all over her dress. I don't think she overreacted."

Harry glared at him. "Whatever, there isn't going to be any more fake blood anywhere except on stage, when needed. The police have everything under control."

"We were going to try reading through the modified script," Dorothy said. "Maybe we should focus on that."

"I'll be directing the read-through," Alfred said from his chair in the corner. "I think that may help."

After a short debate, they all moved onto the stage and took seats on the couches and chairs. When those were full, people sat on the floor. Fenella, Shelly, and Daniel returned to their seats as Josh shouted "action."

An hour later, they'd reached the interval.

"I can almost see what Dorothy is trying to do now," Shelly whispered to Fenella. "I think it's a bit bonkers, but I understand it."

She nodded. "It's an odd story, but done this way, it almost makes sense. I'm not sure why it all falls apart when they start doing it on stage."

"I think part of the problem is the overuse of stage directions," Shelly replied. "There are too many people coming and going and saying random things. Those things are less distracting when everyone is sitting still."

"I wonder what people would think if they did the play like this," Fenella said, nodding toward the group still sitting around on the stage.

"Let's leave it there for tonight," Josh said after they'd finished the play another hour later. "I think we understand the story better now, and we've been through all of the changes as well. Everyone needs to learn the changes by tomorrow night so we can start rehearsing properly."

"Some of us have jobs," Adam said. "I won't have time to learn all of the changes by tomorrow night."

"Do your best," Josh replied. "We'll rehearse every night until our next show on Friday."

A few people grumbled as they got to their feet and began to leave the stage.

"I was completely lost in the second half," Shelly whispered to Fenella.

"I thought maybe it was just me," Fenella replied. "I thought things were going well in the first half, but the second half was incomprehensible."

"How was it?" Dorothy asked as she dropped into the chair next to Fenella's.

"I thought the first half was much better," Fenella told her. "I think I was too tired to properly appreciate the second half."

Dorothy nodded. "I'm exhausted. Even I was struggling with the second half. We'll have to start there tomorrow night, I think. I must tell Josh and Alfred." She jumped up and disappeared behind the curtain.

"Do you think Josh will do what she wants?" Shelly asked.

Fenella shrugged. "I've no idea, and I don't think I really care. I've had more than enough of all of these people for today."

She got to her feet and stretched. Daniel stood up and took the handful of steps he needed to reach her.

"Can I come over when I'm done here?" he asked after the kiss.

"Of course you can," she replied.

"I want to hear your thoughts on the show," he said before dropping a kiss on the top her head.

"Ah, Ms. Woods, just the person I wanted to see," Harry said as he walked down off of the stage. "I was speaking with Josh and the cast and crew. We'd all be delighted if you could invite Mr. Luna to join us for our rehearsal on Thursday evening. We would treat it as a proper performance, just for him, but he would need to understand that it would still be a rehearsal. There might be a few hiccups, if you know what I mean."

"We can certainly ask him to attend," Fenella replied.

"Of course, you're more than welcome to join him for the special showing," Harry told her. "You and any of your friends," he added, nodding at Shelly. "And we'll want a police presence as well," he said, looking at Daniel.

"I'll talk to Forrest and see if he's interested," Fenella said. "Someone will let you know."

"Excellent. And now I must chase everyone away and lock up the theater," he said, walking past them and up the aisle.

"I think that's our cue to leave," Shelly said.

"I think you're right," Fenella agreed. "I'll see you later," she told Daniel.

"I shouldn't be more than half an hour," he replied.

❧ 13 ❧

I t was closer to an hour when Daniel finally arrived at Fenella's door.

"I'm sorry," he said. "Harry had a lot on his mind."

"It's fine," she assured him. She'd spent the hour listening to all of Mona's theories about the letter writer, and she was pretty sure that Daniel had arrived just before Mona was going to start talking about aliens. She pulled him into the apartment and then into an embrace.

When they separated, Mona had disappeared, but Fenella could see wisps of smoke in the air. Daniel walked through them as if he didn't see them, heading for a couch.

"Do you want anything?" Fenella asked. "A drink? A snack?"

"Just you," he told her.

She sat down next to him. He slid an arm around her and she rested her head on his shoulder.

"I don't know if I can stand watching that show again," he sighed. "I'm supposed to go to the rest of their rehearsals, though. I don't suppose you want to come with me?"

Fenella thought for a minute. "I do love you a lot," she said slowly.

He laughed. "But you don't love me enough to sit through yet another performance of *Three Gentlewomen from Bologna*," he concluded for her.

She grinned at him. "I will come, if you really want me to, but I'd rather do just about anything else."

"That makes two of us. Mark was mostly backstage tonight. Tomorrow night, he's going to sit in the theater and I'll stay backstage. It's only fair that he have an opportunity to enjoy the show."

Fenella laughed. "Is that how you're going to sell it to him?"

"I just hope it works. I very nearly said something tonight when the tall man in the cowboy hat started talking about persimmons. What was that about?"

"Yeah, that was something new and different. I can't imagine how frustrating it must be for the cast when Dorothy keeps changing everything."

"It isn't just the cast that's frustrated. As I said, Harry had a lot to say tonight."

"Oh dear. Even her father has had enough, then?"

Daniel shrugged. "He's doing everything he can to support his daughter, but I don't think he'd mind if the production got shut down."

"I don't think anyone would mind if the production got shut down. Dorothy would probably be upset, but she has to realize how many problems there are with the story. Otherwise, she wouldn't keep changing everything."

"I hope you warned Forrest about what to expect."

"Shelly is going to tell him everything when she invites him to the rehearsal. She reckons he'll still want to come since all of the most likely suspects will be there. I suppose it's too much to hope that he'll take one look at someone and realize that they must be behind the letters."

Daniel sighed. "I don't think it's going to work that way, but we can hope. It does seem possible that Forrest might recognize someone from his past in the theater company, but I suspect our letter writer is probably one step or more removed from Forrest."

"Because otherwise, he or she could have just reached out to Forrest directly."

"That's assuming the letter writer's goal is really to meet Forrest, of course."

They sat together, watching the sea, for several minutes.

"Forrest is going to go through his fan mail. Maybe he'll find someone with a connection to the show," Fenella said after a short while.

"I'm going to ring him tomorrow and see if I can go through the letters with him," Daniel told her. "A lot will depend on how many letters we're talking about, though. If there are too many, we may have to give up on that idea."

"I feel as if something is going to happen at the rehearsal on Thursday."

"I do too, which is worrying."

"I don't think our letter writer wants to hurt anyone."

"I don't think our letter writer wanted to hurt Mr. Allen. I'm not certain how he or she feels about Forrest, though. If the entire letter-writing campaign was all about meeting Forrest, then he could be in danger."

"We'll keep him safe," Fenella said.

Daniel nodded. "The company is getting used to having the police at the theater. They won't even notice if we add a few extra constables on Thursday."

"And Shelly and I will be there. I think Shelly is going to invite Tim as well."

"The more the merrier," Daniel muttered.

"It's getting late," Fenella said some time later.

"And I have a lot on my plate tomorrow," he sighed. "At least I'm only a few steps from home."

Fenella walked him to the door. "Do you want me to come to the rehearsal tomorrow night?" she asked.

"I'll ring you during the day when I know more about my plans. In the meantime, remember that I love you."

"I love you, too," she told him.

Of course, Katie was already fast asleep when Fenella walked into the bedroom after locking up behind Daniel. Fenella got ready for bed and then climbed in carefully, trying not to disturb the animal. In spite of her tiredness, she had a restless night. At some point in the middle of the night, Katie disappeared into the second bedroom.

K atie was back at seven to wake Fenella, who was already sitting up in bed.

"I would have thought you'd give me until eight today," she grumbled. "You know I didn't sleep. Of course, I'm wide awake and I was getting up before you came in, so maybe you weren't even going to wake me. Maybe you were just coming to check on me or something. Maybe I'm so overtired that I'm babbling endlessly at a cat."

She sighed and got out of bed.

"I feel as if I've been waiting for something all day, but I don't know what," she told Mona when the woman appeared just before five o'clock that evening.

"I've been busy with Max all day. What have you been doing?" Mona asked.

"I took a long walk on the promenade. I went grocery shopping. I made myself a lovely, healthy lunch and then ate half a tub of ice cream for dessert. Then I took another walk to try to make up for all of the extra ice cream calories. I've been reading this book ever since I got back, but it's not very good, and I was just thinking of tossing it out the window when you arrived."

"You weren't really going to toss it out the window."

"No, of course not. It might have landed somewhere where someone else could find it. That poor unsuspecting someone might even try reading it. I can't be responsible for someone else attempting to read this drivel."

Mona laughed. "What are you going to do with it, then?"

Fenella frowned. "Normally, I donate unwanted books to the library, but I truly don't think anyone should read this one. It's absolutely dreadful. For now, I'm going to put it on the bookshelf in the spare bedroom."

She found some scrap paper and wrote a note to herself. *Reminder, this was a dreadful book,* and then stuck the note inside the front cover before she found a spot for it on the bookcase in the second bedroom.

"What was it about?" Mona asked.

"I'm not talking about it," Fenella replied. "I want to forget everything about it. What were you doing for Max all day?"

"He wants to go to Italy," Mona told her. "You know that he doesn't truly understand that he's dead. He seems to think that I should be able to arrange everything for us to go away for a fortnight. He keeps reminding me that we haven't been anywhere together in years, which is perfectly true, of course."

"Can you actually go to Italy with him?" Fenella asked. As soon as the words had left her lips, she frowned. Mona's answers to questions about the afterlife were unpredictable at best. She seemed to enjoy teasing Fenella about things about which Fenella couldn't possibly know.

"It would be very difficult," Mona replied. "I managed to visit America when you were there, but I get some of my energy through you. I don't suppose you could go to Italy for a fortnight to make things easier for me?"

"I'd love a vacation in Italy, but I don't think Daniel can take any more time off right now."

"You don't have to take Daniel with you. Take Shelly. You'd have a wonderful time together."

"We would, but I'm not sure she'd want to be away from Tim at the moment. They are planning their wedding, after all."

"Jasper can deal with all of that. Shelly would enjoy one last holiday as a single woman."

"You could be right, but I'm not going to Italy for you."

Mona frowned. "Why not? You've nothing else to do."

"I'm right in the middle of a police investigation."

"Is that still going on? I thought Daniel would have solved it by now."

"He hasn't."

Mona sighed. "I don't know what I'm going to tell Max."

"Does he have enough energy to go to Italy?"

"Probably. He doesn't do anything but sit in the ballroom and talk about the past. That takes up very little energy."

"Maybe you should take him to the theater," Fenella suggested. "Maybe he'd enjoy seeing *Three Gentlewomen from Bologna*."

"I know you're only teasing, because it's such a dreadful show, but that isn't actually a bad idea. Perhaps Max and I will come to the rehearsal on Thursday night. He'd enjoy seeing Forrest again as well. I shall have to come up with some excuse as to why he can't speak to him, though."

"Sit in one of the boxes," Fenella suggested.

Mona nodded. "Yes, that's a very good idea. It's just the distraction that Max needs right now. If the play truly is bad, he'll have something about which to complain for at least a week. Maybe, by the end of the week, he'll have forgotten about Italy."

The pair were chatting about books when someone knocked on the door a short time later.

"I'm on my way to meet a friend for dinner," Shelly said when Fenella opened the door. "But I wanted to let you know that I've spoken to Forrest. He and Daniel spent all day going through his letters, and they're going to do the same thing tomorrow and Thursday. He doesn't think they've found anything interesting thus far, though."

"That's a shame."

"Anyway, he's excited about seeing the show on Thursday evening. He wants to take us out for dinner first, though. He had me book the private dining room at the Castaway."

"I've heard good things about the Castaway, but I haven't been there yet," Fenella replied.

"Tim and I went last week, and the food was amazing. I can't wait to go back. Daniel and Tim are invited as well. Tim is going, although he did say he might skip the theater afterwards. He said that seeing *Three Gentlewomen from Bologna* once was probably enough for him."

Fenella laughed. "He's a smart man."

"Anyway, we're meeting at the Castaway at half five. Forrest wants to have an early dinner in case he gets carried away talking again."

"That's also very smart," Fenella replied.

She shut the door and then added the dinner to the calendar that was hanging in her kitchen. As she walked back into the living room, there was another knock on the door.

"Daniel? I wasn't expecting to see you tonight," she said when she opened it.

He pulled her into an embrace. When he lifted his head, he smiled at her. "I spent the day with Forrest, and I have to be at the theater in an hour or so. I couldn't think of anything I wanted to do more than spend that hour with you."

"We should get some dinner," Fenella suggested. "Did you have lunch?"

"Forrest insisted on having lunch delivered. It was a feast as well. I'm not very hungry."

"But you won't want to eat after the rehearsal tonight. Let's go and get something. Chinese?"

"That sounds good."

It took them only a few minutes to walk to one of the nearby Chinese restaurants. It was mostly empty, and their waiter put them at a table in the back of the room. After he took their order, Fenella sat back and smiled at Daniel.

"Did you and Forrest find anything interesting in his letters?" she asked.

He sighed. "I discovered that there are a lot of very strange people in the world, and many of them write letters to famous people."

"But no one had any obvious connection to anyone in *Three Gentlewomen from Bologna?*"

"Not that we were able to determine. What did you do all day?"

Fenella frowned. She had more questions about the letters, but clearly Daniel wanted to change the subject. "I went grocery shopping," she said. "And then I started reading a truly terrible book."

She told him about the book, right up to chapter four, which is where she'd stopped reading.

"Now I'm intrigued," he said when she was done. "Maybe you should lend me the book."

"I'd rather not. I don't think anyone should read it."

"I don't think anyone should watch *Three Gentlewomen from Bologna*, but I'm going to another rehearsal tonight," he muttered.

Fenella chuckled and then gave him a kiss. "People don't truly appreciate how hard your job can be. I'll come with you."

He shook his head. "We're limiting access tonight and tomorrow," he told her. "Mark and I discussed it, and we think it might be better if only the cast and crew were permitted in the theater. I don't know if you noticed, but there were over a dozen people there last night, friends and family members of various people in the company. There's enough tension within the group right now. The fewer people involved, the better, I think."

Over some delicious food, they talked about everything but the case. After they were done, Daniel walked Fenella home.

"Are you spending the day with Forrest again tomorrow?" Fenella asked at her door.

"I am. I should be done in time to have dinner with you again as well, if you don't have other plans."

"If I did, I'd change them," she told him.

He chuckled. "I'll be here not long after five tomorrow, then. Forrest insisted on booking the Castaway for Thursday night."

"Shelly told me. I'm looking forward to it."

She shut the door behind him and then sighed as she leaned against it.

The drum roll started off quietly and got increasingly loud as it continued. Fenella looked around and then sighed again as Mona appeared.

"I didn't want to startle you," she said.

"And it's been ages since I heard a drum roll," Fenella replied.

"I've just been speaking with Max. He's very excited at the thought of going to the theater on Thursday. I've promised to book a box for us and told him everything I know about *Three Gentlewomen from Bologna*."

"You've told him that it's dreadful?"

Mona chuckled. "I've told him that it's experimental and unusual. He may enjoy it."

"I hope he does, but I doubt it."

"I shall be spending tomorrow and much of Thursday resting. If you manage to solve the case, do shout for me, though. That would be worth hearing about. Otherwise, I'll see you on Thursday evening at the Gaiety."

Fenella nodded and then watched as the woman slowly faded away.

"It's too early to go to bed," she said as Katie wandered into the room.

"Meroow," Katie replied.

"Yes, you're right. We could both do with a treat," Fenella replied. "Chinese restaurants don't really offer much in the way of dessert. My fortune was dumb as well. Let's see what we can find in the kitchen."

She gave Katie a treat and then grabbed a bar of chocolate out of the cupboard. "Let's find an old movie," she suggested to Katie, who curled up on her lap when she sat down in front of the television. A moment later, the phone rang.

"Hello?"

"Maggie, darling, it's Jack."

"Hello. How are you?"

"I'm very well, thank you. Being married is quite wonderful. I suppose most of the credit for that must go to Linda, of course. We're truly getting to know one another now, and I'm falling more in love with her every day."

"I'm really happy for you."

"Thank you. How are you?"

"I'm fine."

"You haven't found any dead bodies lately, have you?"

"But you said something about coming for a visit," she replied, eager to change the subject.

"Does that mean you have found a dead body recently?"

Fenella sighed. "I was at the theater when a man accidentally fell from the balcony to the floor below."

"Should I assume that the fall killed him?"

"It did."

"And is Daniel investigating? I know you said it was an accident, but I doubt it's that simple."

"Daniel is investigating. It wasn't that simple. I really don't want to talk about it."

Jack sighed. "What's happened to you since you moved there? In our ten years together, you never found a single dead body. How many have you found since you've been on the Isle of Man?"

"Not long ago, I found one in Buffalo," she pointed out. "And I really don't want to talk about it. When I start to think about it, I don't sleep at night."

"I'm sorry," Jack said quickly. "I didn't mean to upset you. You're one of my favorite people in the entire world. You know that."

"And you know that I'll always love you."

"I love you, too. We were good for each other, even if we weren't meant to be together forever."

"I agree."

"Which is one of the reasons why Linda and I are thinking of coming to the island for a visit."

"How nice," Fenella said, trying to sound sincere.

Jack laughed. "Don't sound so excited to see us," he teased. "This won't be anything like my last visit. I promise. We're planning to stay in a luxury hotel. There are a few I found on the internet that look promising."

"Which ones?" she asked warily.

He named a Douglas hotel.

"You've been there," she told him. "That's the hotel that houses the Tale and Tail."

"It's a wonderful location, right on the promenade. That makes it quite tempting, but the Seaview in Ramsey looks very special."

"It is very special. Shelly, my closest friend on the island, is having her wedding reception there in January."

"I'm just not certain about being in Ramsey."

"The Seaview is right on the beach, but it isn't far from shopping and restaurants. Are you thinking of renting a car?"

"That's the big question," he chuckled. "I'm not certain I could manage driving on the wrong side of the road. Linda is willing to try, but I don't even like riding with her when she's driving over here."

"It does take some getting used to, but to truly enjoy the island, you're probably going to need a car at your disposal. There are buses and taxis, but you can't beat having your own transportation."

"It's something we're going to have to figure out before we come, but not before we start making our reservations," he told her. "Linda likes to spend lots of time researching and planning for her vacations."

"So you aren't coming soon?"

"Not terribly soon. We were thinking about July or August."

Fenella let out a sigh of relief. "That's a long way off."

"Yes, well, that should give Linda plenty of time to plan everything exactly the way she wants it. I hope you won't mind terribly if I call you once in a while for advice."

"Call as often as you like," she said without thinking.

He chuckled. "You don't mean that, but I may take you up on it anyway. The first thing I need to know about, though, is flights. Do you have any advice on where to fly into in the UK?"

They talked for several minutes about the various options. When Fenella put the phone down at the end, she was almost looking forward to seeing Jack again. At least, she figured she would be by the summer.

"And now it's time for my chocolate," she told Katie as she switched on the television.

***

Wednesday seemed to drag as Fenella felt as if she were simply waiting for Thursday to arrive. By the time she was ready for bed that evening, she was feeling a bit jealous of Mona who was, presumably, resting comfortably somewhere before her night out. She slid under the covers and then shut her eyes tightly.

"I wrote the letters," Adam said. "I would do just about anything to get out of this show, including murder. Whom should I kill, do you think? I'd quite like to kill Dorothy. That would get the show shut down, wouldn't it? That's all I want. I want *Three Gentlewomen from Bologna* to end. Is that too much to ask?"

"Why did you come back?" Fenella asked him.

He shrugged. "I suppose I'm a glutton for punishment."

"I wrote the letters," Susan interrupted. "It started out as a joke. I was simply being silly, but then I realized that I'd much rather be in a

Forrest Luna play than the one I'm actually in, and I became much more serious about it all. I can't believe they haven't canceled the show yet. What else do I need to do?"

"I wrote the letters," Victor Miles said. "It was all about getting rid of Mr. Allen, of course. It wasn't easy, setting up the mess at the Gaiety, but I had everything planned for the theater in Ramsey. I still can't believe it worked so well, though. I was afraid the fall wouldn't kill him, but it did."

"I wrote the letters," Daniel told her. "I was bored and I knew I would have to investigate. Not only does it give me some job security, but it gives us something to talk about. What would we talk about if we weren't caught up in the middle of police investigation after police investigation?"

"We'd find lots to talk about," Fenella protested.

"Or we'd get bored with one another," he replied. "It could happen."

"No, it could not," she nearly shouted.

"Merroow," Katie complained.

Fenella sat up in bed and opened her eyes. It was nearly three o'clock and she'd been having nightmares again.

"Sorry," she told the small animal who was standing in her spot in the middle of the bed. She shook her head and then curled up and went back to sleep.

She was awake again before Katie had the chance to wake her. In the kitchen, she started coffee after she'd given Katie her breakfast. The coffee was ready when she got out of the shower.

"That's better," she said after her first sip of the hot liquid.

Katie shrugged and then disappeared into the bedroom.

"She's going to take a nap," Fenella muttered. "I want to take a nap, but I can't because..." She trailed off, unable to think of a reason why she couldn't crawl back into bed for an hour or two.

Someone knocked on the door while she was still thinking.

"Want to take a walk?" Shelly asked.

"Yes, please," Fenella replied eagerly.

They were out of the apartment and walking briskly down the promenade before Fenella spoke again.

"I feel as if I'm waiting for something awful to happen," she told Shelly.

"Do you really think something awful is going to happen at the theater tonight?"

"I don't know. I can't help but feel as if the letter writer's goal has always been to meet Forrest. If that's the case, I'm afraid of what he or she might say or do tonight."

"Daniel will be there, won't he?"

"Yes, with several constables. I'm pretty sure that Mark Hammersmith will be there as well."

"Surely the letter writer isn't going to want anyone to know that he or she was behind the letters, though," Shelly said thoughtfully. "I mean, a man died because of his or her actions."

"So maybe he or she won't admit to having written the letters, but whoever did write them is probably going to try to get close to Forrest."

"Who is going to be surrounded by uniformed constables. Let's talk about something more pleasant," Shelly suggested. "What's new in your life?"

"I talked to Jack last night. He and Linda might be coming to visit in the summer."

"The summer? That's far enough away for you to make other plans."

Fenella laughed. "I don't need to make other plans. I'm looking forward to seeing them again, actually. I'd like to get to know Linda better, and I'll always have a place in my heart for Jack."

They talked about Jack and Linda and how far away the summer seemed as they strolled from one end of the promenade to the other. When they finally got back to their building, they stopped to get their mail.

"Nothing exciting," Shelly sighed as she flipped through the things she'd taken out of her mailbox.

"I got a postcard from an old friend," Fenella said, holding up the card. "She's in New Zealand — or rather, she was when she sent the card. It was postmarked two weeks ago, though. She's probably home by now."

"And now I must spend the rest of today with my book," Shelly said on the elevator. "I'm getting dangerously close to finishing it, and I have about a dozen loose ends to tie up."

"Good luck."

"Thanks. I'd suggest that we have lunch together, but I'm going to have a sandwich while I work. I need to be more disciplined about my writing, and I also don't want to eat much, not when we're going to the Castaway for dinner."

"That's a great point," Fenella said, deciding that she'd have a sandwich for her own lunch when it was time.

She found one of Mona's books on the living room shelves and read for most of the day. Just before five, she headed into the bedroom to find something to wear.

"It's just a rehearsal, so I don't need to dress up too much for that, but dinner at the Castaway needs more than my usual attire," she muttered to herself. "Mona, help me out here," she added as she pulled open the wardrobe.

A blue and green dress that she was certain she'd never seen before was hanging right in the center of the wardrobe. Fenella pulled it out and smiled. "Lovely," she exclaimed.

A minute later, she was twirling slowly in front of her mirror in the dress. "It's perfect," she said softly.

"You look fabulous," Daniel told her when she opened the door to him just before five.

"Thanks. You look pretty good yourself."

He was wearing a dark suit with a lighter shirt and tie. "I thought I should put some effort in for the Castaway," he explained.

Shelly and Tim arrived a few minutes later.

"It's just starting to rain," Shelly said. "I thought we could walk, but I don't know about walking in the rain."

"We could get a taxi," Daniel suggested. "Then we could walk home, assuming the rain stops."

"It's supposed to stop," Tim added.

They rode the elevator down to the lobby and then walked outside. The rain was light, but persistent. Daniel waved down a taxi.

"Terribly sorry, but we aren't going far," he told the driver.

"That's fine with me," the man laughed. "As long as you aren't going to complain about the charge."

"We won't," Daniel assured him.

Two minutes later, he dropped them off in front of the Castaway. Fenella handed him enough money to cover the fare several times over.

"Thank you," she said.

"No, thank you," he told her. "I could just wait out here and take you home again, if you like."

She laughed. "We're hoping to walk home. We're going to need to burn off a few calories."

Inside the restaurant, they were shown to a small private room. Forrest was already there, sipping a glass of water. He got to his feet as they walked into the room.

"Good evening," he said.

"Good evening," Fenella replied.

"I don't know how much Daniel has told you," Forrest said. "But we found a few quite interesting things in my letters today."

Fenella looked at Daniel. "He hasn't told me a single thing," she replied.

Forrest grinned. "Then we'll have lots to talk about over dinner."

❧ 14 ☙

"Should we order a bottle of wine?" Shelly asked. "I feel as if the show will be much better if I've had a drink or two."

Tim laughed. "I'm more than happy to share some wine with you. Daniel is probably working, though."

Daniel nodded. "I am working," he said. "But no one is driving, so please have some wine. I don't mind."

"I came in a taxi," Forrest said. "I can't drive at night any longer, so I may as well have some as well."

They ordered a bottle of wine and four glasses. Daniel requested a soda.

"What's good?" Fenella asked as she opened her menu.

"We've been here only once, but everything was good," Shelly told her.

"I don't think I can eat everything," Fenella laughed.

"We have specials tonight," the waiter told them as he poured the wine. Once he'd gone through those, Fenella knew exactly what she wanted.

They ordered. As the door shut behind the waiter, Fenella turned to Forrest.

"What did you find in your letters today, then?" she asked.

"We discovered that people are strange," he told her. "I always knew it, of course, but seeing so much oddness together in one place was educational."

"You've had the letters for years, haven't you?" Shelly asked.

He nodded. "But they've trickled in, one or two a month, even less frequently in the last decade or so. This was the first time I ever sat down and read through a collection of them at one time."

"We spent three days on the letters," Daniel interjected. "We started with decades' worth of correspondence from educators and students."

Forrest laughed. "Teachers and professors always want to believe that writers have deeper meanings to their work than writers ever intend. How many millions of hours have been spent studying Shakespeare? All he wanted to do was pay his bills and put food on his table. I suspect he'd be appalled to see his work dissected and scrutinized the way it has been."

"My brother wrote a book that's used in college classrooms all over the US," Fenella told him. "He'd agree with you completely."

"We pulled out one or two letters from people who seemed a little bit more, let's say, emotionally invested in the debate than the rest, but the vast majority of the letters seemed completely legitimate and harmless," Daniel said.

"And all of those letters came from people who live far from the Isle of Man," Forrest said.

"We're still verifying the whereabouts of one man, but he was a university professor in Canada thirty-something years ago," Daniel said. "There's no way he's in the cast or crew of *Three Gentlewomen from Bologna*."

"Your starters," the waiter said, delivering delicious looking plates of appetizers. He topped up all of the wine glasses and then left them to eat.

"On the second day, we worked our way through some basic fan mail," Daniel continued as he ate. "Again, there were a few letters that felt a bit off, but most of them were fairly simple."

"They were embarrassing to read, and it was even worse with

Daniel reading them as well. I'm nowhere near as talented as some people seem to think that I am," Forrest said.

"The vast majority of the letters were from Australia," Daniel said. "That includes every one of the letters that we pulled out as questionable. No one involved in *Three Gentlewomen from Bologna* is Australian. We are doing what we can to track down each of the questionable letter writers, but I don't think we'll find anything."

"Didn't you tell me that your agent got most of your fan mail?" Fenella asked Forrest.

"He did, and his agency still does. He used to send the letters from schools and students so that I could see what they were asking. We had a standard form letter that we sent back to any such inquiries, and I used to update it annually to answer any new questions that had begun to be asked."

"That was kind of you," Shelly said.

He shrugged. "I was always more than happy to help students find ways to earn high marks. I was less patient with teachers and professors who wanted to attribute more meaning to my work than it deserved, but if they were going to insist on teaching my plays, I wanted them to get the basics right, at the very least."

"And the other fan mail?" Fenella asked.

"Again, my agent answered most of it, but he used to send me a few of the most complimentary letters now and then. He always said he thought I could read through them when I was having a bad day. I rarely did, but I did keep them."

"Are we finished with the starters?" the waiter asked. He cleared the table and then refilled the wine glasses again. "Everything is just about ready. I'll be right back."

He was gone and then back again as Fenella took a sip of wine. The food, when it was put in front of her, made her mouth water.

"After all of that, we had one box of letters left," Forrest said as the door shut behind the waiter.

"And of course, because we'd left it for last, it was the interesting one," Daniel added.

"Once a month or so, my agent used to send me letters that he felt required a more personal reply," Forrest explained. "When I was in the mood, I'd send off a short handwritten note in reply. I think I probably replied to about half of the letters. In the early days, I did far fewer, because I was busy writing so much of the time. As I got older and started spending less time writing, I began replying to more of these people."

"So what did you find?" Shelly asked.

"It looks very much as if I had a stalker," Forrest said, sounding amused.

"A stalker?" Shelly echoed.

He nodded. "Daniel made the connection. Obviously, I never did."

"What connection?" Tim demanded as Forrest took a bite of his dinner.

"There were about a dozen letters from the same person," Daniel explained. "Except they were all signed differently, as if the person sending them didn't want anyone to know that they had all come from the same person."

"That seems odd," Fenella said.

Daniel nodded. "I spent some time this afternoon tracking down the writer. He's been accused of stalking and harassment before. He's currently serving time in a prison in Rugby for harassing a local radio presenter. Unfortunately, that rules him out of being a part of what's been happening here."

Shelly put her fork down. "This is really delicious," she said.

"I love mine," Fenella told her. "This may be my new favorite restaurant. A lot will depend on what they have for dessert, though."

Shelly laughed. "They had a chocolate cake with a melted center when we were here last time."

"Sold," Fenella said.

"What else did you find in the letters?" Tim asked.

"A man who seems to think that we're long lost cousins," Forrest told him. "I actually remember replying to him, because he insisted that we had to be related because Luna was such an unusual surname. He'd never met anyone else with that surname."

"It is unusual," Fenella agreed.

"Yes, and I had to disappoint the poor man and tell him that it was simply a pen name. My real name is Stanley Fisk, which isn't nearly as interesting as Forrest Luna."

Fenella and Shelly both laughed.

"Was he disappointed?" Fenella asked.

"Very," Forrest replied. "We corresponded for several months, actually. He didn't want to believe me at first, but eventually I managed to persuade him that we were not cousins."

"And where is he now?" Tim asked Daniel.

"He passed away several years ago," Daniel replied. "He never married or had children. I'm reasonably certain there's no connection between him and what's happening here now."

"Is that all you found?" Fenella asked after she'd eaten her last bite.

Forrest chuckled. "That was just the tip of the iceberg. We found several dozen marriage proposals, including some with racy pictures tucked inside the envelopes."

"Oh?" Fenella said, looking at Daniel.

He blushed. "I don't know what some people are thinking. I would never send a stranger a picture of myself naked."

"I understand such things are now common," Shelly said. "There are even smart phone applications that let you send pictures that disappear after a few seconds, I believe."

"Yes, but anyone can screenshot what you send," Daniel told her. "Then they have a picture that will last forever."

Shelly shuddered. "I think I'm fortunate that I grew up before all of this technology. No one wants to send me naked pictures, and they certainly don't want any of me."

Tim took her hand. "I wouldn't say that," he teased.

As Shelly blushed bright red, the door opened, and the waiter walked in, carrying small cards. "The pudding menu," he told them. He cleared the table while they read through the dessert options.

"I need to try the chocolate cake with the melting center," Fenella said.

"I've had it and I need it again," Shelly said.

"Just coffee for me," Daniel said. Then he looked at Fenella. "Unless you'd like me to get something different so you can try it?"

She looked back at the menu and then slowly shook her head. "As tempting as that is, I'm already quite full. I think one dessert is all I can manage tonight."

"Are you going to try to track down all of the would-be Mrs. Lunas?" Shelly asked as the waiter left.

Daniel shook his head. "There were dozens of them. If we don't make any progress tonight, I'll assign a constable to the job of working through them, starting with the ones in the UK and working from there. The vast majority of them came from Australia, though."

"Anything else?" Fenella wondered as she sipped her wine.

"Sadly, there was a large pile of hate mail," Forrest told her with a sigh. "My agent didn't send those to me so that I could reply. He sent me a copy of everything that he sent to the police."

"My goodness, how awful," Shelly exclaimed.

Forrest shrugged. "When you're in the public eye, you attract all sorts of attention, both positive and negative."

"Is another constable going to have to go through and try to find those letter writers?" Tim asked.

Daniel nodded. "We're giving them a higher priority than the others. Most of them weren't too worrying, but a few definitely need investigating."

"What do you mean by 'not too worrying?'" Shelly wanted to know.

Forrest laughed. "He means that most of them just said things like 'you're a terrible writer' and 'your plays are dreadful' as opposed to a few that were somewhat threatening."

"Threatening?" Fenella repeated.

"One person said that if I didn't stop 'churning out rubbish' he'd make me stop," Forrest told her. "Of course, he wrote the letter in nineteen-sixty-three, and I wrote probably a hundred plays after that, so it was a fairly empty threat."

"It's still terrible," Shelly said.

Daniel nodded. "It was investigated at the time, and a constable went and spoke with the man as well. As it happened, he was another playwright, a considerably less successful one. He sent similar letters to several of his competitors. It doesn't seem as if anyone took his threats seriously, and he took a job selling used cars a short while later."

"Was there anything else interesting in the letters?" Fenella asked as the waiter delivered their desserts and coffee.

"There were a few other threatening ones that we're looking at more closely," Daniel said. "We didn't find any letters from anyone who is connected in any way to anyone involved in *Three Gentlewomen from Bologna*."

"Well, that's disappointing," Fenella said. She took a bite of her cake and sighed. "This, on the other hand, is not at all disappointing."

"It's wonderful," Shelly sighed.

They talked about chocolate and cake for several minutes while they enjoyed dessert. As Fenella reminded herself sternly that she couldn't possibly lick her plate in a restaurant, not even in a private room, Daniel glanced at his watch.

"It's almost time to head to the theater," he said. "I wanted to go over a few things with all of you before we get there."

"What sort of things?" Tim asked.

"We've reason to believe that the person behind the threatening letters is involved in *Three Gentlewomen from Bologna*," he told him. "What we don't know is his or her motive for writing the letters. It's possible that he or she simply wants an opportunity to meet Forrest. If that's the case, the letter writer has gone to great lengths to meet the man and will probably be quite excited tonight. Keep your eyes open and let me know if you see anyone behaving oddly."

"They're mostly actors," Shelly said. "Surely, they'll be able to hide how they're feeling."

"You saw the show," Fenella reminded her. "Did any of them seem to be especially good actors?"

Shelly laughed. "Good point."

"Everyone is going to get introduced to Forrest when we first arrive," Daniel continued. "Try to watch how each of them react to that. I'm expecting our letter writer to have a lot to say to him, either positive or negative."

"Is there anything in particular you think he or she might say?" Shelly asked.

"I'm going to be listening for people to say that they've always wanted to meet him," Daniel replied. "I suspect our letter writer has been waiting a long time for this."

"But they're all actors, and they've all heard of Forrest Luna," Fenella said. "Surely, they're all going to be excited to meet him."

Daniel nodded. "We're looking for the person who is just that little bit more eager, someone struggling to keep his or her emotions in check, or maybe someone who forgets his or her lines or gets too flustered to perform in front of Forrest."

Forrest sighed. "This doesn't sound at all enjoyable."

"I want you all to remember as well that this person is already responsible for the death of an innocent man. We'll have constables in place around the theater, and there will be another inspector backstage, but you all need to be very careful while you're in the building," Daniel warned them.

"How careful?" Tim asked, looking anxiously at Shelly.

"As I said, there will be constables in locations around the theater. As long as you stay there, you should be completely safe. If you need the loo, let me know, and I'll send a constable with you. No one will be permitted to sit in the boxes, and the backstage area is restricted to the cast and crew of the show. If I thought anyone was going to be in any real danger, we wouldn't be going. Just stay together in the theater, especially when the lights go down,' Daniel told him.

"I'll hold your hand the entire time," Shelly told Tim.

"I should hope so," he replied with a laugh.

"Should we go?" Forrest asked.

"I need to freshen up," Shelly said. "Especially if we can't go to the loo at the Gaiety without an escort."

"Me too," Fenella said.

When they walked back into the room a few minutes later, the men were all standing near the door.

"We don't want to be late," Daniel told her.

"I'm not so sure about that," she replied as she took his arm.

"I can't be late," he replied. "I enjoyed dinner very much, but technically, I'm working."

She stopped and pulled him into a quick kiss. "I hope that wasn't too much hard work," she teased.

He laughed. "It wasn't too bad."

They walked along the promenade.

"It feels as if the rain must have just stopped," Shelly said.

"The ground is still wet," Fenella replied. "But the skies are clearing." A cold breeze blew in from across the water. She shivered as Daniel put his arm around her.

The group arrived at the theater just a few minutes before seven. The constable standing at the stage door jumped to attention when he saw Daniel.

"Good evening, sir," he said smartly.

"Good evening," Daniel replied. "We're all on the list."

The man nodded and then held open the door for them.

Inside, Daniel led them all toward the theater. As they walked, Fenella could hear raised voices.

"...exactly the way I told you to do it." *That was Dorothy's voice,* Fenella thought.

"Actually, my dear, I'd rather she do it the way that I told her to do it," another voice said. "You may have written the play, but I'm directing the performance."

"I won't have my play ruined," Dorothy snapped back.

"No one is ruining anything," Alfred countered. "I've been very patient with you while you've changed the story over and over again, but we all agreed on Tuesday that there weren't going to be any additional changes. The play is mine now, to direct as I see fit."

As Fenella and her friends walked into the theater, Daniel coughed loudly.

Everyone in the room turned to stare at them. A few people gasped, and then someone started to applaud. After a moment, the rest of the cast and crew joined in.

"Mr. Luna, I can't tell you what a pleasure it is to have you here," Harry said as he jumped up out of his seat and rushed toward them. "I grew up watching your plays. Your stories were one of the reasons why I opted for a career in the theater. I'm not gifted enough to perform, but I do what I can to be a part of the magic."

"This is Harry Gilbert," Daniel told Forrest. "He's the theater manager."

"It's a beautiful old building," Forrest said. "I've probably seen hundreds of plays here over my lifetime, including several since you've been managing the theater. I've thoroughly enjoyed every one of them."

Harry flushed. "You should have informed me when you were coming to see shows. We could have given you special treatment."

Forrest shook his head. "I'm not interested in special treatment. I'm happy to buy my own tickets and sit with the rest of the audience to enjoy the show."

"But we're especially pleased that you were willing to come tonight to see *Three Gentlewomen from Bologna*," Harry told him. "I'm certain someone must have told you that my daughter wrote the script. I think she's very talented, but I'm eager to hear your opinion."

Forrest nodded. "I'm looking forward to the show, but first I'd like to meet the cast and crew."

"Josh?" Harry shouted.

The man rushed forward and was introduced to Forrest. Fenella watched intently as the cast and crew all lined up for introductions.

"For now, let's keep the conversation to a minimum," Josh told everyone. "We'll all have time to speak with Mr. Luna later, after the show."

He then had each person step forward, pronouncing their name and nothing more. Each member of the cast or crew simply nodded at Forrest and then stepped back into the line. Fenella frowned. They weren't going to learn anything this way.

"And now we should get on with the first act," Josh said as the last person nodded at Forrest. "No doubt Mr. Luna will have things to say after he's seen it."

Forrest nodded. "I'm really excited to see what you've created."

"Places, everyone," Josh said.

Dorothy took a step forward as the cast began to make their way toward the stage.

"Mr. Luna, I'm a huge fan," she said excitedly. "I love your plays, and I studied them before I started writing mine. I really hope you enjoy the show. I've poured my entire heart and soul into the production, but I'm not certain that anyone appreciates how hard I worked."

Forrest laughed. "No one appreciates the writer," he told her. "You simply have to do your best and then let the story go out into the world. Once a director gets his or her hands on it, it's never the same again. And don't even get me started on what actors can do to a story. I've worked with actors who have deliberately mispronounced names and ones who've changed my lines on a nightly basis. As I said, all you can to do is write the best script you can write and then leave it with them."

Dorothy nodded. "It's very difficult, though, watching them do things in ways you never intended."

"No one will ever perform your play the way you think they should," he replied. "And it will never be the exact same story twice, either. That's the beauty of live theater."

"Mr. Luna? We're ready," Josh said from the stage.

Fenella and the others took seats in the front row. She found herself sitting between Daniel and Forrest. Dorothy took the seat on the other side of Forrest.

"Don't let me talk too much during the performance," she said as the lights went down.

"My dear girl, you shouldn't speak at all," he replied. "All attention now belongs on the stage."

Having seen the show so many times before, Fenella thought she knew what to expect. She was surprised, however, by how many changes had been made to the script. It wasn't really any more under-standable, but it was confusing in different ways, she decided as the scenes played out.

When the curtain closed after the first act, the lights came back on. Fenella thought that Forrest looked a little bit stunned.

"What did you think?" Dorothy asked. "There were a lot of prob-lems, weren't there? Susan missed her cues twice, and Adam mixed up two of his lines. I still think Brooke's monologue could be improved as well, but I've changed it at least a dozen times, and I still can't get it quite right."

Forrest took a deep breath. "This is your first play, correct?"

She nodded. "Oh goodness, you hated it, didn't you?"

"My first play was considerably worse," he replied. "I hadn't yet learned that writing a play and performing a play are very different things. Did you workshop it for long?"

"I didn't workshop it at all."

"I think that it might have been helpful. Written words and spoken words are often very different things. So much depends on tone and accents and cadence and a dozen other things. I used to spend at least a month sitting around a table with a dozen actors that I knew I could trust. I'd have them swap roles every single time, sometimes having men reading women's parts and vice versa. We'd read through the entire play thirty or forty or even fifty times, and I'd keep rewriting it, over and over again, until we were all happy that the story flowed and the dialogue sounded real."

"My dialogue isn't always the best," Dorothy said miserably.

"I didn't say that," Forrest countered. "There was a great deal of good in what I've seen, and I think you have some talent, but I don't think the story is completely ready for public performances yet. I am aware, of course, that this is simply a rehearsal. No doubt things flow more naturally during actual shows."

Dorothy shook her head. "This was the best they've done," she told him. "I think you're right. I don't think my play is good enough for public performances. I think we should cancel the rest of the run."

"We've sold hundreds of tickets," Harry objected.

"And we'll have hundreds of unhappy theater goers," Adam said as he joined them. "To clarify, I think they'll be unhappy if they actually get to see the show. They'll be much happier if we cancel."

"Thanks," Dorothy said flatly.

"Mr. Luna, I've been wanting to meet you forever," Adam said, turning to Forrest. "I'm a huge fan."

"Thank you," Forrest said.

"I studied your plays at university. Can I ask you about the second act in..."

"This isn't the time or the place for that sort of conversation," Josh interrupted Adam. "Do you have anything you'd like to say to the company before the second half of the show?" he asked Forrest.

Forrest hesitated and then shook his head. "I'll speak with everyone at the end," he told him.

Josh nodded. "Places, everyone. We're starting again in five minutes."

"Why bother?" Dorothy asked as Josh and Adam headed for the stage. "We're going to cancel the rest of the performances, aren't we?" she asked her father.

"I don't know," he replied. "I'm going to have to think about it."

"If you continue, you'll do so without my support," Dorothy warned him. "And I'll go public with that as well."

"My dear, I understand how you feel, but you must remember to always behave as a professional," Forrest said.

Dorothy flushed. "What would you do if a theater insisted on putting on a show and you wanted to cancel it?"

"Once I've licensed a theater to perform my play, it's out of my hands. If you signed a licensing agreement, then it's up to the theater to decide what to do," he replied.

"I never signed anything," Dorothy said angrily.

"You did," her father corrected her. "But let's not argue. Not now, anyway. I think they're ready to start."

The lights went down again and the second half began. Within minutes, Fenella realized that things were falling apart on stage. Susan started to speak and then stopped and frowned at Adam who began to laugh and then shook his head. Brooke walked out and tried to talk, only to stop as Adam continued to laugh. Eileen had been sitting quietly on the couch since the curtain had gone up. Now she sighed loudly and rose to her feet.

"This isn't working," she said. "No one knows what they're doing."

"We have an audience," Josh reminded her. "Carry on."

"Carry on?" Eileen replied. "I don't think that's possible."

Behind her, Adam was still laughing. Brooke looked close to tears, and Susan seemed to have given up. She'd dropped into a chair and was staring off into the distance, seemingly ignoring everything around her.

"All right," Alfred shouted as he stood up from his seat. "Let's take a break."

The lights came back up. Dorothy was crying in her seat. Harry looked completely fed up. Josh stood up and walked to the stage.

"What is wrong with you?" he demanded. "And that's addressed to each and every one of you. You were all told to treat this as a proper performance. You all know that we have a very important guest in the audience. There's no excuse for this level of unprofessionalism."

"I forgot my line," Susan told him. "That's hardly surprising since it's been six different lines in as many rehearsals. I've been involved in community theater for forty years, and I've never been involved in such a ridiculous train wreck. Dorothy wants to cancel the show. I think she's right."

"I'm sorry," Adam said. "Susan got her line so badly wrong that it struck me funny. Once I'd started laughing, I couldn't seem to stop. It was very unprofessional of me, though."

"You can blame me for bringing the rehearsal to a screaming halt," Eileen said. "We muddled through the first half, but I truly don't even know where I'm meant to be or what I'm meant to be saying in the second half. I'm afraid I'm going to have to agree with Susan. It might be best if we simply cancel the rest of the run."

"We have to finish," Brooke said loudly. "We have to finish tonight."

"I don't think that's going to happen," Adam said. "As much as I hate to say it, this show needs to be canceled."

"Whatever, we have to do the second half tonight," Brooke said insistently.

"I'm done," Susan said. "The only way I'm going to get through the second half is with a script in my hand."

"Fine," Brooke told her. "Sit on the couch with a script and read your lines. I have to do my part. My monologue truly shows my talent as an actor."

"We all know you're a wonderful actor," Adam said dryly. "If you'd like, we can all applaud for you as well. Then we can all go home and get some sleep and start working on forgetting that we were ever a part of *Three Gentlewomen from Bologna*."

"We have to finish," Brooke said.

Fenella could see tears in her eyes.

"This is my big chance," she said. "My chance to show the great Forrest Luna my talent."

"My dear," Forrest said, getting to his feet and walking toward the stage. "I've already seen your talent. You were the brightest part of the first half of the show, and watching you was what I was most looking forward to in the second half."

Brooke blushed bright red. "I knew it," she said. "I knew you'd see my talent. You see the truth, don't you?"

"The truth?" he asked. "I see a very beautiful and talented actor. I'm afraid I no longer have any connections anywhere, though. There's nothing I can do to advance your career."

She shook her head. "This isn't about my career. This is about me. Look at me. Truly look."

Everyone in the theater stared at Brooke. Daniel got to his feet. Fenella could see him sending text messages as he walked toward the stage. Mark and a uniformed constable walked out from behind the curtain. As they walked up behind Brooke, Forrest smiled at her.

"What am I meant to be seeing?" he asked.

"You know. If you don't want to say anything here, in front of all of these people, that's okay, though," she replied.

"I'm sorry, my dear, but I don't know what you mean," Forrest said after a moment.

"You must recognize me," Brooke said. "I look a lot like my mother, but I think I look like my father, too."

"And I know your parents?" Forrest asked, sounding confused.

Brooke laughed loudly. "You knew my mother. You are my father."

❧ 15 ❧

As a few people gasped and Mark moved closer to Brooke, Forrest frowned.

"My dear, I can assure you that you're mistaken," he said softly.

Brooke shook her head. "Mum told me everything. You don't have to lie to me." She glanced around at the crowd. "You don't want to say anything in front of all of these people. I understand. We can talk privately later."

"There's nothing to discuss," Forrest said firmly. "I'm not your father."

"Of course not," she said with an exaggerated wink. "My mother told me everything, even the things you told her not to tell me. I understand why you've lied for all these years, but I truly think it's time for you to tell the truth, not just to me, but to everyone."

"I think we should take this conversation elsewhere," Daniel said. "Ms. Blake, I don't know if you want to change clothes or anything before we go."

She shook her head. "But we should have this conversation here," she argued. "This is a theater, and a theater is where my story begins. Daddy, do you remember it? Of course you do."

"I'm so very sorry," Forrest said. "But I think someone has been telling you things that simply aren't true."

"Mum never lied to me," Brooke replied firmly. "She told me every-thing, and she always insisted that I must never, ever, under any circumstances, try to speak to you."

Forrest sighed. "Did you ever think that maybe she didn't want you to speak to me because she wasn't being entirely truthful?"

Brooke laughed. "Of course not. You're married. If your wife found out about your relationship with my mother, she would get all of your money. That's the law in Australia. That's why it was so important that no one know about me."

"Your mother was mistaken," Forrest replied. "That is not the law in Australia, and I can assure you that I would have divorced my wife if I'd ever met another woman with whom I'd wanted a relationship. That never happened."

"But here I am," Brooke said.

"Let's continue this conversation in my office," Daniel said. "Mr. Luna, I'm going to ask you to come to the office as well."

"Of course," Forrest replied.

"He is my father," Brooke insisted. "Mum told me not to contact him in any way, but I knew that he'd recognize me when he saw me. I knew that he'd know the truth the moment he laid eyes on me. Of course, he can't admit to that here, in front of everyone, because he'd lose all of his money, but I know the truth."

"You've been sending the threatening letters," Adam said.

Brooke flushed. "I had to find a way to get my father to see me," she explained. "I knew that he always came to his own shows, so I thought it would be easiest if I could get someone on the island to put on one of his shows. I was going to audition for the show, but if I didn't get a part, I thought I could just be in the audience every night until my father turned up."

"What did you think was going to happen next?" Susan asked.

"I knew what was going to happen," Brooke told her. "My father would see me, either in the show or in the audience. He'd recognize me, of course, and then he'd invite me to get a coffee or a drink after the show. I know he wants to apologize for not being there for me during my childhood, but I'm not angry. I understand. The law in Australia made it impossible."

"There is no such law in Australia," Eileen said.

"Well, there must have been, back when I was a child," Brooke replied.

Forrest cleared his throat. "I'm terribly sorry, but I never had a relationship with your mother. Even though my wife and I aren't together, I've been faithful to her for our entire marriage."

"We'll talk later," Brooke said, winking at him again. "I do understand."

Forrest muttered something under his breath and looked at Daniel. He took a step forward and nodded at Mark.

"You're going to have to come with me," Mark said to Brooke.

"Why?" she asked.

"You just admitted that you've been writing threatening letters," Adam snapped.

"They were harmless," Brooke replied. "I had to do something. I had to meet my father."

"The letters may have been harmless, but the other things you did weren't," Susan countered. "A man is dead because of you."

Brooke flushed. "That was rather awful," she said after a minute. "I had it all planned perfectly. During the interval, I was going to lean on the railing. Of course, I wouldn't lean too hard, just hard enough to make it drop out of place. Everyone would have been terribly sympathetic."

"You don't sound the least bit sorry about causing Mr. Allen's death," Adam said.

"Of course I'm sorry, but it wasn't intentional. No one can be upset with me. It was just an accident," Brooke replied.

"And a crime," Harry muttered.

Brooke shook her head. "Daddy, you shouldn't let them say such horrible things to me. I did this for you."

Forrest took a deep breath. "I don't know what to say to you. Perhaps your mother was lied to by someone pretending to be me."

"It was you. Please stop pretending it wasn't. You met my mother at the Star Theater in Derby. Sadly, it isn't there any longer. She had a small part in one of your shows. It was the summer of nineteen-ninety-two."

"I spent the entire summer that year in Australia," Forrest countered. "One of my children was poorly, and I went and stayed there for six months or more."

"You must have the year wrong," Brooke told him.

"I don't, but I don't intend to argue with you," Forrest replied. "We can take DNA tests. That will settle the matter."

"My mother was Suzanna Blake," Brooke continued. "She was nineteen that summer, and she was beautiful."

Forrest held up a hand. "I was nearly fifty that summer. There is no way I would have become involved with a young woman still in her teens."

"Love has no age," Brooke argued. "My mother told me that you weren't her first lover, but that she hadn't had much experience before she met you. You were her last lover, though. She never so much as looked at another man after she ended the relationship."

"I think that's enough for now," Mark said.

"She ended things before I was even born," Brooke continued. "She told me that she knew that you'd fall in love with me the moment you met me, and that then you would end up losing everything so that you could be with me and with her. She didn't want to cause you to be penniless, so she ended your relationship right after she found out that she'd fallen pregnant."

"Did she tell him about the baby?" Susan asked.

"She did," Brooke told her. "And she sent him a picture of me when I arrived. He wrote back and told her that he would carry the picture everywhere he went for the rest of his life. Show everyone the picture, Daddy," she said.

Forrest sighed. "I never wrote to your mother. I never met you mother. I never received a letter from your mother. That last part may not be true. My agent handled my post. He may have a letter from your mother somewhere in his files, but if she did actually write to me, he didn't think the letter was important enough to forward on to me."

"I have the letter you sent back," Brooke said. "And other letters that you wrote to my mother over the years. They're my proof."

"I don't know who your mother was corresponding with, but it wasn't me," Forrest replied.

Fenella shook her head. She'd started out thinking that Brooke had been lied to for her entire life, but the more Brooke talked, the more she wondered if Forrest was the one who was lying.

"Where are the letters?" Mark asked.

"In a locked box in my makeup case," she told him. "I carry them everywhere I go so that I always have a bit of my father with me."

"We'll want to take a look at them," Mark replied. "Maybe take copies of them."

She nodded. "They're proof that he's my father."

"With all due respect, anyone can write a letter and sign my name to it," Forrest said. "I'd much rather rely on the DNA tests."

"We can take DNA tests," Brooke replied. "If that's what it takes to convince you, I'm happy to do them."

"The results are going to upset you," he warned her.

"How will you feel if you find out that Mr. Luna isn't your father?" Adam asked.

"But he is," Brooke replied. "If he isn't, then I've wasted my entire life. I studied theater, just so that I could become an actor, because I knew being in one of his shows was the best way to meet him. Then I discovered that he doesn't really leave the Isle of Man any longer, so I had to find a way to move over here. It took me years to save up enough money and get a job over here. Once I was here, though, I couldn't find anyone interested in doing one of his shows. That's why I started sending the letters. I thought one of them would do the trick before I actually had to start causing disruptions to shows, but no one seemed to take my letters seriously."

"Okay, that's enough," Mark said. "We're going to take this to the station now."

Everyone watched as he escorted Brooke back behind the curtain. As they disappeared from view, all eyes shifted to Forrest.

"Are you quite certain you aren't her father?" Adam demanded.

"I've never been to the Star Theater in Derby," he replied. "I don't recall ever meeting anyone named Suzanna Blake. I certainly wasn't in the UK in nineteen ninety-two. Besides all of that, I've never cheated on my wife," he replied.

"So either her mother lied to her, or someone was pretending to be you in Derby in the early nineties," Adam replied.

"I'm not certain which is worse," Forrest said with a sigh.

Daniel took Forrest down to the station to get his statement. Shelly, Fenella, and Tim stopped at the Tale and Tail for a drink on their way home.

"That was all very sad," Shelly said once they were all sitting together on the upper level.

"It was," Fenella agreed.

"I wasn't at all disappointed that we didn't get to see the second half of the show," Tim said.

Someone knocked on Fenella's door not long after she'd arrived at home. "Daniel, hello," Fenella said as she opened her door. "Come in."

"I can't stay long. I just needed to see you," he said, pulling her into a kiss.

"Was it awful?" she asked when he released her.

"She's convinced that she's right, that Forrest is her father, and nothing anyone says can change her mind. She's going to need some serious help when the DNA tests come back."

"The poor girl. What about the letters?"

He sighed. "There were only three of them. She had them together with a few notes from her mother, who passed away when she was sixteen. To my eye, the handwriting looked very similar to her mother's, but I'm not an expert."

"So her mother wrote a few notes, pretending to be Forrest, to give her daughter a father," Fenella guessed.

"I believe so. I don't think she ever imagined that Brooke would come looking for the man."

"Especially not after she told her not to."

"I'm going home to get some sleep," Daniel told her. "Mark and I both have mountains of paperwork to get through tomorrow before anyone can work out what charges should be brought against Brooke."

"Poor Mr. Allen," Fenella sighed.

"Max isn't pleased," Mona said when she appeared in Fenella's living room a short while later. "He wanted to see the rest of the show."

Fenella shrugged. "I could try to tell you the rest of the story, but I didn't understand it, not any of the times that I saw it."

"At least we know who was behind the letters," Mona said. "That poor girl. I think her mother should have told her the truth."

The next day the *Isle of Man Times* announced that the remaining performances of *Three Gentlewomen from Bologna* had been canceled. The paper also had a lengthy interview with Adam, who repeated nearly everything that had been said at the rehearsal. The headline read: "Who's the Daddy?," and Fenella felt a rush of sympathy for both Forrest and Brooke.

The story was the talk of the island for the next week while everyone waited for news to leak about the DNA test results. Fenella's phone rang on a Tuesday morning.

"Good morning," a voice said when she answered. "It's Forrest."

"Hello, how are you?"

"I'm struggling a bit with all of the press attention," he replied. "There's been a great deal of ugly speculation about my love life, both on the island and across. Actually, it's been quite a bit uglier across. It's been decades since I've been on the cover of the tabloids, and I hadn't missed it."

"It's been a slow news week."

He chuckled. "Yes, of course. Why couldn't a member of parliament get caught doing something naughty last week? Never mind. I've rung to let you know that I'm taking a long holiday. I'm going to visit my children, one after another, for at least a few months each. My doctor isn't happy, but even he had to admit that being on the island is causing me stress right now."

"I'm sure it will do you good to get away. I hope you have a wonderful time."

"I've sent a press release to the local paper for publication tomorrow. The DNA test results are back and they've proven that I'm not Ms. Blake's father. I feel terrible for her, but there's nothing I can do to help her."

"She's going to be devastated."

"Indeed, but I can't allow myself to feel guilty for any of this."

"None of it was your fault."

"The police in Derby have done some investigating, and they don't think that anyone was impersonating me in the city in ninety-two. It appears that Ms. Blake's mother simply selected me at random to name as the father of her daughter."

"It's all very sad, especially for poor Mr. Allen."

"Yes, we mustn't forget that a man lost his life in all of this," Forrest sighed. "Please tell Shelly that I'll ring her when I get back. I'm afraid I shall have to miss her wedding, but I'd very much like to celebrate with her and Tim once I return."

"I'll tell her," Fenella promised.

She put the phone down and then sighed. "It's all so sad," she said to Mona as the woman appeared on the couch next to her.

"Your brother is about to ring," she replied. "He wants to come for a visit."

"Which brother?" Fenella asked.

Mona disappeared as the phone began to ring.

UMBRELLAS AND UNDERTAKERS

Release date: February 18, 2022

All Fenella Woods wants is to have a nice lunch with her fiancé, Police Inspector Daniel Robinson. When the café's owner manages to start a fire, though, things get complicated very quickly. As if the fire isn't enough for Daniel to investigate, a local undertaker wants to make a deathbed confession.

Alfred Beck claims that while he was arranging for Kent Thomas's funeral, he overheard Kent's wife, Tammy, talking about how she'd managed to murder him. Kent's been dead and buried for over ten years, his death attributed to a heart attack. Of course, Tammy denies having done or said any such thing, but the police still exhume the body. When it turns out that Kent was poisoned, Daniel finds himself in the middle of another murder investigation.

Can Fenella help Daniel work out who killed Kent Thomas? Can she discover the truth about Karl Carlson, the man behind the café fire? And can she go anywhere on the island without bumping into someone involved in one case or the other?

ALSO BY DIANA XARISSA

The Durand File

The Markham Sisters Cozy Mystery Novellas

The Janet Markham Bennett Cozy Thriller Series

The Armstrong Assignment

The Blake Assignment

The Carlson Assignment

The Doyle Assignment

The Isle of Man Romance Series

Island Escape

Island Inheritance

Island Heritage

Island Christmas

The Later in Life Love Stories

Second Chances

Second Act

Second Thoughts

Second Degree

Second Best

Second Nature

Second Place

ABOUT THE AUTHOR

Diana started self-publishing in 2013 and she is thrilled to have found readers for the stories that she creates. She spent her childhood and teens years wearing out her library card on a regular basis and has always enjoyed getting lost in fictional worlds.

She was born and raised in Erie, Pennsylvania, and studied history at Allegheny College in Meadville, Pennsylvania. After years working in college administration in both Erie and Washington, DC, Diana moved to the UK following her marriage.

While living on the Isle of Man, Diana had an opportunity to earn a master's degree in Manx Studies, focusing on the fascinating history of the island. Eventually, she and her husband and their two children relocated to the US, where they are now settled in the Buffalo, New York, area.

She also writes mystery/thrillers set in the not-too-distant future as Diana X. Dunn and Middle Grade and Young Adult fiction as D.X. Dunn.

Diana is always happy to hear from readers. You can write to her at:

Diana Xarissa Dunn
PO Box 72
Clarence, NY 14031.

Find Diana at: DianaXarissa.com
E-mail: Diana@dianaxarissa.com

Made in the USA
Monee, IL
30 November 2021

83485763R00129